DISCO DEAD

Also by Marcia Talley

The Hannah Ives mysteries

SING IT TO HER BONES
UNBREATHED MEMORIES
OCCASION OF REVENGE
IN DEATH'S SHADOW
THIS ENEMY TOWN
THROUGH THE DARKNESS
DEAD MAN DANCING *
WITHOUT A GRAVE *
ALL THINGS UNDYING *
A QUIET DEATH *
THE LAST REFUGE *
DARK PASSAGE *
TOMORROW'S VENGEANCE *
DAUGHTER OF ASHES *
FOOTPRINTS TO MURDER *
MILE HIGH MURDER *
TANGLED ROOTS *
DONE GONE *

* *available from Severn House*

DISCO DEAD

Marcia Talley

**SEVERN
HOUSE**

First world edition published in Great Britain and the USA in 2022
by Severn House, an imprint of Canongate Books Ltd,
14 High Street, Edinburgh EH1 1TE.

Trade paperback edition first published in Great Britain and the USA in 2023
by Severn House, an imprint of Canongate Books Ltd.

severnhouse.com

British Library Cataloguing-in-Publication Data
A CIP catalogue record for this title is available from the British Library.

ISBN-13: 978-1-4483-0795-1 (cased)
ISBN-13: 978-1-4483-0796-8 (trade paper)
ISBN-13: 978-1-4483-0794-4 (e-book)

This is a work of fiction. Names, characters, places and incidents are either the
product of the author's imagination or are used fictitiously. Except where actual
historical events and characters are being described for the storyline of this novel,
all situations in this publication are fictitious and any resemblance to actual
persons, living or dead, business establishments, events or locales is purely
coincidental.

All Severn House titles are printed on acid-free paper.

Typeset by Palimpsest Book Production Ltd.,
Falkirk, Stirlingshire, Scotland.
Printed and bound in Great Britain by
TJ Books, Padstow, Cornwall.

After ten years and ten novels together, this one is for my splendid editor, Sara Porter, without whom . . .

ACKNOWLEDGEMENTS

A million thanks to my husband, Barry, who enjoys playing Beethoven on the Steinway, but when I'm on deadline, happily dons a pair of headphones and moves to the electronic keyboard.

And to Blue Apron, the outstanding meal kit company that is teaching him how to cook.

To Hobie, the Lynx Point Siamese who keeps wandering into my life and my stories. Thanks, Gary and Melanie Tisdale, for sharing a cat who is clearly too fine an animal to be wasted on just one novel.

To my crack team of military advisors:

Michael Burt, for planting the seed.

Al 'Blues' Baker for the loan of his Naval Academy yearbook, the 1978 *Lucky Bag*.

And especially to David Fuquea, who constructed a career for one of the most sinister villains I never want to meet outside the confines of these pages.

If I got anything wrong, it's entirely my fault, not theirs.

To my Facebook friends on DNA Detectives, you are all search angels.

To Jenny Nordstrom, artist and photographer, for the hairstyle.

To Spotify, for the disco playlist.

To friend and partner in crime, writer Elaine Viets, for the perfect title.

To Sherriel Mattingly, beta reader and Hannah's Number One Fan.

And, as always, to Vicky Bijur.

'Pop music, disco music and heavy metal music is about shutting out the tensions of life, putting it away' —Peter Tork

ONE

Dancing Queen (ABBA)

1978

A my slipped a Marlboro between her lips and lit it. She inhaled leisurely, holding the smoke in her lungs until they began to burn. She closed her eyes, shutting out everything in the bar, everything except the music.

Get up, get up, let nothing get you down . . .

Her head swam. The music swirled around her, the passionate notes of the electric guitar seducing her, drawing her down, sucking her in. She took another drag and held it, riding the chords that floated from the jukebox on a rainbow of sound.

. . . Ooh, babe, your heart is not a hand-me-down.

'Aren't you afraid someone will notice?'

Amy opened one eye and squinted at Donna, the bartender, a girl she knew from her seminar at St John's. She took another drag and held her breath for half a minute. She frowned, irrationally hating Donna's flawless complexion and shoulder-length blonde hair, perfectly parted in the middle, that framed the bartender's face with feathery, fly-away wings.

'So what?' Amy drawled at last, smoke escaping from her lips in a thin, blue stream.

Donna flapped her hand, waving the smoke away. 'Jeeze, Amy. You're out of your freaking mind.'

Amy leaned forward, resting her elbows on the polished red cedar countertop that Doots, who owned the bar, was so proud of. It had been salvaged from a sloop of war, circa 1813. 'Anybody can see it's only a Marlboro,' Amy whispered.

'And anybody can smell . . .' Donna began.

Amy cut her off, shoving the pack across the bar. 'Have one.'

'No way, José. I'd like to graduate tomorrow, thank you

very much. Besides, I'm working.' As if to demonstrate, Donna lifted Amy's glass and wiped under it with a damp cloth.

Amy shrugged and continued to smoke. Reflected in the mirror behind the bar, a guy materialized from the crowd as if beamed down from the starship *Enterprise*, except nobody on the *Enterprise* would have been caught dead in a chocolate brown double-knit leisure suit. Carrying a bottle of Miller that glistened with sweat, he slid onto the barstool next to her. 'What are you drinking?'

Amy addressed his reflection. 'Gin and tonic. It's too damn hot for beer.' His close-cropped hair was dark and curly, and he was cute as all get out, in spite of the leisure suit.

'Another Miller for me, then, and a G and T for the lady.' He twirled his beer in a wet ring on the bar. 'I'm Nick.'

Amy turned to face him and smiled.

'From University of Maryland.' Nick's head bobbed to the disco beat of 'Car Wash'. With his beer, he pointed to a pony-tailed guy wearing a ball cap who was feeding coins into the jukebox near the dance floor. 'Me and my friend over there? We usually go to Georgetown on Saturday nights, but thought we'd check out the action in Annapolis.'

'Boy have you come to the wrong place! Annapolis is Deadsville.' Ignoring Nick, Amy concentrated on her cigarette, observing dispassionately as the paper burned down another centimeter. It had taken her an hour to fix those fags, massaging them between her fingers over a sheet of notebook paper until the tobacco fluttered out. Mixing the tobacco carefully with what was left of her stash. Tapping the filter ends gently on her desktop until Philip Morris's best settled in nicely alongside the Acapulco Gold. She sighed, smoked the joint down to the filter, then snubbed the partially melted filter out in the ashtray. 'Nothing ever happens in Annapolis,' she complained, peering at Nick through the haze.

'I don't know about that,' he said. 'The president's coming next week.'

'Carter?'

'We got another president?'

'Nooooh.' She punched him on the arm. 'You know what I mean.'

'Yeah.' He sipped his beer silently for a moment then added, 'He's speaking at the Naval Academy graduation.'

'Super,' Amy deadpanned.

'Wanna blow this joint? Check out Georgetown?' Nick asked gently.

Amy wasn't in a Georgetown mood. 'Nah. I'm waiting for my boyfriend.'

Nick laid a hand lightly on Amy's sleeve. 'You sure?'

'Sure I'm sure. Keith'll be here any minute.' She slipped her arm out from under Nick's hand and peered at her watch, twisting the face sideways until it caught a flash of light from the mirrored ball rotating in the rafters overhead and she could read the time. Eight-oh-five. Keith was supposed to meet her at seven-thirty, the rat. 'I wonder what's keeping him?'

'Maybe he changed his mind,' Donna chimed in.

Amy glared at her friend. 'He's not allowed to change his mind. It's my fucking birthday, for Christ's sake!'

Donna snapped her towel on the edge of the bar. 'Shit, Amy! Why didn't you tell me?'

Amy shrugged and drew another cigarette from the pack. 'You didn't ask.'

Nick produced a matchbook from his breast pocket. Cupping the match in his palm to protect the flame from the blast of the air conditioner, he leaned forward and lit Amy's cigarette. 'If I had a girlfriend pretty as you, I wouldn't stand her up.'

Amy blew out the match. Nick's eyes were ice blue, his lashes thick and dark. 'He'll be along.'

Nick flicked the spent match into an ashtray. 'Where're you from, Birthday Girl?'

'St John's College,' she said, but when Nick smiled and shook his head, she laughed. 'Oh, you mean where do I *come* from? New York City. At least that's where my dad lives when he's not jetting off to Rio or someplace with wife number three. You?'

'You'll laugh.'

'No, I won't.'

'What if I said Ho-Ho-Kus?'

'In New Jersey?' She giggled. 'Then we're practically neighbors.'

Nick waggled a finger at her. 'You promised you wouldn't laugh.'

Amy arranged her face into a frown. 'Better?' She was beginning to like this guy, even if his hair was too short. If Keith didn't show up in five minutes, he could go to hell.

'Car Wash' segued into 'Dancing Queen'. Suddenly, so suddenly that the barstool teetered dangerously, Amy hopped to the floor. 'Let me make it up to you,' she said. Still holding her cigarette, she grabbed Nick's hand and pulled him toward the dance floor. 'This is one of my favorite songs.'

While Nick took the time to remove his jacket and toss it to his friend, Amy found a spot on the edge of the crowded floor and began swaying, her head swimming as it struggled to keep up with the rest of her body. *She* was the dancing queen!

Lights kaleidoscoped past her eyes. She was speeding through the galaxy at warp speed, then Nick was there, his hands resting lightly on her pink polyester shoulders, running down her arms, lifting her hands and raising them high until the two were dancing fingertip to fingertip, perfectly in synch.

'Are you a teaser?' Nick crooned in a throaty tenor, inches from her ear. 'You gonna leave me burning like the girl in the song?'

'I may be spaced-out,' Amy whispered into the V of flesh formed by his open collar. 'But I never tease.'

Two gins and tonic and quite a few songs later, it seemed to Amy that she and Nick danced alone. Maybe she'd fallen for his crooked smile and straight, white teeth, the well-developed biceps that rippled under his silk-smooth shirt. And if she could get a close-up of those abs, she'd even forgive him the ugly white belt.

'Oh, babe,' she whispered, her breath warm against his cheek. 'Light my fire.'

Nick's hands found her waist and turned her, gently guiding her back to him until they were nestled together as comfortably as matched spoons.

Reaching back, her hands found his butt, hard with muscle. Something else was hard against her, too. While Nick's fingers traced slow circles on her thighs, Amy smiled, feeling her skirt ride up as she kneaded herself against him.

'Oh . . . my . . . God.' Amy's legs began to tremble.

Nick's breath was hot in her ear. 'Let's get out of here.'

'We can crash at my dad's,' she whispered. 'He's got a summer place on the Magothy.'

Nick spun Amy around, buried his hands in her thick, auburn hair and kissed her, hard. She went limp, arms dangling at her sides like a rag doll. 'Where you parked?' he mumbled, his lips still touching hers.

Amy tried to remember. It seemed like days had passed since she pulled her TR6 into a parking space outside of, outside of . . . She kissed Nick back, her tongue just tickling his lips. 'In front of the hardware store,' she mumbled at last.

Making no move to go, Nick kissed her cheek, her nose, her chin. Amy laid her palm flat on Nick's chest and pushed him away. 'Steven's Hardware!' she caroled. 'Last one there is a rotten egg!'

Dodging and weaving, Amy cleared a path through the throng of bodies gyrating along with Freddie Mercury to 'We Will Rock You.' Just as the familiar stomping and clapping chant began, she grabbed her purse from behind the bar and shot out the door.

Doots' Bar was halfway up Fleet Street, not far from the barbershop where George Washington got his hair cut, or so Amy'd always been told. She had sprinted all the way to Middleton's Tavern and was crossing Randall Street when Nick caught up with her, laughing and gasping for breath.

She pointed. 'There it is. I left the top down. Sure glad it didn't rain.'

Nick whistled. 'Far out!' He turned to Amy, his mouth slack. 'A '76. What a beaut! They don't make them any more, do they?'

Amy shrugged.

'Where'd you get it?'

'It's a guilt gift. My dad's terrible with holidays and birthdays, so he gave me the Triumph new, two years ago. Birthday, Christmas and Valentine's Day all rolled into one' – she trailed her fingertips along the bright canary-yellow hood – 'for the next million years. C'mon. Get in.'

Without opening it, Nick threw his long legs over the door and settled comfortably into the passenger seat, grinning.

Amy was pissed to see that Nick's friend had followed them from the bar. He leaned negligently against Steven's picture window, partially blocking a display of picnic coolers and window fans – twenty percent off – and still nursing a beer. 'No room,' she said, hoping he had his own set of wheels. Perhaps it was rude not to ask his name, but she didn't care. She didn't want him tagging along.

'No sweat.' Nick twisted in his seat and patted the luggage rack. 'Hey, Vegas! You can sit up here, like Queen of the Rose Bowl Parade.'

Amy scowled. 'Vegas? What kind of name is that?'

'He's got a real name, but he digs the nightlife, so everybody calls him Vegas.'

'Does he *have* to come?' Amy complained.

'Don't worry. Vegas knows how to make himself scarce.'

Vegas, still carrying Nick's jacket, tossed it casually over Nick's head. 'Fuck you, man.' A few seconds later, he planted his narrow backside on the luggage rack, bracing his legs between the bucket seats. 'How 'bout I buy the booze?'

Amy put the car in reverse and, without looking, backed out of the parking space. 'Shit, no,' she said. 'Dad's liquor cabinet is full of stuff.'

She shifted into first and careened around Market House, roaring up Main Street at thirty-five miles per hour. At Church Circle she floored it, taking the right turn by the Governor's Mansion on two wheels, before shooting out of town on the straightaway – Rowe Boulevard. At the Route 50 exit, Amy geared down but took the turn so fast that Vegas shouted, 'Crazy bitch!'

Amy laughed. Checking him out in the rear-view mirror, she couldn't help noticing that he hadn't been frightened enough to drop his beer.

At College Parkway, she ran the red light. Between Robinson Road and Baltimore-Annapolis Boulevard, she steered for a while with her knees, raising her arms over her head as if she were riding a roller coaster. Glancing sideways, she noticed that Nick had raised his arms, too. 'I love you!' he shouted into the wind.

At the intersection of Route 2 and Magothy Bridge Road, Amy slowed, turned, then sped on, swerving left and right until the road narrowed and she found herself on a winding, tree-lined lane. As she snaked down it, Amy counted mailboxes – seven, eight, nine – before finding what she was looking for: two narrow dirt ruts, far too primitive to be dignified with the title 'road'. A teeth-jarring mile later, she slammed on the brakes. 'My dad likes privacy,' she said. 'He sometimes brings his assistant here. To, um, work.'

Amy closed her eyes and leaned her head back against the driver's seat. She cherished privacy, too, and often came to her family's waterfront cabin to mellow out, unwinding from the rigors of her academic schedule. Just Amy and the sheltering trees, the cicadas gently chirring and the frogs grumping away in the marshes. Amy climbed out of the car and waved vaguely. 'The water's down there.'

Nick held out his hand. 'Got a key?'

'Oh, the door isn't locked.' She giggled. 'You'd have to find this place before you could rob it.'

Amy felt exhilarated by the drive and the salt-fresh air, but once she entered the cottage, the pent-up heat hit her like a wall. Pointing toward the liquor cabinet, she set Vegas to making drinks and assigned Nick to the record player while she bustled about opening windows.

Her father's stereo system was built into a pine bookcase near the door; stereo speakers dominated either side of the fireplace. Nick pulled an album from a stack sandwiched between two marble bookends on the oversized mantle. 'ABBA. Cool.' He continued flipping through the pile and selected another. 'Hey! You got the new Stones album.'

'Yeah. Dad got me an advance copy. Somebody he works with in DC. Put it on, why don't you?'

Nick considered the jacket. '*Some Girls*!' He laughed. 'Lucy, Raquel, Liz, Marilyn . . . and get this! Mick Jagger in a wig. Far out!' Nick slipped the record out of its sleeve and centered it on the turntable. When the music started, Amy watched as

Nick listened critically for a few seconds, turned up the volume, then boogied toward her, snapping his fingers. Grinning, she turned to concentrate on shoving aside the sliding glass doors that led to the balcony. Nick kissed the back of her neck.

'Hey! I'm almost completely sober, Nick. Make yourself useful and tell your friend to fix me a drink.'

Amy hauled an afghan off the back of the sofa and laid it on the floor in front of the fireplace. She lay down on it, then patted the space next to her. 'Come here, Nick. Keep me company.'

She lit another cigarette, smoking it slowly, staring up at the ceiling while Nick squatted at the edge of the blanket, watching her, his arms resting on his thighs, quietly sipping the pale yellow concoction Vegas had prepared for them. Nick drained his glass and set it on the flagstone hearth, then leaned toward her. He ran a finger down Amy's arm, removed the cigarette from her fingers and threw it into the fireplace. He kissed her softly, easing his tongue between her lips. Amy opened her mouth and melted into him, trembling as he drew the breath right out of her. *God! How could his hands be everywhere at once?* Lifting her blouse, unhooking her bra, easing up her skirt and drawing down her pantyhose, then her panties. Nick's mouth found her breast, and then he was in her, gently thrusting. She arched into him, completely on fire. She could even hear it roaring in her ears: so respectable, so delectable!

Mick . . . Nick . . . Mick . . . Nick. What difference did it make?

Nick shuddered, then moaned, collapsing lightly on top of her, breathing warmly into her neck. In the breeze coming in from the window, Amy felt his sweat cooling on her body.

When Amy opened her eyes, she was creeped out to see Vegas watching them. She'd forgotten about Vegas. He was perched on the kitchen counter, still wearing that stupid hat. Amy wondered what the hell Nick saw in him, who, unlike his friend, was dressed casually in faded jeans and a M*A*S*H T-shirt.

Nick rolled over onto his back. 'Shit,' he said to the ceiling. 'What did you put in that drink?'

'Mixed some stuff together,' Vegas drawled.

Amy turned on her side and propped her head up on her hand. She ran her finger down Nick's chest and walked little circles around his navel. 'Oh, baby, don't go to sleep on me *now*.' But Nick had passed out, snoring lightly.

Amy pulled her blouse down and sat up, hastily rearranging her clothes. 'Hey, Vegas!' she called. 'Bring me my purse and some more of that shit you mixed up.'

Vegas hopped off the counter, snagged the strap of her purse as he passed the sofa and sauntered over to the fireplace. He knelt down on a corner of the blanket, laying Amy's purse to one side.

Too late, Amy noticed the bulge straining Vegas's jeans. Not daring to move, she watched as he unzipped and pulled his erection out. Amy shook her head and scooted back against the hearth. Vegas reached out and grabbed her hand. *Gross! He's going to make me touch it!* Feeling sick and helpless, she closed her eyes . . .

He reeked of Brut and crème de menthe. She tried to pull her hand away and fight him off, but he was much stronger than she was and more than capable of pinning her to the floor. She stared at the rough-hewn beams of the ceiling; watched the ceiling fan slowly rotate; noticed a spider web shimmering in the Tiffany chandelier she'd helped her mother pick out at an antique store on Long Island. Long ago. Far away. In some other life.

It was the rhythmic flick of his ponytail against her bare shoulder, like a sweaty horse swatting flies, that dragged her back, gasping.

'Nick! Nick! Help!' she screamed.

Vegas's forearm pressed heavily against her neck.

She tried to scream again, but the sound died in her throat. *Stop! I can't breathe!* Bright lights exploded in the darkness inside her head, swirling and spiraling like leaves in a storm, a sparkling whirlpool sucking her down and down.

Then it was all darkness.

TWO

We Are Family (Sister Sledge)

Present day

After everything that happened, I swore I would never shop at Trader Joe's again.

But that was before I pulled the last package of spicy Italian chicken sausage out of the freezer. Before my husband mooned around the kitchen clutching the last bag of Cheese and Pepper Puffs like a life preserver, puppy dog eyes begging for more.

'There's Seasoned Kale Chips,' I offered helpfully.

Paul shot me a look that left no doubt how he felt about kale in any form.

So, I caved. Put on my big-girl pants, grabbed my handbag and drove out to the Annapolis Mall, taking deep, steadying breaths as I pulled into the vast parking lot and circled round, carefully avoiding the spot where a maniac had shot up my car and my friend Trish and I had nearly died.

After parking the Volvo in front of Joann's Fabrics, located a relatively safe distance from the scene of the crime, I took a diagonal across the lot, grabbed a shopping cart and trundled it into the iconic grocery store. Following my customary serpentine route counter-clockwise along the aisles, I loaded up on our favorites: southwest chopped salad kit, multi-colored carrots, teeny-tiny avocados. I snagged a free sample of Trader Joe's Bay Blend coffee in a two-ounce cup, then steered the cart down the frozen food aisle where two bags of Mandarin orange chicken and frozen cauliflower gnocchi joined the growing pile. Turning left at the cold case where they stored the fontina, triple crème Brie and other highly agreeable cheeses, I aimed for the shelves where I knew I'd find Thai lime and chili cashews. That's when I noticed a familiar profile reaching for a jar of Trader Joe's peanut butter, organic, natch. I gently tapped my cart against hers. 'Emily.'

She started, then grinned. 'Mom!' She added the peanut butter to the jumble in her cart. 'I'm surprised to see you here after, well, you know.'

'Your father was running low on acceptable snacks,' I explained. 'I had to face it sometime.'

'What's wrong with Dad?' Emily scoffed. 'Can't drive the car? Got two broken legs or something?'

'You know how he feels about grocery shopping.'

Emily puffed air out her lips. 'Wimp.'

As I trailed along behind my daughter, she turned her head to ask, 'How's Trish doing, anyway?'

'Great under the circumstances,' I said. 'She's home from rehab, getting around on a walker. When I popped across the street for a visit yesterday, Peter told me she'll be graduating to a quad cane in a couple of weeks.'

Emily's eyebrows disappeared under her bangs. 'Quad?'

'Four-legged,' I explained. 'The fancy ones have seats.'

While waiting our turn at the checkout counter, I ripped into a packet of chocolate crème cookies and offered one to my daughter. 'No thanks,' Emily said, rolling her eyes. 'Give me credit for a little self-control.'

'No calories in food sampled at the grocery store,' the cashier offered with a grin as cheerful as the retro-Hawaiian shirt she wore, decorated with surf boards and hula girls.

'It's the law,' I added. 'No calories in food eaten while leaning over the sink, either.'

'Ha ha ha,' Emily said. 'I wish.'

'Want to stop by the house for coffee on your way home?' I asked as the cashier began to run my purchases over the scanner.

'Sorry, can't. Timmy's got soccer practice today. He just got his learner's permit and I'm what the Maryland Department of Motor Vehicles calls the qualified supervising driver,' she said, making quote marks in the air with her fingers.

I couldn't believe my grandson, Emily's youngest, was already old enough to drive. 'Lordy,' I said.

Emily leaned toward me and tapped her head. 'See all the gray?'

If there were any silver strands among her shoulder-length, ash blonde tresses, I couldn't see them. 'Just as well,' I said, as we approached her car a few minutes later. 'As I kinda sorta had plans.'

'Oh?'

'A genealogy project.'

'You really got sucked down that rabbit hole, didn't you?' Emily remarked as she aimed a key fob at her SUV and pressed the button that would open the hatchback.

'I enjoy it, Em,' I said as the hatch yawned wide. 'And if I hadn't gotten hooked on GenTree back then, we never would have learned about our Native American roots, nor met our Lakota cousins.'

'So, what kind of trouble are you getting into now? Don't tell me more of Uncle Scott's sperm donor kids have turned up?'

I laughed. 'Not that I know of. Isn't sixteen enough?'

'One would think,' she said as she heaved a cooler bag into the back of the van. 'But you know Scott. His motto should have been *je séme à tout vent* – I cast my seed all over the place.'

I had to laugh at Emily's loose translation. 'It's "I sow to all winds,"' I corrected. 'French major, remember? On behalf of Pierre Larousse and his encyclopedia, I'm setting you straight.'

Emily leaned in, chasing down a canteloupe that had escaped from the bag, then said, 'I never thought much of him anyway.'

'Who? Larousse?'

'No, silly. Uncle Scott. He could be a shit.'

I started to agree with her, then thought better of it. 'It's not nice to speak ill of the dead.'

'Well, it's the truth, Mother. In the boyfriend department, I much prefer Zack, to be honest.'

'I think your Aunt Georgina does, too,' I said with a grin.

'Zack treats Georgina like an intelligent human being, for one thing. Too bad she didn't marry him in the first place.'

'Then where would Sean, Dylan, Julie and Colin be?' I said, naming my baby sister's four children, only the youngest of whom, Colin, still lived at home.

Emily locked her car and insisted on escorting me to mine. As we crossed the parking lot, shopping cart clattering along the tarmac, she said, 'So, what *are* you doing?'

'You'll mock.'

'No, I won't.'

'I'm visiting cemeteries. Taking pictures of headstones.'

Emily frowned. 'That's seriously creepy, Mom.'

'You wouldn't believe how many people on GenTree are looking for photos of their ancestors' headstones,' I informed her. 'I've gotten requests from as far away as Thailand.'

'How . . .?' Emily began, but I anticipated her question.

'A while back, I signed up with FindAGrave.com.' I slotted the shopping cart between my Volvo and a pickup truck, dug my iPhone out of my handbag and tapped the FindAGrave app. 'Requests are sorted by zip code. You can choose to claim them or not. Look,' I said, turning the screen in her direction. 'Here's the list of requests for the 21037 zip code I'm working with today.'

Emily shielded her eyes from the noonday sun and squinted at the tiny screen. 'St Luke's Cemetery I know, but where's Bayview?'

'Just off Central Avenue, down in Mayo.'

'Honestly,' Emily said after a moment. 'Couldn't you have a hobby like *normal* mothers. Scrapbooking? Candlemaking? You like to garden. Why don't you take up *bonsai*?'

'I knit,' I protested.

'You know what I mean.'

'Don't sell it short,' I said. 'I stroll around outside, get sun, fresh air and exercise. It's quiet, nobody to bother you and nobody to talk to but dead people.'

Emily raised both hands, palms out. 'And everybody always says *I* march to a different drummer.'

'The acorn doesn't fall far from the tree,' I said, matching her cliché for cliché. 'Wanna see how it works?'

When Emily nodded, I drew her attention to the app again, swiped a couple of screens forward. 'I locate the headstone, take a picture and upload it to the database while I'm standing right there in the cemetery. It's a slick piece of software.'

Emily studied the photo on my screen – a 1943 headstone for a woman who had lived to be 102 before 'falling asleep in the arms of Jesus' – then surprised me by laughing out loud. 'It's still weird, Mom.'

'My good deeds for the day,' I said.

Emily helped load groceries into the Volvo, then turned to go. 'St Luke's. Isn't that where that famous general is buried?'

'James Taylor Johnson,' I said as I opened the driver's side door and slid onto the seat. 'Yes. Old Bloody Jim.'

'Well, say hello to the good general for me, will you?'

'Of course. But he won't be saying much. He's been dead for one hundred and sixty years.'

THREE
Mamma Mia (ABBA)

Twenty minutes later, I dropped the groceries off at home, restocked the freezer, fridge and shelves. Before leaving the house on my mission to the cemetery, I propped a bag of trail mix against the microwave where Paul could find it when he came home from teaching his afternoon advanced calculus class at the Naval Academy. Back in the Volvo again, I headed out of town, driving south on Old Solomon's Island Road. At Central Avenue I hung a left at the intersection and drove straight east toward Mayo. Just past the Old Stein Inn – draft beer and spaetzle to die for! – I slowed, watching for the turn-off.

St Luke's was just as I remembered from previous visits. The church and its cemetery sprawled over several acres of valuable waterfront property, a section carved out nearly two centuries ago from the old Nicholas Gassaway estate. Gateposts, set wide apart, marked the entrance to the church parking lot, but if there had ever been a gate, it had long ago disappeared.

I parked in a spot reserved for visitors, then headed for the church portico where I consulted the laminated loose-leaf notebook St Luke's keeps chained to a post there, wishing as always that they'd put the darn directory online. I located the first of my assignments in the alphabetical listing, a Thaddeus Q Wilson, 1799–1875, checked his coordinates on the over-sized map attached by rivets to the stone wall, then set off to find the old gentleman himself.

It is impossible to enter St Luke's cemetery without passing the memorial to Union General James Taylor Johnson, who had perished in September of 1862 in a little-known skirmish in western Maryland, early in the Civil War. For the past 160 years or so, the good general – thanks to his well-to-do family

– had sat astride his war horse, Magnus, riding in triumphant bas relief across a bronze memorial plaque the size of an eighty-six-inch television screen. A troop of rifle-bearing foot soldiers trailed like ducklings behind him. A preposterous memorial, I thought, considering Johnson had distinguished himself by being shot by his own troops, accidently it is said, not far from Antietam. His burial plot was so large, in fact, I wondered if Magnus had been buried there, too.

As I passed the general, I paid my respects, as countless others had done before. Magnus's flank gleamed in the afternoon sun, burnished bright by thousands of fingertips. I'm not particularly superstitious, but some folks rub the bronze testicles of the charging bull on Wall Street to ensure good fortune on the stock market; the town fathers of Verona, Italy were forced to remove the statue of Juliet Capulet whose right breast was receiving far too much attention from love-seeking tourists; and senior midshipmen at the Naval Academy rub the bronze beak of Admiral Hiram Rickover, father of the nuclear Navy, for good luck before their final exams. What did Johnson's visitors wish for? I wondered.

I located, photographed and uploaded old Thaddeus to the FindAGrave.com database, then moved on to the final resting place of Lillian Brelsford who was 'Once Met Never Forgotten,' at least not by her grateful granddaughter who texted me back almost immediately when she received the picture. *OMG, you rock!*

After searching for more than ten minutes, I determined that the headstone of Clifford Conway had gone AWOL, if it had ever existed, a situation not unusual for people who died in the early 1700s. It was nearly two o'clock and the late spring sun was still high in the sky, so I sat down on a marble bench in the shade of a sugar maple, took off my sunhat, and twisted the cap off a bottle of water I'd brought with me. The bench had been provided courtesy of Mary Yardley, who must have been a young widow in 1967 when her husband, Robert, died in Vietnam. Presumably, Mary still visited him here – her name, too, was engraved on the tombstone opposite, but her death date remained blank.

I was checking my phone for emails, appreciating the

solitude and the gentle breeze, when a sudden movement caught my eye.

I wasn't alone.

Several yards away, near the rock wall separating the cemetery from a high-end housing development, a woman knelt before a grave, fussing with an arrangement of pink and white carnations. Slim and fit, she was dressed in navy blue jogging pants and a matching zip front jacket. She wore her dark hair scrunched into an untidy bundle at the top of her head, secured with a lipstick-red claw from which blonde-tipped ends exploded like an astonished bird.

Perhaps she sensed my eyes boring into her skull, because she turned her head and nodded.

I nodded in acknowledgement, wondering where the heck I'd seen her before.

At church? Definitely not. St Katherine's congregation was on the small, intimate side and as a newcomer, she would have stood out.

The Naval Academy Spouses and Civilians Club? Mentally, I restyled her hair and dressed her in a little black dress and a double strand of pearls. Not there either.

Maybe the breast cancer support group I helped facilitate at the medical center? Nope. We dressed casually there, too, and that hairdo would be hard to forget.

As I was considering what to do next, the woman stood and took a few steps back, signaling that her task was done. Then she turned toward me, smiled and waved.

Ah, I thought. She recognizes me, too. Busted! Time for some fancy tap-dancing. I rose from the bench and headed her way.

'Beautiful bouquet,' I said as I neared the grave.

'It is, isn't it? Blooms in Mayo does a super job.'

In the lengthening silence, I took time to study the headstone, its inscription neatly framed by the flowers:

Amy Lynn Madison
May 27, 1958 – May 27, 1978
DANCE, THEN, WHEREVER YOU MAY BE

Only twenty when she died, I noticed, and then suppressed a gasp. 'She died on her *birthday*?'

My companion nodded. 'Sad, isn't it? Tragic, really.'

I did a quick calculation based on my companion's apparent age and asked gently, 'Your sister?'

She smiled wistfully. 'No. Actually, I never even met the girl.'

'Then why . . .?' I began, but she raised a hand, cutting me off.

'Why am I putting flowers on the grave of someone I don't even know?'

'Something like that,' I said.

'I've done it every year since 1979, on Amy's birthday. She deserves to be remembered, and if I don't do it, there's nobody left who will.'

'You said tragic?'

'Her body was found floating in the Magothy River.'

'She drowned?'

'Murdered, according to the medical examiner. Most likely strangled during a rape gone bad.'

Even though the sun shone hot against my skin, I shivered. 'Whoever did it, I hope they locked him up and threw away the key.'

She shook her head. 'Never tracked the guy down, although I have to give the cops credit for trying. Amy was a senior at St John's,' she explained. 'She was celebrating her birthday at a disco bar on lower Fleet Street called Doots. It's long gone now. Turned into a pizza parlor.'

'I know the place,' I said. 'They make a shrimp and fontina pizza to die for.' I paused. 'Sorry, that was an unfortunate choice of words.'

If the woman noticed, she gave no sign of it. 'Doots was a happening place back then. Long bar, dance floor, big disco ball, DJ, jukebox, the works. Witnesses say Amy was dancing with a guy about her age, although nobody saw them leave together. Her father had a summer place on the Magothy, so that's where they ended up, the cottage where investigators say the poor girl was actually killed.'

'Any suspects?' I asked. 'Persons of interest?'

'Case is colder than cold,' she said with a sigh. 'That's one of the reasons I come here. Years ago, I promised Amy that I wouldn't rest until her killer was brought to justice.' She paused, shrugged and looked me straight in the eyes. 'Obviously, I'm doing a terrible job.'

I suddenly realized where I'd seen the woman before. 'You're Isabel Randall!' I exclaimed. 'That investigative reporter on WBNF-TV.'

'For my sins,' she said, extending a hand. 'And it's Izzy.'

I took her hand and gave it a firm squeeze. 'I'm Hannah Ives,' I said. 'I knew I recognized you from somewhere! I had narrowed it down to someone in my Zumba class at the Y when I noticed you standing over here.'

'Zumba?' She laughed. 'Hardly, although I could probably use it.' Using her thumb and forefinger, she seized a bit of excess skin around her waist and gave it a playful jiggle.

Thinking about Amy's murder, I said, 'You covered the story?'

'Yes. Still am, at least on my own time.' She bobbed her head toward the grassy spot under which Amy's body lay. 'I keep my promises.'

'I haven't seen you on TV recently,' I said. 'That other reporter, Brenda Boyce? She's been all over that double murder in Highlandtown. Are you on vacation?'

'Not exactly,' she said. 'Do you want the long story or the short story?'

'I'm in no hurry. You?'

'All the time in the world. Let's sit,' she said, indicating the bench I had recently occupied.

'Bad things always come in threes,' Izzy said after we'd gotten settled. 'My mother is fond of saying that.'

'Do statistics bear your mother out?'

'Dunno, but if bad things really do come in threes, I figure I'm fucked.' After a moment, she began to speak again, ticking items off on her fingers. 'First, Quigley pulls me off the Highlandtown story,' she said, giving it the local pronunciation: *Hollantown.*

'Who's Quigley?'

'News director, a.k.a. an SOB. Shouldn't have argued with

him, of course. Lost my cool. Told him he couldn't be *serious* taking me off a story I'd been working on for three months. Unfortunately, he was. Ever since TechnoMedia took over the station . . .' She paused. 'I'm sure you noticed that Brenda Boyce is a few centuries younger than I am. 'Nuff said.'

'You could sue for age discrimination,' I suggested.

Izzy shrugged. 'I should have seen it coming. My gender and my age painted a bullseye square on my back. Judy Woodruff and Andrea Mitchell are the exceptions rather than the rule.'

'You said threes.'

'Two is the aforementioned mother. She's in assisted living up at Symphony Manor in Roland Park. You know the place?'

'I do. Posh, isn't it?'

'It'll do. Two days after Quigley took me off Highlandtown and had me covering the school board meetings – which are torture, like watching paint dry – I got a call from the Manor that Mom had slipped in the bathroom, fallen against the toilet, maybe broken her hip. I interviewed a guy in traction once, with steel pins screwed into his leg bones like some invention out of the mind of Frankenstein, but that guy had been in a motorcycle accident. How much damage could an ordinary toilet do?' She turned her head to address me directly. 'A lot as it turns out.'

'Ouch,' I said. 'How's she doing?'

'Amazingly well,' Izzy said. 'Johns Hopkins replaced her hip, and she was out of the hospital in three days. Rehab, that takes a little longer, but Mom's a tough old broad. After only four weeks, she's up and about on a walker, driving me the usual crazy.' She tapped her forehead with an index finger. 'Vascular dementia.'

'I'm sorry,' I said.

'It is what it is,' Izzy said with a shrug. 'You still got parents?'

'My dad. He and his girlfriend spend a lot of time on cruise ships, which to my way of thinking is the way to go, assisted-living wise.'

Izzy laughed. 'I hear you. Round-the-clock food, quality entertainment, lectures, someone to clean your room and make your bed every morning, Raoul bringing you poolside drinks with umbrellas in them.' She placed her hands on her knees, leaned forward and stood. 'Well, I guess I'd better let you get back to whatever you were doing.'

I explained about FindAGrave.com.

'Keep up the good work, Hannah,' she said. 'I enjoyed our chat. Maybe we'll run into each other again.'

'Hope so,' I said. 'And you, too,' I said, thinking about her job issues. 'Keeping up the good work, I mean.'

'Count on it.'

FOUR

Shake Your Groove Thing
(Peaches and Herb)

B ack home on Prince George Street, I took a package of ground beef out of the freezer and set it on the counter to thaw. I stared at it for a while, long enough for the plastic wrap to grow slightly frosty, while I pondered what to turn it into for dinner. Bolognese? Burgers? Sloppy Joes? But every recipe that sprang to mind was instantly shoved aside by what Izzy had told me about Amy Madison.

Leaving the beef to thaw unassisted, I headed for our basement office where I sat down at the desk and powered up the computer. While I waited for the desktop to populate with the usual icons, I thought hard. I didn't remember the Amy Madison case. What had I been doing back in May of 1978?

Paul had been in grad school at M.I.T. We were newly married and living in a one-bedroom apartment in an elderly, ten-story building in Cambridge, Massachusetts. In May of that year, we were having a heatwave, I had been heavily pregnant with Emily and wishing that our building had an elevator and central air conditioning. If Amy's murder had made the national news, I was too busy sitting in front of a cranky, second-hand window unit feeling like an overheated beached whale to have been aware of it.

I logged into the comprehensive newspaper database that I had access to through the Naval Academy Library portal and searched the *Annapolis Capital, Baltimore Sun* and *Washington Post* for the story.

It had made all three.

According to a brief article in the *Annapolis Capital* on May 28, 1978:

Natural Resources Police recovered the body of a young woman early today from under a private pier on the Magothy River just north of Annapolis. Her body was taken to the Office of the Chief Medical Examiner in Baltimore. Identification of the victim is being withheld pending notification of next of kin.

Two days later, the *Sun* picked up the story:

The body of a young woman found yesterday floating in the Magothy River near Annapolis has been positively identified as Amy Lynn Madison, 20, a senior at St John's College in Annapolis. According to the medical examiner, the cause of death was manual strangulation. The death has been ruled a homicide.

Miss Madison was last seen at Doots' bar, a popular disco bar in downtown Annapolis, in the company of a young man. Witnesses describe the man as of medium height, slim build, dark-haired and clean-cut, wearing a tan leisure suit. The victim was reported missing on Sunday when she failed to show up for graduation ceremonies at St John's, the 282-year-old liberal arts college, popularly known as the Great Books School.

'She didn't come home last night,' Miss Madison's roommate told police. 'But it was her birthday, you know, so I figured she was still out celebrating with Keith.'

Keith Ritchie, a friend of the victim from Alexandria, Virginia, told investigators that he planned to meet Amy for dinner, but his car got caught in a rush hour backup on the Woodrow Wilson Bridge, and by the time he arrived at the bar she had already left.

Efforts to reach the victim's family for comment have been unsuccessful.

Anyone with information is invited to call the anonymous police tipline at 410-280-CLUE.

Amy's obituary didn't appear in the papers until over a week later. In the interim, someone who apparently knew her well had taken time to do a proper job of it. The *Washington Post*, much to my surprise, had given Amy's obituary twice as much space as they gave to announce the death of Carl Reynolds, a seventy-five-year-old Major League Baseball player (eighty home runs, they said, and 699 RBIs over 1222 games!) who had played for the Washington Senators in the 1930s.

Out of a photograph at the head of the long, narrow column Amy grinned, almost impishly, left eyebrow slightly raised as if contemplating a bit of youthful mischief. Her abundant, shoulder-length hair was parted on the side and layered, curling away from her cheeks in an explosion of ringlets.

> Funeral services for Miss Amy Lynn Madison who died suddenly on May 27 were held today at St Luke's Episcopal Church in Mayo, Maryland, the Reverend Thomas E. Pace presiding. At the time of her death, Amy had completed the requirements for a Bachelor's Degree from St John's College and would have graduated the following day. An exceptional student, her senior essay, 'Power, Authority and Truth in Sophocles's *Antigone'* was shortlisted for the Senior Essay Prize.
>
> After graduation, Amy planned to work as a veterinary assistant at South County Animal Hospital prior to her enrollment at the University of Pennsylvania's School of Veterinary Medicine in the fall.
>
> The popular redhead was an accomplished horse-woman who enjoyed reading, playing the flute in community theater productions, and tossing a Frisbee with the family dog, Buster.
>
> She is survived by her loving parents, Mrs Susan Whittaker King of Chicago, Illinois and Mr Patrick J. Madison of Annapolis and West Palm Beach, Florida, her maternal grandparents, several uncles and aunts, and numerous cousins. A sister, Cecelia, predeceased her.
>
> In lieu of flowers, contributions may be made to St John's College Greenfield Library. Arrangements by Kramer and Sons.

'I can't even,' I muttered as I flopped back in my chair. *Two* daughters dead. One murdered, and the other . . . who knew?

I wondered if Cecelia's death had anything to do with the break-up of the Madison's marriage. I was only three when my infant sister, Mary Rose, died in her sleep, but I still remember the toll it took on my parents. In some ways, my mother never got over it, until a fatal heart attack at the age of sixty-six relieved her of the grief and the guilt.

I did the math. If Amy's parents were still alive, they'd be well into their eighties by now.

I consulted Professor Google, starting with Patrick J. Several candidates got eliminated right away, including a Patrick N., age sixty-six, who 'roared off to heaven on his Harley to be with his Heavenly Father' back in 2015. We should all be so lucky! A police officer who died of Covid in St Louis, Missouri was way too young, and so was the creep currently serving a twenty-year sentence in Kentucky State Prison for forcible sodomy and a string of other sexual offenses. Ugh.

I took a refreshing break from dangerous felons and wandered upstairs to open a Coke and pour it over ice into an insulated tumbler. Back at my desk, I sipped thoughtfully as I continued browsing the Madisons, wishing Patrick had been born with a more unusual surname, like Bidelspatch. I'd half-finished the Coke when I stumbled upon him, at least six screens down and with a different middle initial, but clearly my guy. I followed the link to the *Palm Beach Post*. Patrick Ian Madison had been a successful real estate developer in Florida. He died in 2010 at the age of seventy-one, and 'two daughters, Cecelia and Amy, predeceased him'. No mention of a wife or an ex-wife, but once again I'd been sucked down the research rabbit hole, so I knew I'd wander back to his ex once I finished stalking him.

From Zillow I learned that Patrick had done very well for himself. At the time of his death he owned a development company that bore his name, and was living in a charming, mission-style home on Palmetto Drive in West Palm Beach. The house was back on the market, so I took a virtual tour. I would have bought the place in an instant if I had an extra one million seven gathering dust. I closed Zillow and made a pit stop over at GenTree where I jotted down the information that Patrick had been born in Oak Park, Illinois, a wealthy suburb of Chicago, and had attended DePaul University which is probably less staunchly Catholic now than it was then.

Amy's mother was a bigger challenge. Like Elizabeth Taylor Hilton Wilding Todd Fisher Burton Burton Warner Fortensky, Susan Whittaker had added several additional surnames to the string following King on her marital résumé by the time I finally located her and Carleton Oakes, husband number four, living in The Villages, a sprawling, age fifty-five-plus golf cart community in central Florida about ninety miles north of Orlando. Courtesy of the comprehensive online collection of telephone directories at the Library of Congress, I jotted down Susan's address and phone number, at least one that had been current two years prior. According to the online edition of *The Villages Daily Sun*, the staunchly conservative local rag, neither Susan nor Carleton had appeared among the frequent obituaries, so I assumed they were still happily tooting around the village in a pimped-up golf cart, enjoying golf, mahjong and daily two-for-one cocktail hours like their neighbors.

I set my empty tumbler down next to the computer, tilted my chair far enough back so I could prop my sock-clad feet up on the desk and ask myself why on earth I was poking around in Amy's life. Her father was beyond reach of all but the angels, and I wasn't about to telephone Amy's mother and say, 'Hello, you don't know me, but I was just visiting your daughter's grave in Maryland and decided to track you down for no particular reason and intrude upon your life.'

I was still mulling it over when I heard the thud of the front door and Paul's cheery, 'Hello, sweetie, I'm home!' I logged off the computer and wandered upstairs to greet him.

'How was your day?' I asked, as I always did.

'Fair to middlin,' he responded as I turned my face up to receive the usual peck on the cheek. 'What's for dinner?' he asked.

My eyes wandered over to the ground beef, sitting thoroughly thawed on the kitchen counter, but stubbornly refusing to turn itself into burger patties or anything remotely resembling dinner.

'Ask me again in five minutes,' I said, as I opened the pantry door and started rummaging.

FIVE

Ring My Bell (Anita Ward)

By the time Paul returned to the kitchen, he had changed into shorts and a T-shirt. From my position crouched in front of the fridge, pawing through the vegetable drawer, I answered his earlier question. 'Oriental beef, if I can find the ginger that's gotta be in here somewhere.'

Paul reached over my shoulder and liberated a bottle of chilled pinot grigio from a shelf in the door. 'May I pour you a glass?'

'Tah dah!' I said, holding up the fresh ginger root for his inspection. 'And yes to the wine.'

I measured jasmine rice into the rice cooker and set the timer, then set to work with a chopping knife. By the time the beef was nicely browned and fragrant with the aroma of sauteed garlic and ginger, I'd filled Paul in on my visit to the cemetery, my conversation with Isabel Randall and what I had been up to in the basement all afternoon.

'You can't help it, can you?' Paul grinned when he said it, to let me know he was pulling my chain.

'Guilty,' I said, as I stirred a blend of brown sugar, soy sauce and toasted sesame oil into the beef mixture. I bobbed my head in the direction of the refrigerator. 'Can you throw a salad together? If you look hard, you might even find an avocado in there.'

'My pleasure.' Paul stood, shook the kinks out of his long legs, then wandered over to the fridge. While he balanced an assortment of leafy greens, celery, scallions, carrots and a pint of cherry tomatoes in an orderly row along his arm, I sprinkled an extra eighth of a teaspoon of red pepper flakes over the beef. We like Asian food spicy.

Paul dumped the salad ingredients on the counter nearest the microwave, then dove shoulder-deep into the back of the fridge in an effort to locate the wayward avocado. 'If I'm not back in five minutes, send in a search party,' he quipped. I was cheering him on from the sidelines, waving a wooden stirring spoon like a baton, when he emerged, triumphant, holding the avocado aloft like a trophy.

That's when my cell phone burbled.

With the hand holding the wooden spoon, I leaned over the table to tap the display. The call was coming from a number I didn't recognize, but it was from the 667 area code reserved for Baltimore. My Robo-Killer app hadn't blocked the caller as potential spam, so I decided to pick up.

'Hello?'

'Is this Hannah Ives?' The voice sounded vaguely familiar.

'Who's calling, please?'

'This is Izzy Randall. We met at St Luke's Cemetery earlier today.'

'Oh, yes?' I took a breath and was about to ask 'and how did you get my number?' before realizing that, duh, Izzy was an award-winning investigative reporter. Of course she knew how to track down my phone number.

'I enjoyed our conversation, Hannah, and a couple of things you said rang some bells, so I've been reading up on you.'

I had to laugh. 'Surely you have more important things to do, Izzy.'

'I'm serious. Based on your background, I have a proposal for you.'

'My background?' I asked, genuinely perplexed.

'May I refresh your memory?' When I didn't answer, she plowed on. 'The young girl dumped down the well in South County? That ballroom dancer who died of thallium poisoning? The pedophile who fell overboard while you and your sisters were sailing aboard that cruise ship? Some dead guy in a fish tank out at Calvert Colony?' Izzy went on to remind me of situations where, like a Jessica Fletcher wannabe, I'd found myself stumbling over a body and getting deeply involved in a murder investigation. Surprisingly, Izzy even knew about my run-in with Bigfoot out in Flat Rock, Oregon. A tip of the hat to the woman for that. She'd also probably heard about the incident in Denver where I solved a case while being a mile high on marijuana (by accident, I swear!), but if she did, she was polite enough not to mention it. Recreational marijuana was still illegal in Maryland.

'But the work you did on that viatical and life settlement fraud case,' Izzy continued, 'that was a real eye-opener for me.'

I felt my face flush. 'It was news for a lot of people,' I said. 'Investing in the life insurance policies of terminally ill people seems like a creepy way to make a buck. And I lost Valerie, a good friend, because of it. She was way too young to die.'

'I'm sorry,' Izzy said. And as the silence lengthened between us, I imagined she was thinking about Amy Madison's life cut short, too.

'So, what kind of proposal?' I asked after a moment.

Paul had been listening to my end of the conversation calmly, but when the word 'proposal' came up, he laid the vegetable peeler down on the cutting board and gave me his undivided attention.

'I'm wondering if you might have time over the next couple of days to join me for coffee. There are some people I'd like you to meet,' Izzy said.

'What kind of people?' I asked warily. Just because I used to watch this woman every night on the *Six O'Clock News* didn't mean I *knew* her.

'Citizen detectives, like you,' she said. 'Volunteers. In our spare time, we work on cold cases. Cases like Amy Madison's.'

'Depends,' I replied, glancing at my husband. 'When my husband travels with the offshore sailing team as kind of a glorified chaperone, he cautions the midshipmen to stay out of three places: hospitals, newspapers and jail.' As I spoke, I noticed Paul nodding vigorously. 'But it hasn't always worked out that way for me,' I confessed.

'From what I hear, you hit the trifecta,' Izzy said.

As a cancer survivor, I'd had my fill of hospitals, thank you very much, and it's true that my name had appeared in newspapers from time to time, as Izzy had clearly discovered. 'You must be referring to the Jennifer Goodall case,' I said, recalling the time I'd spent as a guest of the Feds, held in the custody of the US Marshall's Office in Baltimore on suspicion of her murder. I hadn't bludgeoned Lieutenant Goodall to death with a hammer, of course, but I'd hated her so much for her false sexual harassment accusations against my husband that if I'd been the FBI I would have arrested my ass, too.

'There are three of us,' Izzy explained. 'A small group, but we take on orphan cases and are kind of passionate about it. I've got connections in the media, natch, and I think your online research skills will complement the background and experience of the two others.'

'Who are?' I asked.

'Jack's a former Baltimore homicide detective and he's expert at sweet-talking police departments out of evidence and official case files. The other member is Mark Wallis, a retired Navy chaplain. He's got a master's degree in criminal psychology.'

Paul was making a time-out motion with his hands, but I was so intrigued by the credentials of Izzy's team and the potential of its collaborative efforts, that I waved him off and said, 'Let's talk. When and where?'

'How about Barnes and Noble,' she said. 'Thursday at ten?'

'I'll be there,' I said, then added with a sideways glance at Paul, 'but absolutely no promises.'

'Understand completely,' Izzy said, then she chuckled. 'I'll leave it to the boys to convince you.'

'Tell them I might be a tough nut to crack,' I said before ending the call and turning my attention back to the stove.

'Let me guess,' Paul said before I had the chance to brief him.

'She's asked me to join her cold case group,' I explained while giving the beef another stir. 'I imagine they're working on the Amy Madison case and need a bit of help. There's just the three of them.'

At the mention of cold case, Paul seemed to relax. He picked up the peeler and began scraping carrot shavings into the salad. 'Families who have lost loved ones to violence certainly deserve closure,' he observed. 'But seems to me that's the job of law enforcement.'

'Cold cases,' I reminded him. 'Stone cold. Law enforcement gave up on them a long time ago.'

'I get it,' Paul said while giving the salad a toss with the tongs. 'Just be careful, Hannah.'

'I wouldn't worry. Amy's case is so old, I suspect the perpetrator's already dead.' I plated up the rice and beef and topped each serving with a scattering of finely sliced scallions. 'Besides, I haven't agreed to anything yet.'

'It'll be interesting to hear what Izzy has to say,' Paul said as he pulled out a chair and sat down in front of his plate.

'Chopsticks?' I asked.

'*Dui,*' said Paul in his elementary Chinese, so I grabbed two pair of *kuaizi* from the utility drawer and sat down to join him.

'Yummy,' I sighed as I dug my chopsticks into dinner, 'if I do say so myself.'

'*Hen hao chi,*' Paul said. '*Xie-Xie,* Hannah Ives.'

SIX

Take a Chance on Me (ABBA)

Thursday finally rolled around, and for some insane reason, I dithered in front of my closet, unable to decide what to wear. I'd obviously impressed Izzy, but what about the two guys? I'd long ago sent my Dress For Success suits and sensible Cole Hahn block heel pumps to Goodwill, so which of my remaining outfits conveyed intelligence and competence with a *soupçon* of relaxed congeniality?

I chided myself for harking back to grade school insecurities as our family moved from school to school, following the peripatetic naval career of my officer father. Until I settled down in Annapolis with Paul, I'd never lived anywhere longer than two or three years. First impressions were important, I had learned that, so I found myself hoping that Jack and Mark would like what they saw and heard, even if I decided not to join their group.

I finally settled on a white, scoop-neck, long-sleeved T-shirt and fresh-from-the-dry-cleaner chinos. After another minute of indecision, I slipped my feet into a pair of comfortable black flats. Before leaving the house, I plucked a denim jacket, heavily embroidered in a *Dia de los Muertos* motif, out of the coat closet. The air conditioning at the bookstore was often set on freeze.

The Annapolis Barnes and Noble is in the Harbour Center, which is not central to anything nor anywhere near the harbor, although the entrance was decorated with a dinghy gloomily marooned on a grassy traffic island. I parked in front of Old Navy, grabbed the bookbag containing my purse and a notebook, and entered the bookstore. I turned left past the table of new releases stickered at twenty percent off and, just past the CD racks, mounted the short flight of stairs that led to the Starbucks concession.

Izzy and her gang were already there, grouped around a table at the far end not far from the bakery case. Izzy caught sight of me and waved me over. As I neared their table, both guys stood up. Contrary to popular belief, I thought with a grin, chivalry is not dead.

'Hannah, this is Jack Shelton,' Izzy said, 'the retired cop I told you about.'

It had taken Jack a few extra seconds to unfold his long legs from under the table, push back his chair and extend himself to his full height. He was so tall that I had to take a step backwards in order to meet his eyes, which were hazel.

'Pleased to meet you, Hannah,' Jack said. His hand devoured mine, but his squeeze was gentle.

'Ditto,' I said with a smile, still holding his hand while I took in his abundant silver hair, laced here and there with strands of the dark brown it used to be. Bushy eyebrows matching his hair shaded his eyes like awnings. Jack was dressed in a red polo shirt tucked into a pair of Levis and secured by a belt embroidered with the distinctive logo of the Eastport Yacht Club. When he released my hand, I pointed at the belt. 'You sail?'

He gave me a bright, gap-toothed smile. 'Busted.'

'My husband does, too,' I said. 'With the Naval Academy offshore team.'

Turning to the guy who had to be Mark, Izzy said, 'And this is Captain Mark Wallis, Chaplain Corps, You-Ess-Enn, retired.'

I had to smile at her use of Mark's full title. I nodded and extended my hand. 'Nice to meet you, Captain.'

'Mark, please.'

Mark stood a few inches taller than me, maybe five foot eight, built straight up and down, solid as a fireplug. Like me he was dressed in chinos and a T-shirt, although his tee was patterned in blue-gray camo. 'I haven't seen blueberries in a while,' I said, indicating his shirt.

His dark eyes twinkled behind round, wire-frame eyeglasses. 'The Navy declared that uniform obsolete in 2019. Turns out they made sailors harder to see only when they fell overboard. Back to the regular green camo these days,' he said with a chuckle, 'but I held on to a couple of blueberries for sentimental reasons.'

It was hard to tell the color of Mark's hair because it was buzz-cut, shorn high and tight, a style he had favored, I later learned, since serving with the 3d Marine Battalion in Iraq. A pair of dog tags hung around his neck. I suspected it was not a fashion statement. 'We'll wait while you get yourself some coffee,' Mark said. 'Nobody's on a time clock here.'

I readily agreed and headed for the counter where I placed my order and waited while the barista whipped up a vente mocha frappucino, no whipped cream. At the fixings bar, I plopped a straw through the hole in the clear plastic lid, wrapped one of the cardboard sleeves around the base of the cup to soak up any moisture, and returned to the table.

Once I got settled, Izzy wasted no time getting down to business. 'I've already briefed the guys on your background, Hannah.'

'Such as it is,' I said.

'Don't sell yourself short,' Jack cut in. 'You've obviously got the curiosity and dogged energy required for the job.'

'And the research skills,' Mark added. 'Librarian, right?'

'Close,' I corrected. 'Records manager at Whitworth and Sullivan, a big DC accounting firm.' I smiled. 'But that was ages ago. I don't miss the commute one bit.'

'I hear you.' Jack raised his cup, toasting me with what looked like a latte. 'Before the kids came, my wife worked in DC.' He took a sip of his latte. 'Department of Interior, Bureau of Indian Affairs, although it's just Indian Affairs now.'

'My niece, Julie, is teaching school on the Pine Ridge Reservation in South Dakota,' I said. 'Gap year. Part of our heritage, as it turns out.'

Izzy's eyebrows shot up. 'Oh?'

From her expression, I gathered she'd missed that tidbit of information while delving into my bona fides.

'Long story,' I said, as my eyes scanned my companions' faces over my straw. I didn't know these people, but surely . . .

'Nancy, my wife, is half Navajo,' Jack said. 'Shall we compare notes?'

'And my mother was an ensign on the starship *Enterprise*,'

Izzy said in a let's-get-down-to-business voice. 'Life stories later,' she added with a grin, leaving no doubt who was in charge.

'So,' she began, laying her hands flat on the tabletop. 'Let's see if we can't talk Hannah into joining us.'

I raised my hand, waved it a bit, like a kid asking for a bathroom break. 'First, please tell me why you need me.'

'In a minute. But, before we get into all that, let's give you some background information. Jack?'

Jack, sitting to Izzy's right, got an encouraging nudge with her elbow. 'I'm your go-to guy for police records. If a case is cold enough, it's pretty easy to get the files you need, but for more recent cases, say in the last ten years, it takes a bit of sweet-talk, particularly if you want to examine the evidence left at the crime scene or send it out for independent analysis.'

'Jack goes over everything with a fine tooth-comb. We all do, actually, but he's got the policeman's eye for details we might overlook.'

'Worked Baltimore County homicide for twenty years,' Jack explained, 'until I got between a suspect and his estranged girlfriend and took a bullet in the back.' He winced. '*She* shot me, not him,' he added. 'The guy was a scumbag, but he was her meal ticket. In any case, I had to retire on disability.'

'Ouch, I'm sorry,' I said.

Jack waved my concerns away. 'Only hurts when it rains. Over to you, Mark.'

'I'm not sure what you'd call me.' Mark paused, brow furrowed.

'A witness whisperer,' Izzy chimed in. 'Mark is super tuned in to issues that people are going through, like mentally or physically. It's uncanny, like he can read people's minds, empathize with what's bothering them and draw them out.'

Mark's face flushed. 'Izzy makes it sound like I'm psychic, Hannah. I'm not.'

Izzy flapped a hand, dismissing his modesty. 'Call it whatever you want, as long as it works.

'Me?' she rattled on. 'I track down old leads and follow up

with new ones. Witnesses are sometimes more comfortable speaking to reporters than they are to cops, and relatives are grateful that their loved one hasn't been forgotten. Mostly they're hoping that you'll get their story back out there. That somebody, somewhere, will see it and remember something that will crack the case wide open.'

I leaned forward, resting my arms on the table. 'So, how did you all get together?'

Izzy smiled, then glanced at Jack. 'I ran into Jack two years ago February while standing in the ticket line at the Lyric to see *My Favorite Murders*. We got to talking . . .' She shrugged. 'Jack brought Mark along a couple of months later. They're golf buddies.

'We've been coasting along for a couple of years,' she continued, 'but recent developments in DNA have greatly expanded what we can do. Have you heard of forensic genetic genealogy searching?'

I nodded. 'Solved a lot of cold cases recently, like the Golden State Killer.'

'Joseph DeAngelo. Exactly. Before FGGS, any DNA profile you got would have to match up with one already in CODIS. If the perpetrator or a close relative didn't have a record in the FBI system, you'd come up empty.

'Recently, though,' she continued, 'we've sometimes been able to get ahold of case DNA and run the profiles through recreational genetic databases like GEDmatch. You might recall that DeAngelo was identified by a partial match to his great-great-great-grandparents. Researchers built a family tree and drilled down from there. Collected a surreptitious sample of his DNA and bingo!'

'I'm familiar,' I said, 'but didn't Maryland recently pass a law that you have to have a warrant to access those genetic databases for law enforcement purposes? Invasion of privacy and all that?'

'Total bullshit,' Jack spat out. 'DNA genetics is the best tool law enforcement ever had to get at the truth.' He paused. 'Just think about it. If you could catch a rapist after his first or second attack, you could take the word "serial" out of serial rapist.'

'It's the Wild Wild West out there right now,' Mark added. 'Inevitable that somebody will try to tame it.'

'Frankly,' I said, 'if my cousin were a serial killer, I'd be the first person standing in line holding the DNA sample that would turn him in.'

'We all would,' Jack muttered.

Mark laughed. 'I hear you. The new laws won't make it easy, for sure, but it's better than what we had before, which was nothing.'

'Besides,' Izzy added, 'Maryland's law doesn't go into effect until October, so that's one reason we're eager to push ahead now. Long-range familial searches, building those family trees, can be a tedious process requiring close attention to detail.'

'Is that where I come in?' I asked.

'Primarily, but we work as a team. Share the load.'

'How many cases are you working on?' I asked.

Mark spoke first. 'Solved two, so far. Tracked down the identity of a sixteen-year-old girl who was murdered on the WB&A bike trail more than fifteen years ago.'

'Wanda Hudson? I remember reading about her. And the other?'

'That was a heart-breaker,' Mike said. 'Aberdeen Baby Doe, found in a suitcase behind the Maryland House Travel Plaza. M.E. said she'd been shaken to death.'

'The victim's older sister always wondered what happened to her baby sister,' Izzy added. 'Kept having flashbacks she couldn't understand. Got tested, put her family tree up on Ancestry. Even had a Facebook page, called Justice of Francine.'

'That's how we first got our name,' Mark said.

'Name?' I asked.

'The Chesapeake Justice League.'

I must have looked surprised because Izzy said, 'What? You don't approve?'

'Oh, no, the name's great,' I chuckled. 'I just had this sudden image of you wearing superhero uniforms.'

'I left my shield at home this morning,' Mark said with a grin.

'And my cape's at the dry cleaners,' Jack added.

Izzy pouted. 'Sadly, a philanthropist out in Las Vegas was already using the term justice league, so if we refer to ourselves as anything at all, it's the Silent Sleuths.'

'The SS,' Mark cut in. 'Has a nice ring to it.'

'Very funny, Mark,' Izzy said.

'We're entering a bit of new territory here,' Jack said, drawing everyone's attention back to the matter at hand. 'Both previous cases involved identifying homicide victims, but this is the first time we've attempted to use FGGS to track down a killer.'

'And I've built family trees before,' I confessed to the group, 'but never anything very elaborate.'

'We live in hope that a perp has a father, mother, brother, sister, son or daughter who has a DNA profile up on Ancestry,' Izzy said, 'but that rarely happens. Usually, you're working with third and fourth cousins on branches of a tree that sprawl all over creation.'

'Or a spreadsheet,' Mike cut in.

'So, say you're able to ID the perp. What do you do next?' I said, looking directly at Jack. 'Clap plastic cuffs on the guy and haul him in?'

'Nope. We turn the evidence we've collected over to the police. They handle it from there.'

During our discussion, I'd completely forgotten about my frappuccino. To gain time to think about what I'd heard, I picked up the cup and took a leisurely sip. Then another, studying their faces over the rim of the cup. After what seemed like minutes but was probably only seconds, I said, 'Meticulous record-keeping is my middle name.'

Izzy smiled. She arched an eyebrow. Her eyes wandered from Jack to Mark and back to me again. 'Good. Then let's get started.'

'Let me guess,' I said. 'Amy Madison.'

Izzy nodded.

'Tell me how far along you are in the process,' I asked.

'About a month ago, Anne Arundel County Police sent the DNA from the crime scene out for comprehensive analysis at Hexagon Labs over in Frederick. Fortunately, there was plenty of it: hair, saliva, semen, fibers. We're hoping that after forty-some years it's not too badly degraded. We won't see any results for a couple more weeks, at least.'

'We know that Amy had sex with two men that night,' Jack said. 'Whether consensual or not is anybody's guess.'

'As I mentioned to you earlier,' Izzy said, 'Amy's father had a summer place near Pasadena on the Magothy. It's long gone, of course. Nothing but a high-end housing development up that way now, but that's definitely where the poor girl was murdered. From the evidence, there had been quite a party going on in that cottage.'

'You all are way ahead of me,' I said. 'I'll need to be brought up to speed. Police file?'

Izzy spoke first. 'I'll email it to you. The autopsy report, too. We'll be interested in what you think, fresh eyes and all that.'

'Have you ever seen a police report?' Jack asked.

I nodded. 'Once or twice,' I admitted, shading the truth just a tad. 'My brother-in-law was a cop down in Chesapeake County. Lieutenant Dennis Rutherford. Retired now. Did you know him?'

Jack shook his head. 'Never had the pleasure. My patch was up in Baltimore County, so our paths never crossed.'

'One more thing,' I said. 'You said you're working locally with Hexagon Labs. Are they anything like Parabon, Orthrom, or Verogen?'

'Cutting edge,' Izzy said. 'Parabon is even experimenting with software that predicts the physical appearance of a suspect from an analysis of his DNA.'

'Pure fucking magic,' Jack said.

'Then why do you need me? Don't those companies have people who do the FGGS for you?'

'They sure do,' Jack said. 'But . . .' He rubbed his thumb vigorously against his index and middle finger.

I grinned. 'Ah, money. Why am I not surprised?'

'It costs one thousand five hundred dollars just to process a sample,' Izzy explained. 'More if they need to rescue it using mitochondrial DNA analysis. FGGS adds another three thousand five hundred dollars to the tab.'

'Some families have the means to pay outright, but

others . . .' Izzy paused. 'It breaks my heart to see how easy
it is to crowd-source a DNA profile for a dead child, but a
black teenager, especially a young male . . .' Her voice trailed
off.

'Who's paying for Amy's analysis?' I asked.

Izzy's face flushed. 'I am.'

After a moment of silence, I asked, 'Do you have a preferred
service?'

'In the past, we've used a combination. GEDmatch has
some pretty powerful autocluster and autotree tools, but
since their users are required to opt-in in order for us to access
their profiles, and less than twenty-five percent of users
have done so, it's clearly not ideal. Ancestry and 23andMe
severely limit how police can use their data, requiring a
search warrant, yada yada yada. Fortunately, FamilyTree
has no such restrictions. Yet . . .' She paused. 'In general, we
start with Ancestry, which has the larger database by far.'

'I know some people avoid using Ancestry because it's
expensive,' I said, 'but I have a full subscription, including
World, Newspapers and the military files, so I'm good to go.
I always check the free sites, too, starting with GenTree and
moving on to MyHeritage, FamilyTreeDNA, GEDmatch,
LivingDNA and Geneanet. Who am I forgetting?'

Izzy grinned. 'That about covers it.'

Mark turned to Izzy. 'Hire this woman before she gets away.'

'I'm in complete agreement,' Jack said.

I felt my face flush. 'OK, then. Sounds fascinating. If I sign
up, do I get a free cup of coffee?'

SEVEN

The Second Time Around (Shalamar)

When the email from Izzy came through, as promised, I was sitting in front of the computer waiting for it, killing time by playing Words With Friends on my iPhone. I downloaded Madison.zip to my desktop, clicked on its icon and then sat back in growing horror as file after file after file began to populate the computer screen. Crime scene log. Death report. Evidence report. Lab report. Vehicle report. Victim information. Witness statements. Officer at scene notes. On and on and on. Twenty-five files in all by the time the Zip file ran out of steam at Miscellaneous.

Had I bitten off more than I could chew?

I responded to Izzy's email with a simple thank you, promising that I'd look at the files in the morning when I had a brain, then wandered upstairs to whine about the situation to Paul. I found him sprawled on the sofa watching a docudrama about Vikings on TV. Hobie, the Lynx Point Siamese cat, who in spite of the late hour was visiting from across the street, was curled up on his lap.

I plopped down next to Paul, reached out to give Hobie a gentle scratch behind the ears, then filled Paul in on my meeting with the Sleuths. 'I told them that I'd seen police reports before,' I said, as Hobie arched his neck into my hand and purred with contentment, 'but obviously I've seen only *parts* of police reports. The darn thing is massive. I hardly know where to begin.'

'Begin with what you need to know.'

'That's just it, I won't know what I need to know until I need to know it.'

Paul laughed out loud, causing Hobie to open his eyes in languid alarm. 'If it were me, I'd want to know the police theory of the crime, probably take a look at the crime scene

photos if they have any, and check out the autopsy report.' He
reached for the remote and pressed mute, cutting Ragnar
Lothbrok off in mid primal scream. 'From what you've told
me, there's not much you can do on your part until the DNA
results come back, anyway.'

'True,' I said. 'And I figure it's not too late to back out.'

'When have you ever backed out of anything, Hannah?'

'The curse of the A-type personality,' I said. 'Besides, they're
genuinely nice people doing important work, and I want to be
a part of it. Working quietly behind the scenes, volunteering
my time, seeking justice, not recognition, really appeals to me.'

'Then you have your answer.' Paul gave my knee a squeeze.

'Still, I'll sleep on it,' I said, then stood to go.

Paul aimed the remote. Ragnar went back to slaughtering
terrified villagers, Hobie resumed dozing, and I headed
upstairs to bed.

I slept fitfully. Nightmares fueled by my imagination, and
what the Silent Sleuths had already told me about what must
have been Amy's final, fearful minutes, kept me popping in
and out of bed, first to use the bathroom, then to get a glass
of water – a vicious cycle if there ever was one – until I gave
up around five. Leaving Paul to sleep until his alarm jolted
him awake at seven, I wandered down to the kitchen, popped
a K-cup into the Keurig and waited for it to brew, then
carried the steaming mug of coffee down to the office.

Four hours and two mugs of coffee later, I had not learned
much more about the theory of the crime than I'd already
managed to glean from articles that came out in the *Sun* and
the *Capital* back in 1978.

After several hours of drinking and dancing, around nine
o'clock, Amy had been seen leaving Doots' Bar in the
company of a young man. One of the witnesses, a bartender
named Donna Crowe, told police that the guy said he was
a student at the University of Maryland or maybe Georgetown,
and she might have heard Amy call him Rick or maybe
Nick. The bar had been packed that night, so if there had
been anyone else paying particular attention to Amy, Donna
didn't notice.

Somehow, Amy ended up at her father's summer cottage where a party took place, attended by three, possibly four people – Amy, the two men and, based on synthetic blonde hair fibers found behind the bar, another person, probably a woman. Hair samples and semen left on a blanket spread out on the floor near the fireplace confirmed that Amy had sex with the two men. At some point, the sex turned violent. Skin samples under Amy's fingernails indicated she tried to ward off her attacker, but in the struggle, her hyoid bone was crushed and she suffocated. Police speculated that the killer dragged her body to the end of the pier and dumped it into the Magothy River. It was discovered early the following morning caught under a neighboring pier by a fisherman, who recognized the victim and called police.

Amy was found fully clothed, but barefoot. Her bra was unfastened and her panties on backwards, indicating that the killer had re-dressed the body post-mortem.

The crime scene photographs showed the interior of the Madisons' summer cottage, tented yellow number cards completely spoiling the interior designer's airy, laid-back, coastal-chic decor. Liquor bottles, highball glasses and ashtrays overflowing with cigarette butts littered the furniture, and record album covers lay strewn across the carpet. When crime scene investigators arrived, the stereo system was still on, a Rolling Stones LP rotating on the turntable.

Although the killer, or killers, had made a decent attempt to wipe up behind them, partial fingerprints, none of them deemed useable, were collected at the scene.

Police had interviewed Amy's date, Keith Ritchie, and his story about being delayed in rush hour traffic had checked out. He was not a suspect.

Amy's car, a yellow, late-model Triumph TR6, was located parked at the lower end of King George Street, across from the St John's boathouse. It had been left unlocked, its ignition keys tucked under the front seat. Amy's roommate, Alice Watts, told police Amy usually parked in the college's gymnasium parking lot, but if spaces were full, she'd park on the street until a space on campus opened up. It was her habit to leave the keys inside the car in case she needed to

send someone else, like Alice, to move it. On May 29, the
few fingerprints in the car were Amy's, which didn't surprise
Alice because Amy was anal about wiping down the dash
and upholstery with ArmorAll. Police speculated that Amy
had not driven her car at all that night, but had accepted a
ride to the cottage with her killer.

After reading the evidence report, I felt confident that
Hexagon Labs would have plenty of material on which to
work their magic. As Jack had mentioned, the partiers had left
partial fingerprints, hair, semen, saliva, and wig and clothing
fibers strewn all about the cottage. Although no tire tracks
appeared in the gravel driveway, someone wearing a size 12C
Nike 'waffle racer' had stepped into the mud at the base of
the pier leaving a dandy impression.

The reports, for the most part, were written in English
just about anyone could understand, but there were a few
notes that needed clarification. Rather than showcase
my ignorance to the Sleuths at this early stage of our relationship, I decided to telephone my brother-in-law, Dennis
Rutherford, the retired cop.

When Dennis picked up, he was out in the field, discussing
the weather (he said) with Buttercup, one of the cows. Dennis
and Connie tended a herd of Dexters, pint-sized cows –
averaging 600 pounds – originally from Ireland, that produce
rich milk, high in butterfat. Dexters are also known for
their lean, well-marbled beef, but we don't discuss that in
front of Buttercup.

When he finished his chores, Dennis returned my call via
Facetime.

Facetime! Ack! I was still in my PJs!

I answered the call anyway, doing my best to angle the
camera so that my Betty Boop sleep shirt stayed out of
camera range.

Connie was teaching an art class at the West River assisted
living facility, Dennis explained, so he was fending for
himself for lunch, with the telephone propped up against the
toaster.

While he fixed himself a ham and cheese sandwich with
lettuce and sliced tomatoes, I described what I knew about

the Amy Madison case and how I would be involved with the Sleuths in the genetic tracking effort. 'Are you shocked that I'm not up to my usual tricks? Meddling, or sticking my nose into somebody else's business?'

'Gold star for you,' Dennis said, brandishing a mayonnaise-covered knife. 'Seriously. I vaguely remember the Madison case, but it was a long time ago.'

'More than forty years. It'll be a while before the DNA results come back from Hexagon, but Izzy emailed me copies of the police files, and I'm kind of overwhelmed. I've spent the morning going over everything, but there are a couple of things that I thought you might be able to help me understand.' I paused. 'The autopsy report is particularly hard going.'

'They always are. Just be thankful it's not about a six-year-old who got shot up by a maniac with an AK-47.'

I shuddered, drew a deep breath. When the Sandy Hook massacre happened in 2012, my grandson, Timothy, had been six, the same age as all of the young victims. I'd had nightmares for weeks. 'I didn't need that, Dennis.'

He'd finished assembling the sandwich. A yellow bag of potato chips hove into view. 'I didn't think. Sorry.'

'I'll get back to Amy's autopsy in a minute. But first, I want to ask you about the toxicology report. Apparently, Amy was high on drugs. According to the medical examiner, her blood alcohol level was 0.17 percent. There was a THC reading of 3.7, which is Greek to me, and 25 mg of methaqualone in her blood plasma.' I paused. 'Methaqualone. That's Quaalude, right? What they used to call disco biscuits or 714s?'

Dennis's brow furrowed, then he gave a long, slow whistle.

'What's that whistle mean?' I asked.

'It means, I hope she wasn't driving.'

'Would Amy have been conscious?' I asked.

'Maybe. How much did she weigh?'

I knew the answer to that. 'Around one-twenty-two.'

'If she had built up a tolerance for the drugs, she might have been staggering around, but seriously, a combination like that could prove fatal.'

'It wasn't the drugs that killed her. She was strangled, remember?' I paused for a moment as an idea occurred to me.

'Maybe she drove to the cottage and *then* somebody spiked her drink with a 'lude when she wasn't looking.'

Dennis furrowed his brow speculatively. 'If so, it certainly would have made her more vulnerable to a sexual attack. It'd be harder to resist when your limbs are as boneless as jello.'

'Ugh,' I said.

'Agreed.' After a moment of silence, Dennis spoke again. 'You said there were a couple of things.'

'True. According to the autopsy report, Amy's hyoid bone had been crushed, and not in the usual way I would think about strangulation, you know, somebody wraps his hands around your neck and squeezes, with the thumbs pressing in and making bruises. There were no ligature marks, either, like there would have been if she had been hanged, or the guy had strangled her with a rope or a belt. I've tried to visualize the scene, and it seems to me that while the guy was raping her, she fought back, and so he held her down by putting a lot of pressure on her neck, like with his forearm, maybe?' I paused for breath. 'How much pressure do you think it would take to crush a small woman's hyoid bone?'

On my iPhone screen, I watched Dennis take a bite of his sandwich and chew thoughtfully. 'Not much. Seven pounds, max.'

'That's kinda what I thought.'

I waited until Dennis set his sandwich down on a paper plate before asking, 'Could you do me a favor?'

'Oh, oh,' he said with a teasing smile. 'Here it comes!'

'Stop it!' I laughed. 'What if I send you some of these reports so you can look them over. See if there's anything that leaps out at you.'

'I'm retired, Hannah.'

'Seriously, Dennis. It's really overwhelming.'

'I was teasing. Of course I'll do it. Connie's away the rest of the day, so other than the cows, I don't have any distractions. Bring it on.'

'Thank you!' I blew a kiss into the phone.

'I'll call you back in a day or two. Is that OK?'

'Perfect! You're a *mensch*.'

'That's what all my girlfriends say.'

EIGHT

Where Do We Go From Here (Trammps)

O ver the course of the next two days, while I waited for Dennis to call me back, I decided to do some prep work. Even though I had no DNA profiles to attach to them yet, I signed on to GenTree and created family trees for each of the two suspects, calling one family 'Lewis' and the other 'Clark'. Both were males, of course, and I made a guess about their ages, settling for a birth year of 1958, the same year as Amy's.

Although there are a number of online tools to help researchers organize DNA matches, I prefer to use good, old-fashioned Excel spreadsheets that can be printed, taped together and spread out, accordion-like, over the kitchen table in preparation for some serious pondering.

Back in 2018, while working with an adoptee to help identify her biological father, a 'search angel' named Dana Leeds developed a brilliantly simple method of clustering second-, third- and fourth-cousin DNA matches by color, making it easier to identify common ancestors. Using Leeds's format, I created two blank templates and saved them as Lewis and Clark in a new desktop folder called 'Amy'.

With nothing more to do until the DNA results came in, I decided it was time to wash the living- and dining-room curtains, a project that had been on my Spring Cleaning To-Do List for at least three of the previous four springs. Before leaving for class, Paul helped wrestle the curtains off the rods and lugged them down to the laundry room where I stuffed them, two panels at a time, into the washing machine. An hour later, I was mourning the disintegrated remains of the sun-damaged damask panels that had hung over the windows at the south side of the house, when the landline rang. I hustled upstairs and managed to answer it on the fourth ring with a breathy hello.

'Did I get you at a bad time?' Dennis asked.

'Not really,' I panted. 'Was down in the basement washing curtains. It didn't end well.'

'Who won, you or the curtains?'

'Definitely the curtains. They dissolved. It's a good thing I have a fistful of Bed Bath and Beyond coupons tacked to the bulletin board. Twenty percent off.' I paused to catch my breath. 'In other bad news, now that the curtains are down, I can see how badly the windows need washing.'

Dennis clucked sympathetically. 'As I reminded Connie just the other day, there are people who will wash windows for you.' He paused. 'Just to be clear, I am not volunteering.'

'I wouldn't dream of asking,' I said. 'Besides, if we were keeping score of favors, it would be Rutherford 20, Ives 3.'

'Twenty-one,' Dennis corrected. 'I've gone over Amy Madison's case file pretty thoroughly. For the most part, it's good, solid police work, even by today's more technologically advanced standards.'

'You said "for the most part,"' I said, 'which implies there might be a least part.'

'Could be something, could be nothing,' Dennis said. 'But if this were my case, I'd want to take a closer look at the fiber analysis. As you know, the techs collected a number of Kanekalon modacrylic fibers at the scene, commonly used in wigs. This led to speculation that another woman was at the cottage that night, or maybe sometime shortly before.'

I thought back to the transcripts of the witness interviews in Amy's file. 'But, according to the cleaning lady, the cottage had been thoroughly cleaned just two days prior to the party. And, what's more important, the cleaning lady didn't wear a wig, and neither did Amy.'

'I registered that, too. But, here's the thing, Hannah. I think they may have made a mistake by discounting so early on in the investigation the possibility that Amy's killer might have been a Naval Academy midshipman. Just because the bartender thought she overheard the guy mention he was from

Georgetown or from the University of Maryland, doesn't mean he was telling the truth.'

'That really narrows it down,' I grumped. 'Only four thousand five hundred suspects then, unless . . . but, wait a minute. Women were relatively new at the Academy in '78. The first class to graduate women was 1980, but there couldn't have been more than one hundred or so among the brigade.'

'Fifty-five,' Dennis corrected. 'But that's not the point. The wig probably belonged to a guy.'

'A guy,' I repeated dumbly. 'A guy?'

'Think back to the seventies, Hannah. The Vietnam war had been grinding on for years, anti-war demonstrations erupted all over the country, and the military was held in very low esteem.'

'Oh, yeah. Kent State. Ohio. Tin soldiers and Nixon,' I said, referring to the wildly popular song by Crosby, Stills, Nash and Young.

'Four students dead and nine wounded,' Dennis reminded me.

The song triggered a memory. 'A little before my time at Oberlin, late sixties maybe? But they say cops had to use tear gas and water hoses on a couple of hundred demonstrators in order to free a Navy recruiter from his car, which the students had surrounded, then overturned.' Picturing the chaotic scene, I suddenly understood where Dennis was going. 'Midshipmen are naval officers, clean-shaven, close-cropped. In a decade dominated by flower children, a midshipman would have stood out.'

'Exactly. Can't blame them for wanting to blend in in social situations, so quite a few mids wore wigs when they went out on the town.'

'You're not kidding, are you?'

'Sideburns and all,' Dennis chuckled. 'There used to be a wig shop at 151 Main Street. Colonial Wigs it was called. Something like that anyway.'

I knew the area well. 151 Main was a few doors down from Mother Earth, the New Age shop owned by my older sister, Ruth, who had never outgrown her flower child stage. 'Gone,' I told him. '151 has been a paint-it-yourself pottery shop for quite a while now.'

'I'm not surprised. But you might try tracking down the former owner. The shop probably had a lot of military clients back in the day. Don't know if anyone kept a record of who bought what, but if the detectives at the time had pursued that line of inquiry, there's no record of it in the files.'

'From the bartender's description, we know the guy Amy left with wasn't wearing a wig, so it must have been the other one.' I paused. 'I've given them names, by the way. Lewis and Clark. Lewis is the cute one Amy was seen dancing with. Clark is the mystery man.'

'Cute?' Dennis scoffed.

'Even Ted Bundy was cute,' I said. 'It's part of their toolkit. Keeps women off guard.'

'And here's another thing for your group to consider,' Dennis continued. 'If Amy drove her TR6 to the cottage where she was murdered, and Lewis or Clark, or maybe both, drove it back, what more natural place to park than the end of King George Street where it was an easy walk to Gate Eight where they'd need to check in before curfew.'

'Wow,' I said. 'And in that case, one or both of them must have wiped the car clean of fingerprints.'

I could see Dennis nodding. 'This is all speculation, of course, but something I would have followed up on.'

'We are all shaped by our prejudices,' I mused, 'especially back then. My doctor, he, for example, not my doctor, she, and guys don't wear wigs unless they're tee-totally bald or belting out arias in Saint-Saëns's *Sampson and Delilah*.'

That made Dennis laugh. 'Guys' egos are fragile, Hannah. Some soldiers in my National Guard unit were so desperate to blend in when they showed up for their monthly training that they had *short* wigs made to hide their work-a-day locks.'

'The Kanekalon fibers at the scene were five or six inches long,' I reminded him. 'So more likely a long-wigged mid than a short-wigged weekend warrior.'

'Agree,' he said. Then after a moment, added, 'How about your guy – Mark? Did he have a full career in the Navy? Would he have known about the wigs?'

I made a quick calculation, based on Mark's age which I

took to be in his mid- to late-fifties. 'By the time Mark enlisted, grooming standards for the fleet were far more relaxed. You could even grow a mustache or beard. Back at the Academy, though, male plebes still got their hair cut billiard ball short. Pretty much still do.'

'Did he go to the Naval Academy?'

'Who? Mark? Don't know, but Izzy's set up a Zoom session for tomorrow night, and I can't wait to ask him.'

NINE

Bad Luck
(Harold Melvin & the Blue Notes)

I couldn't think of anyone who knew more about Main Street Annapolis than my older sister, Ruth. She had opened her new age shop at number 157 almost twenty-five years before in partnership with her ex-husband, Eric Gannon, a philandering do-nothing who had now, thankfully, moved on – *way* on. To Thailand, last we'd heard.

From our house on Prince George Street, Mother Earth was a short stroll around the corner, down Maryland Avenue, around State Circle and through a narrow alley that spit me out on Main Street between a boutique and the lobster roll shop, directly across from Café Normandie, another one of my go-to restaurants when I felt too lazy to cook. A short walk downhill toward the harbor and I reached Mother Earth, where I paused outside for a moment to admire the window display.

This month's theme was 'Wellness,' as announced by a hand-painted sign propped up on an easel. Daddy's significant other often helped Ruth at the store and I recognized Neelie's decorative style immediately – a Goddess Moon Box Gift Set nestled in a basket of straw strewn with dried lavender stalks. A 'vegan and cruelty-free' House Cleansing Kit perched on a pedestal of stacked chakra candles. Crystal suncatchers suspended on almost invisible fishing line from a multi-branched piece of bleached driftwood, twisting and sparkling in the beam of a spotlight camouflaged by an oversized scallop shell. Zen stacking stones in one corner and geodes scattered about.

I opened the door and was immediately engulfed in a suffocating wave of *nag champa*, a heady combination of sandalwood and frangipani that I knew would cling to me for hours after I left the shop. Ruth was busy with a customer, explaining how to use the dowsing rods she was about to purchase to help locate a leak in the water pipe leading from her house to her detached garage. Meanwhile, I browsed through Ruth's selection of novelty mugs. After the woman left the shop carrying her purchases in Mother Earth's signature violet hundred percent recyclable tote, I called out, 'What does it take to get a little service around here?'

Ruth grinned and emerged from behind the cash register. 'Good to see you, too, Hannah.'

'I can't make up my mind,' I said, holding up a mug in my right hand that said, *Self care is cancelled. We're doing mushrooms and yelling at the moon naked* and in my left hand one imprinted with, *I'm in a really good place spiritually, so please fuck off. Namaste.*

'It's a tough choice,' my sister said. 'Yelling at the moon naked is more you, I think, but likely to scandalize the neighbors.'

'You've changed your hair,' I said as I returned the mugs to their places on the display shelf.

Keeping up with my sister's hair styles was a moving target. Over the decades since the Summer of Love, she'd traded the stick-straight, salt and pepper tresses that once streamed behind her like a banner for elaborate braids like Daenerys Stormborn, Mother of Dragons, to, at one point not so many years ago, a bronze crop with stiffly jelled spikes. That disaster had eventually grown out in favor of an upswept twist secured at the crown with a decorative chopstick. But today's look – a shaggy pixie cut with neon-streaked side bangs – was out there, even for Ruth.

She raised a hand and swept the unicorn-colored bangs out of her eyes. 'Do you like it?'

'What does Hutch think?' I asked, evading the question.

One expected Maurice Gaylord Hutchinson III, Ruth's attorney husband, to be as conservative as his Ivy League name, so I was surprised when she said, 'Hutch picked out the colors.'

'How's Hutch doing?' I asked. 'Last we heard he was handling a messy custody battle over a Pomeranian.'

'Oh, that finally settled,' Ruth tossed over her shoulder as she headed back toward the cash register. 'Peaches made her wishes known. She bit the wife. Bang the gavel. Case closed.'

I had to laugh.

'Just browsing?' Ruth asked after a moment, 'or do you have something on your mind?'

'I promise to buy something, honest,' I said, as I checked out Ruth's display of aromatherapy candles. I selected an attractive candle that had been poured (by hand, according to the label) into a black-matte recycled glass container, then sealed with a cork top. 'An uplifting blend of orange blossom, petitgrain, and bergamot top notes, with a heart of neroli, amber, and jasmine, and a grounding base of musk, cedar and sandalwood,' I read aloud, then took a whiff. 'Honestly, Ruth, it smells divine, but what the hell is petitgrain . . .' I paused, '. . . or neroli?'

'Extracted from bitter orange,' she explained with the patience of a nun. 'The former extracted from the leaves and twigs, the latter from the blossoms.'

'Who writes these descriptions, by the way? Retired wine makers?' I handed the candle over. 'OK, you've talked me into it. It's for the downstairs powder room, so you can visit it often.'

'Perfect,' Ruth said as she began ringing up my purchase.

When prompted, I slid my credit card into the machine and held it there while waiting for the beep of approval. 'And you're right, there is something I wanted to ask you about.'

Ruth reached under the counter for a shopping bag, but I held up a hand. 'Save the bag, Sis. I'll just tuck the candle into my backpack.'

Ruth passed the naked candle across the counter, along with the credit card receipt. 'So, what did you want to ask me?'

'Do you remember a wig shop that used to be down at 151, where the Clay Bakers are now? I'm trying to get in touch with the owner.'

Ruth's face wore that puzzled expression where her eyebrows almost met, then her face brightened. 'Oh, you must mean Pauline House. But it wasn't a wig shop when I first knew her. She'd turned it into Polly's Pot Shop.'

'You're joking.'

'Pauline had a wicked sense of humor. I don't know what buyers expected when they walked in the door, but it really was a shop that sold decorative pots, house plants and supplies for their care and feeding.'

I smiled, thinking I'd like to have known this woman.

I explained Dennis's theory about Colonial Wigs supplying wigs for socially insecure military personnel and how that might be connected to the cold case the Sleuths and I were working on. 'It's a long shot, I know, but I'm wondering if Pauline kept any sales records.'

Ruth snorted. 'I doubt it, Hannah. It was four decades and at least that many businesses ago. And, sadly, Pauline isn't around to ask, either. She died just a couple of years after I opened Mother Earth. It was around the time of the new millennium, as I recall, so, um, 1999. I went to her funeral. She was eighty-seven years old.'

'Oh, damn,' I said, although I wasn't surprised.

'Don't beat yourself up about it, Hannah. From conversations I had with Pauline, I'm pretty sure she didn't sell custom wigs, just over-the-counter synthetic kinds that sat around her shop perched on creepily blind Styrofoam heads. I remember her telling me she had a private room in the back, separated from the rest of the shop by a curtain. That's where she'd fit the guys up with wigs made for women, but she'd snip and shape until they looked like John Travolta or David Bowie or whatever celebrity happened to be popular at the time.'

'How long are you required to keep business records?' I asked.

'Three years for sales records and seven for bank and credit statements.' She rocked her hand from side to side. 'More or less.'

'Ah, well, we're well and truly screwed on records, then.' I patted the candle-shaped lump in my backpack. 'Thanks for the information, Ruth, and for the candle.'

Ruth followed me to the door and held it open for me. 'When are we going to resume the monthly gourmet dinner nights? It's our turn, Hutch and me. French theme, if I remember correctly. Hutch has been revisiting Julia Child's recipe for French onion soup.'

'Yum,' I said. 'Peter thinks Trish may be ready as early as next month, but says he'll be doing the cooking. Let me check with him and get back to you. *Ces soirées délicieuses m'ont vraiment manqué.*

She brushed her lips against my cheek. '*Pour moi aussi, ma chère.*'

TEN

And the Beat Goes On (The Whispers)

The following night, after a dinner featuring my late mother's award-winning meatloaf with mashed potatoes and gravy, I left Paul to the washing up and headed downstairs to the computer. In the few minutes I had before Izzy's Zoom session was scheduled to begin, I fussed a bit with the angle of my computer and the location of my office chair so that the Sleuths would see more of my bookshelves than the open doorway behind me that led to the laundry room where my curtains still lay, heaped in disgrace.

I was glad I made the effort.

Jack's study had the look of a well-consulted library where books were returned to the shelves willy-nilly after use, lying at haphazard angles or resting on top of one another. Mark owned fewer books, but they were arranged in tidy groups by subject, propped up by heavy bookends made from what looked like howitzer shell casings. Empty space on his shelves gave pride of place to several ship models – one three-masted schooner in wood and a smaller one carved from ivory – and souvenir beer steins. Framed citations, pennants and boxed flags hung on the wall.

Meanwhile, Izzy seemed to be Zooming from a New York City penthouse overlooking Times Square.

'Green screen,' she explained, waving vaguely behind her when I asked her about the view. As we watched, she clicked a few keys and suddenly materialized in Paris, sitting in her comfortable swivel office chair at the foot of the Eiffel Tower.

I laughed out loud. 'I want one of those!'

Two more clicks, and Izzy's chair was perched on the edge of the Grand Canyon, overlooking Bright Angel trail. 'Better?' she asked. She adjusted her reading glasses and leaned closer to the screen. 'I've been to all those places at one time or another, mostly for work.'

'The Navy owns a lot of beautiful waterfront property, too,' Mark said. 'Doesn't get much prettier than senior officer's quarters on a hillside overlooking Naples.'

Jack moaned. 'You guys are killing me! Until we moved to Glen Burnie, my view consisted of the old Sparrow's Point steel plant and an army of loading cranes that march across the waterfront like AT-AT walkers in *Star Wars*.'

I decided not to weigh in, or mention the curtains.

As she turned to gather her papers, Izzy's image shimmered, as if she were about to beam down to planet Vulcan with Captain Kirk. 'Let's get started.' She sat up straight and the image stabilized. 'Jack?'

'No DNA results yet, I'm sorry to say. By next week, maybe. They've been swamped by a request from Fort Meade. POW remains take priority.'

Izzy had spent her free time trying to locate and re-interview witnesses. Through Facebook, she'd tracked down Donna Crowe, the woman who had been tending bar at Doots' bar that fateful night. Neither Donna, nor Keith Ritchie, Amy's former boyfriend who now lived in Santa Fe, New Mexico, could add anything to what they had told police back in 1978. Mark took down their contact information and promised to do deep, follow-up interviews in a couple of days.

Izzy had also completed another important step. Based on the information I'd given her earlier, she'd located and spoken to Amy's next of kin, her mother Susan Oakes, née Whitaker, who gave the Silent Sleuths carte blanche to investigate her daughter's case. 'Susan's eighty-seven,' Izzy told us. 'But still sharp as the proverbial tack. Living in The Villages and married to a golf pro twelve years her junior. Susan told me she owes her longevity to yoga, mahjong and a bi-weekly game of pickleball.'

'Pickleball,' Jack mumbled. 'I just don't get it.'

I didn't get pickleball either, but figured a discussion of the pros and cons of a game played on an outdoor court with ping pong paddles and whiffle balls would do little to move

Amy's case forward, so I changed the subject. 'I remember reading in Amy's obituary that there'd been another daughter who died. Did Susan mention anything about that when you spoke to her?'

Izzy nodded. 'Cecelia. Died in a downhill skiing accident when the poor girl was fifteen. Amy and her sister were born only eighteen months apart, and were close in other ways, too. It was a terrible blow. Susan believes it's what broke up her marriage to Patrick. He blamed her for allowing the girls to go on the ski trip.'

Out of the respectful silence that followed, I heard Izzy calling my name. My turn at bat.

I confessed to sending Amy's police file to my brother-in-law for a consultation.

'Brava,' Jack said to my relief, giving me a high five. 'Every little bit helps.'

I wasted no time passing on Dennis's compliments to the group and his comment that the original investigation seemed to have been properly handled. Then I explained Dennis's theory about the origin of the wig fibers.

'Well, I'll be damned,' Mark said. 'I should have picked up on that.'

'Did you go to the Academy, Mark?'

He shook his head. 'No. I joined right out of seminary. The Navy whipped me into shape at the Naval Chaplaincy School in Newport, Rhode Island.' He paused thoughtfully, then added, 'I've met a lot of officers in my career, as you can imagine, and most of the balding ones either shaved their heads or wore toupees. Bad ones, too. Like hamsters crawled on top of their heads and died there.'

Jack laughed out loud. 'I can do you one better, Mark. Worked with a police chief once, naming no names. He had wigs made in three different lengths which he'd rotate. After wearing the long one for a couple of weeks, he'd stand in front of the mirror in the incident room, run a hand over his wig and announce, "Golly, looks like it's time for the old man to get a haircut." The next day he'd show up wearing the short wig.'

'You are making that up,' I said.

Jack flourished a three-fingered Boy Scout salute. 'Scout's honor.'

I smiled. 'And they say women are vain.'

I went on to tell the group how I'd followed up on Dennis's suggestion to check out the Colonial Wig Shop. 'It's a dead end, I'm afraid. The wig shop is long gone, and I can't interview the owner because she died more than twenty years ago.'

'Good work, though,' Izzy said. 'Thanks for closing that loop.'

Mark waved to get our attention. 'So, we could be looking for a couple of midshipmen.'

'Or, company officers,' I suggested. 'They're only around thirty years old.'

'Swell. That really narrows down the field,' Jack grumbled, ticking them off on his fingers. 'Four thousand five hundred midshipmen back then, give or take a handful of women, and thirty-six company officers.'

'It might,' I said, 'once the DNA data comes in and we can analyze it for possible matches.'

As we were talking, Mark seemed distracted, flipping through papers on the desk before him, head down so far that I could see the beginning of his bald spot. 'Bingo,' he said at last.

'What?' Izzy wanted to know.

Mark beamed into the camera. 'I've got a bit of homework to do, but I may be on to something. Give me a couple of days?'

'Any hints?'

Mark shook his head. 'Nah, I don't want to embarrass myself if I'm barking up the wrong tree. But, stay tuned, OK?' His screen vanished from the chat.

'Well, OK then,' Izzy grumped.

'I'm done, too,' Jack said. 'Until the DNA results come in, we're pretty much in a holding pattern.'

'I'm ready to go whenever,' I said. 'Just wish they weren't taking so long.'

'Amy's been waiting a long time for justice,' Izzy reminded me. 'She can wait a couple of weeks longer.'

ELEVEN

Shoot Your Best Shot (Linda Clifford)

*A**re you sitting down?** Jack texted just a week and a half later.

I texted back: *No. I'm standing in line at the Navy Federal ATM.*

He replied: *DNA results are in.*

I replied with a hands clapping emoji.

Sending them over now.

I decided I didn't need one hundred dollars in cash that badly. I returned to my car and headed home, running the red light at Taylor Avenue in my eagerness to get there.

My hands were shaking as I powered up the computer, opened up my mail and downloaded the raw data files Jack had emailed: AncestryDNALewis.txt and AncestryDNAClark. txt. A quick peek at one of the files revealed five columns of letters and numbers that seemed to stretch southward forever. Before proceeding I made copies of each data file and backed them up to the cloud.

There are too many sloppy genealogists in the world today – those who list children born when their mothers are five, or worse, after they're dead, or post photographs of ancestors who died in 1680 – but I am not one of them. Following a careful protocol I'd worked out over the past couple of years, I began by uploading the files to the trees I'd built for each man, beginning with GenTree.com. With fifteen million records, it was one of the largest of the databases by far. Next came GEDmatch.com with its sophisticated one-to-one and one-to-many matching algorithms, followed by MyHeritage, FamilyTreeDNA, LivingDNA and Geneanet. Two other popular genetic databases, Ancestry and 23 and Me, required proprietary testing, so I had to skip them, but their public family trees would prove invaluable later for research purposes.

Processing times at each of the sites varied widely, but I knew there'd be nothing to see for several hours at the earliest, so I took a long walk down Prince George Street and around the Naval Academy sea wall to keep my head clear.

The DNA files still hadn't populated by the time dinner rolled around, so I poured myself a glass of pinot noir, threw together a pot of chili, assembled a green salad out of the pitiful contents of my refrigerator's vegetable drawer, and warmed up a frozen loaf of garlic bread in the microwave. 'Do you mind if I stick you with the dishes again?' I asked my husband as he ladled up a second helping of chili.

'My pleasure,' he said, making shooing motions with his free hand. 'I know you're anxious to get on with the files, so scram!'

After the dishes were done, Paul came down to see how I was getting along.

'Status report?' he asked from the doorway.

'GenTree files are up!' I hooted. 'I'm reviewing Lewis's matches right now.'

'Do you mind if I look over your shoulder?'

'Not at all. Just don't breathe down my neck.'

Instead, he raised my hair and kissed the back of my neck before pulling up the spare chair we keep in the corner. I grinned. 'Rogue.'

Paul leaned in, his arm warm against mine. 'What am I looking at?'

I tapped the screen. 'This is a pretty good match for Lewis,' I said. 'Four hundred and thirty-three centimorgans.'

'Centi-who?'

'Centimorgans are a measure of the total length of your chromosomes. In a normal person, that's about seven thousand four hundred centimorgans. It's a math problem, professor. If you inherit half of your DNA from each parent, that means you get about three thousand seven hundred centimorgans from each. A grandchild of those same people would share about one thousand seven hundred and fifty centimorgans with them.'

'That sounds pretty straightforward.'

'Well, yes, it would seem so, but you'd be wrong. Let me

give you another example. Let's say you match another person at one thousand seven hundred and fifty-nine centimorgans. Based on these formulas, that person could be a half-sibling, a niece or nephew, an aunt or uncle or even a grandparent or grandchild.'

I pointed to the color-coded chart that I'd taped to the bottom of the monitor. 'That's called DNA Painter, and it's really helpful in determining possible relationships from centimorgan counts, but you still need more information before coming to a decision. Obviously, if the one thousand seven hundred and fifty-nine centimorgan match is to an eighty-five-year-old, it's not going to be a grandchild.

'Also,' I continued, 'it's not exact science. You notice on the chart that there's quite a range of centimorgans in each category. DNA can be a bit messy, and you don't inherit equally from any particular ancestor. Ruth and I match at two thousand three hundred and fifty centimorgans, while Georgina and I are at two thousand three hundred and two, for example, even though we have the same mother and father, but that's super close. Also, my sisters and I have known first cousins that range from the low seven hundreds to the high nine hundreds, so it's not always easy to sort relationships out.'

'My head is starting to hurt.'

I patted Paul's knee. 'The good news is that Lewis has this really good four hundred and thirty-three match, which could be a first or second cousin, and thirty-eight additional matches in the third-cousin range – roughly two percent of their DNA in common – which means they probably share a great-great grandparent. Fingers crossed that some of these matches are linked to proper family trees.'

'Don't they all have family trees?'

'Nope. You can simply get your DNA tested and uploaded, but not link it to any family trees, dammit.'

'The nerve!' Paul said.

I had to laugh. 'Exactly. But to be fair, a lot of people are not interested in finding genetic matches. They're simply interested in their ethnicity estimates. Take you, for example,' I said, tapping a few keys. 'You're sixty-three percent English, twenty-three percent Scottish, nine percent Norwegian – those pesky Vikings, I imagine – four percent Irish and a weird little one percent from Sardinia that's probably a hangover from Julius Caesar's invasion of England back in 55 BC.' I smiled. 'But I haven't gotten around to building a family tree for you yet, so that's all there is to go on.'

'No rush,' Paul said with a grin.

Turning back to the screen, I said, 'So I start by tracking the strongest DNA matches up their family tree if there is one, and then drilling down, looking for someone who might match with Lewis.'

'And if there isn't a tree?' Paul asked.

'Well, you can try emailing the person who manages the DNA profile through the GenTree website, but in my experience, if they haven't put up a tree, as I said, they're probably not interested in connecting.'

'So, how about the other guy, Clark?'

'Not so fast, professor. Let me finish printing out what I need to start working with Lewis, first. One step at a time.'

I pressed a few keys and took a screen shot of the display.

'Why did you do that?' Paul wanted to know.

'Insurance. Sometimes when a match pops up unexpectedly, people panic and take their results private, or even delete them altogether.' While he watched, I moved the image into the folder I'd made for Lewis.

'How did you get to be so smart, Hannah Ives?'

'Good genes,' I told him.

TWELVE
Take Your Time: Do It Right
(S.O.S. Band)

After several days of listening to Paul suggest (gently!) that I might be hogging the family computer just a teeny-tiny bit, followed by a half a day of 'some of us have jobs we are *paid* to do, sweetheart,' I took the hint and drove to the Apple store, arriving just after it opened.

I didn't need one of the Apple techs to tell me what I wanted. I'd been lusting after a MacBook Air for some time, so I whipped out my credit card and bought one. In rose gold.

Back home, I set up shop on the dining-room table where Paul found me when he got home from work around four-thirty.

'Well, well, well,' he said.

Fingers poised over my brand-new keyboard, surrounded by notebooks and printouts, I didn't even glance up. 'Hello to you, too.'

'Let me guess,' he said. 'No hosting of dinner parties for the foreseeable future.'

I favored him with a scowl. 'You planning any dinner parties?'

'No, sweetheart. Just trying to be funny.'

'Ha ha,' I said.

'Nice laptop,' Paul said as he breezed past me on his way to the kitchen.

'I succumbed,' I said.

'Good for you, Hannah. If you hadn't done it yourself by September, I was going to buy you one for your birthday.'

'*Now* you tell me,' I grumped. 'And while you're in the kitchen, fix me an iced tea, please.'

Two minutes later, my husband was back, holding a diet

Coke in one hand and a glass of tea, decorated with a generous wedge of lemon, in the other. 'How's it going?' he asked.

'Slow, but steady,' I said, reaching out for the tea. 'I made screen shots of Clark's DNA results, but I'm working on Lewis right now.'

Paul pulled out a chair opposite me and sat down. 'How did Lewis's pretty good first cousin match turn out?'

'Dead end,' I said. 'Linked to a skimpy family tree of six individuals, all marked private. Thanks a bunch. I emailed MHQ29, the person who manages the account, but when I checked the listing, it told me he or she last signed in over a year ago.' I picked up the tea and gave the lemon wedge a good squeeze. 'I always hope to hear back, of course, but not getting an answer is fairly typical, I'm afraid. I suspect people upload their data, don't see anything unexpected and forget about it.'

'And yet you persisted,' Paul said.

'Well, it certainly helps to have someone like WindyCityCathy waltz into your life,' I told him. 'She's a strong one hundred and fifty-seven centimorgan match to Lewis across nine segments, but more importantly, she's built a family tree with . . . hold on a minute . . .' I consulted my notes. 'Eleven thousand four hundred and seventy-three people in it. If she walked into the dining room right now, I'd kiss her.'

'It's helping then?'

'Ohmahgawd, yes. She's really into genealogy, big time. Several of her kids have tested, too. They show up as matches to Lewis further down in the fourth to fifth cousin range, but WindyCityCathy is still my best match at approximately the third cousin level, and the detail on her tree is amazing.'

'Have you contacted her?'

'Gosh, no. Not until I'm one hundred percent confident of the identification. Not everyone is going to be thrilled to learn that they might have a murderer in the family. Her tree is a treasure. I can't afford to scare her into taking it private.'

'Point taken,' Paul said. 'So, if I'm doing the math correctly, if Cathy and Lewis are third cousins, they probably share great-great grandparents. Since each of us is allotted sixteen great-grands, your job is to sort out which two they have in common.'

'Exactly,' I said. 'That's what all the color-coding using the Leeds method was about, tagging shared matches to identify the four grandparent lines. I applied the technique to each of Lewis's matches and that's what led me to WindyCityCathy's family tree where I eventually narrowed it down to a Henry and Sarah Miller.'

Paul rose from his chair and made his way around the table. 'Can I see?'

'Sure.' As he leaned over me, I back-arrowed to the main display, then tipped the screen up a bit. 'Henry was born in Cincinnati in 1852 and Sarah née Wiley in Pennsylvania in 1856. It would have been a lot easier if Henry had spent more time concentrating on the mining company he was doing accounting for out in Utah than visiting his wife in Mercer, Pennsylvania, but, hey. Over the course of the next fifteen years, he managed to sire seven children.'

'Reminds me of the nursery rhyme, as I was going to St Ives, I met a man with seven wives, and every wife had seven sacks, and every sack held seven cats, and every cat had seven kitts—'

I pinched his forearm, hard, cutting him off. 'Exactly. By the time you work your way down the family tree to the year 1958 or so, we're talking enough potential offspring to popu-late a small town.' I paused, then added, 'Are you sure you want me to go on? It can get complicated.'

'Hit me,' he said. 'I'm tough. I can take it.'

'I've been able to narrow it down quite a bit,' I continued. 'WindyCityCathy's great-grandfather was the oldest son, also named Henry. He was born in 1879 and died in 1973. So he's out of the competition.'

'How do you know Lewis's great-grandfather wasn't Henry, too?'

I shot a withering glance over my shoulder. 'Because then Lewis and Cathy would test out closer, as second cousins, maybe.'

Paul raised his hands in feigned self-defense. 'Never mind! Go on.'

'A girl, Ann, was born in 1884 and died the same year, so she's out, too, obviously. Ditto Matthew who died at age two of what his death certificate listed as scarlet fever.'

I clicked on the icon for Clarence, the next son, born in 1891, and moused over to the gallery view where I brought up an image of his 1914 US passport application. Clarence stared out at me with the darkly handsome intensity of a silent screen matinee idol. 'Sadly, Clarence was killed in action in France on July 15, 1918 at the Second Battle of the Marne.' I sighed. 'Just look at him! Any number of women would have been happy to have caught Clarence's eye, but as far as I can tell from the records, he never married. John, on the other hand . . .' I closed Clarence's image and moused to the right across WindyCityCathy's family tree. 'John was the youngest, born in 1894. He served during the First World War as a lieutenant in the Twentieth Balloon Squadron. In spite of being gassed and shot down twice, he managed to survive the war. Ironically, it was the gas that killed him. Later, though, in 1924.' I clicked on the image of John's obituary in the *Cincinnati Enquirer* and enlarged it a bit so Paul could read the print. 'His story's all here. It says he is survived by a wife and daughter, so I'll definitely need to work down along that line. If John was Lewis's great-grandfather, then the daughter would have been his grandmother.

'So, who does that leave you with?'

'In addition to John, that leaves James, the second oldest, who was born in 1881 and his sister, Sophie, who joined the happy family in 1889.'

Paul squinted speculatively. 'How do you know Henry and Sarah didn't have more children after John was born in 1894? Sarah would have been only, what, thirty-eight years old, so it's possible, right?'

I frowned. 'Puh-leeze! She'd been pumping them out like clockwork almost every two years. Poor woman deserved a rest, don't you think? In any case, I checked out the 1900 census, and everyone's still unmarried, living at home. By the time the 1910 census rolled around, Clarence and John were eighteen and fifteen, respectively, and still at home, but everyone else had flown the nest.' I elbowed him in the ribs. 'And no new babies.'

'How about the 1890 census?' Paul wondered.

'There is no 1890 census,' I explained. 'Almost all of it was destroyed in 1921 by a fire at the Department of Commerce.'

'Yikes,' he said.

'A tragedy on so many levels,' I said, 'and a brick wall for many genealogists. There's a something-something-great aunt on my Alexander family tree who was born in 1881, so she doesn't appear on the 1880 census, but by 1900, she was nineteen, had married and moved away. If she hadn't attended a family wedding in 1912 and been identified in the local newspaper as Mrs Southworth, sister of the bride, she might have been lost to history altogether.'

Paul stood, leaned over and kissed the top of my head. 'I feel my eyes starting to glaze over.'

I grinned. 'Don't say I didn't warn you.'

'If you want me, I'll be in the living room catching up on the news.'

'Have fun,' I said, and returned to the task at hand which was . . .? In the twenty minutes I'd spent explaining all the nuts and bolts to Paul, I'd completely lost track.

I sighed, checked my watch, then shut the laptop down. Tomorrow morning I might have a brain, and it was almost time for dinner.

Did Nano Asian still deliver? I wondered. I made the phone call. They did.

THIRTEEN
Dynamite (Stacy Lattisaw)

Saturday morning. Too damn early.

Paul had already left to make a seven thirty tee time with his buddies at the Naval Academy Golf Club, so the house was eerily quiet. I polished off the oatmeal he'd left congealing in a saucepan on the stove – after decorating it with raisins and brown sugar and drowning it in half and half – then brewed myself a second cup of coffee and carried it into the dining room. I sat down, opened my laptop and thought, now where the hell was I?

I consulted my notebook which, after yesterday's mini-tutorial with Paul was now a mess of scribbles, and turned to a fresh page. I wrote:

James Miller, 1881–1953.
Sophie Miller, 1889–1970.
John Miller, 1894–1924. Wife and daughter?

Where to begin?

For no particular reason, I started expanding Lewis's tree with Sophie. Beginning with the 1900 census, where she was listed as ten years old, I tracked her through the decades. In 1910, now twenty, she lived at home in Mercer. Her occupation? Music teacher. By 1920, she was still single and living at home, but in 1930, all that changed. Sophie had purchased a house on Jackson Street in Pittsburg and was listed as head of the household. Her elderly parents had moved in with her. After they passed away a few years later, Sophie ran the house with the help of a servant with the improbable name of Zipporah Virtanen and took in borders. According to Zillow, Sophie's four bedroom, two bath, all brick home had been built in 1911 and would list for a quarter of a million dollars today. The school district sucked, nowadays at least, but that probably wouldn't have concerned Sophie, as there was no evidence she'd ever had children. But she was beloved. In 1970, according to her obituary in the *Pittsburgh Post Gazette*, dozens of former students attended her funeral including one who'd gone on to attend Julliard and play piano at Carnegie Hall.

I scratched Sophie off the list.

Sophie's older brother, James Miller, attended medical school at Western Reserve University in Cleveland and by the time the 1910 census rolled around, had set up a general medical practice in Ashtabula, Ohio. According to his World War One draft card, he was part of the third registration wave in September of 1918, but perhaps his age (thirty-seven) or maybe his occupation saved him from conscription, because I couldn't find any evidence he had ever served in the military. In late 1919, he married a woman named Lucinda Babcock and their first child, also named James, was born a year later, followed by Matthew, Mark and Luke, *bing-bing-bing*. It took me the better part of two days, late into Sunday night, to research and add James and Lucinda's progeny to Lewis's family tree. By the time I was done, the Miller family tree was sprawling east to west across my monitor and I had learned a lot about Cedar Point Amusement Park (one of their sons supervised the Tumble Bug construction in 1934); the 1952 polio epidemic (two of their grandchildren succumbed to the disease); and the year the Cuyahoga River caught on fire (1969), but was no closer to finding a match for Lewis among James and Lucinda's fifty-four grand- and great-grandchildren, a surprisingly large proportion of them turning out to be women. Vincent Gunter (his mother was a Miller) generated brief excitement. Born in 1959, Vince was attending the University of Maryland in 1978, but he moved to New York City in the early eighties, attended Pratt, became a commercial artist and gay rights activist before dying of AIDS in 1992.

After regretfully eliminating poor Vincent, I was back to square one.

Depression set in.

On Monday morning, dressed in my finest jogging attire, I drove to Emily's house in Hillsmere where I picked up my grand-dog, Coco the Labradoodle, and took her for a two-hour walk in Quiet Waters Park. Watching Coco frolic with her canine companions at the dog beach always had a soothing effect, and it's cheaper than a therapist.

Afterwards, I treated myself to lunch at Grumps Café – a tuna melt to die for – then headed home, feeling refreshed and ready to dive back in.

'When you're looking for something, you'll always find it in the last place you look,' my mother used to say. 'Well, duh,' I remember answering back. I smiled, thinking of Mom as I sat down and powered up my laptop.

'*Please, please, please,*' I chanted as icons populated the screen, 'may John Miller and his wife and daughter be the last place I will have to go searching for Lewis.'

After John Miller died of his war-related injuries in 1924, his wife, Ruth, moved back to West Virginia with their infant daughter, Louisa, and by the time the 1930 census-takers showed up, were living with Ruth's parents in Morgantown. Ruth never remarried. According to the tombstone photograph on FindAGrave.com, she died nearly thirty years later and was buried back in Ohio alongside John, which I found touching and rather sweet.

World War Two rolled around, and John and Ruth's daughter Louisa, just seventeen, married a guy named Nicholas Forsythe who, according to his draft card, was also seventeen. The US Navy immediately shipped Nicholas out to a destroyer in the South Pacific and, as reported by the local newspaper, there was much rejoicing in Morgantown when he returned home to his wife and two-year-old daughter relatively unscathed. Nicholas moved his family to Dorset, Vermont where his father owned a car dealership. He and Louisa made up for lost time and, like Adam and Eve, had been fruitful and multiplied. Louisa was a good sport, you had to hand it to her for that: *if at first you don't succeed, try, try again.* Five daughters later, in 1955, Nicholas junior was finally born.

I sat up straight. Three years older than Amy, and yet . . .

My fingers flew over the keyboard.

Because his family lived in Dorset, Vermont, Nicholas had been privileged to attend the prestigious Burr and Burton Academy in Manchester where he excelled at baseball and lacrosse. Immediately after his 1973 graduation, for reasons known only to Nicholas, he enlisted in the US Navy. After serving a couple of years as a lowly seaman, an officer recognized his potential and encouraged him to apply for admission to the Naval Academy through the Naval Academy Prep School in Newport, Rhode Island. Nicholas did, impressed the heck out of everybody in Newport and entered the Academy as a plebe with the class of 1978. On service selection night, four years later, he'd gone Marine.

But I'd find all that out later.

What had the bartender, Donna, told Izzy? *Oh, I would recognize the guy again anywhere. Those eyes! Ice blue, you know, so sexy, like Peter O'Toole in* Lawrence of Arabia.

At that moment, those ice blue eyes were staring steadily at me from a strong-jawed, handsomely chiseled face. An eagle, globe and anchor pin shone from each side of the high, mandarin collar of his dress blues; captain's bars gleamed on his shoulders; marksmanship medals and service ribbons decorated his chest.

Nicholas Edward Forsythe, Junior, Captain, US Marine Corps had died in October of 1983, along with 240 others, when a Lebanese suicide bomber drove an explosion-laden truck into the Marine Corps barracks in Beirut.

FOURTEEN

I'm So Excited (The Pointer Sisters)

When I called, Izzy picked up right away.

'I've found Lewis!' I bubbled, effervescent with excitement.

'No shit!' she exclaimed. Then, more softly: 'Sorry, Mom.'

'Not a good time, I take it,' I said, feeling deflated. Where were the fireworks, the balloons, the party favors?

'You could say that,' Izzy replied. 'We have a bit of a situation here.'

I didn't have my phone set to speaker, but even so, Izzy's mom blasted into my eardrum loud and clear. 'Terry! Where's Terry? He'd never allow this to happen, missy, I can tell you that.'

Keeping my voice low I asked the obvious question. 'Who's Terry?'

'I'll be back in a minute, Mom,' Izzy said. 'I'm sure we can straighten this out.'

I heard the sound of a door opening, then closing. Then footsteps, followed by several beeps, then another door opening and closing. 'Sorry about that,' Izzy said. 'I've escaped to the garden. Mom's accused one of the nurses of stealing her pearls.' She sighed deeply. 'And Terry is James Terrance Campbell, my ex, by the way. No matter how many times I remind Mom that Terry and I split for good over eight years ago, it doesn't stick.'

'I'm sorry,' I said at a loss for better words. 'Terry Campbell the WBNF weather guy?'

'It was a stormy relationship,' she said.

I giggled. I couldn't help it.

'And for the record, Mom's pearls are kept in a bank safety deposit box, along with the rest of her jewelry. I took her there once, but . . .' She sighed deeply into the phone. 'But to hell with *that*,' she continued. 'Tell me about Lewis!'

'Do you want the good news first or the bad news?'

'Don't toy with me, Hannah Ives. I'm not in the mood.'

'So I gathered. Hopefully, what I've found will lift your spirits. I've been working flat-out on the DNA matches for Lewis and I'm ninety-nine-and-one-hundredth-percent certain I've identified one of the two guys who were at the scene of Amy's murder. My brother-in-law was right. The guy *is* a Naval Academy grad. Unfortunately, he was killed in Lebanon in 1983.'

'Marine barracks?' she asked, clearly familiar with the incident.

'Bingo,' I said. 'But I'm guessing you don't have time to talk details now.'

'Let's schedule a Zoom call for later tonight,' she said. 'I'll check with Jack and Mark and send everyone the link.'

'Can't wait,' I told her. 'I've been running around the house giving myself high fives. Maybe I'll have settled down by then. Tell everyone to bring champagne.'

That made her laugh. 'Later, and Hannah?'

'Yeah?'

'Thank you. You're amazing.'

'Who knew?' I said with a chuckle.

The Zoom link pinged into my inbox just ten minutes later, punctuated by a smiley face tooting a party horn. Izzy's timing gave me between four o'clock and seven-thirty that evening to get my presentation organized, and I'd need to squeeze dinner in somewhere.

My famous turkey tetrazzini was invented precisely for such occasions. Made with heavy cream, ladies and gentlemen, gruyère, and actual sherry – Oloroso. I liberated one of the casseroles from the chest freezer in the basement and set it out on the kitchen counter to thaw. I'd microwave the green beans with slivered almonds left over from the night before. Open a can of tropical fruit salad. Perfection!

Dinner sorted, I sat down at my laptop and got busy.

*   *   *

Other than Izzy, I was the first to arrive for the meeting; she
linked me in at seven twenty-eight. This time, Izzy was calling
in from Waikiki. 'Where's your lei?' I asked.

'Got one lying around somewhere,' she said. 'The flowers
light up and it plays *Aloha Oe* when you press a button.'

'Everyone needs one of those,' I said.

Mark was the next to join followed by Jack. Both were
wearing dark blue polo shirts, almost as if they'd coordinated
their outfits beforehand. Nobody'd brought champagne, but
Mark was sipping coffee from an *I Got This*, signed *God* mug
and Jack was enjoying a frosty Heineken 0.0. He tipped the
neck of the bottle and tapped the camera. 'Well done, Hannah.'

Mark and Izzy joined him in a brief round of applause.

I felt my face flush. Maybe they wouldn't notice in the
greenish light reflecting off my screen.

I gave the group a concise summary of how I'd started with
WindyCityCathy's DNA match and used it to wind my way
up her meticulous family tree, weave around the numerous
branches, stripping them of leaves one by one until I ended
up with Nicholas Forsythe who, it turned out, happened to be
in the right place at the right time: Annapolis, Maryland.

Jack whistled, long and low. 'Izzy said you were good.'

I laughed. 'Maybe, but it's not rocket science, just pure
doggedness. It's all out there, you know. From the minute
you're born until the minute you die.'

'Maybe we should start wearing tinfoil hats,' Jack said.

'One day soon we'll have access to the 1950 census,' I went
on, 'but thanks largely to the Church of Jesus Christ of Latter
Day Saints I wasn't without resources. A good bit of recent
data comes from the US Index to Public Records that the LDS
compiles.' I took a breath, ticked them off on my fingers.
'Phone directories, address lists, residential records, voter
registration lists, on and on. More high school and college
yearbooks are showing up online every day, too, as well as
church directories. I've got a subscription to Fold3, the historical military database, but one of the most useful resources
I've found is local newspapers. The *Manchester Journal*
has come out every Friday since 1861. That's where I first
found Nicholas's obituary, although his name was pretty much

everywhere after the DOD officially released the names of the Beirut bombing victims.'

I clicked on the green 'share screen' icon and opened Nicholas's obituary. Nobody said anything for several minutes as they studied his picture and read the article through.

Mark was the first to speak up. 'Sounds like a helluva guy.'

Jack didn't seem totally on board. 'Ever read an obit that wasn't complimentary?'

"'Although gravely injured,"' Mark read to emphasize his point, "'Forsythe managed to pull four of his fellow Marines out of the rubble before collapsing. He was evacuated, along with thirty-five others, to an army hospital in Wiesbaden, where he died several days later of chest and lung injuries due to severe burns."'

'I'll bet he earned a Purple Heart for that,' Jack admitted. 'Posthumous, sadly.'

"'Greater love has no one than this, that he lay down his life for his friends,"' Mark quoted. 'John 15:13.'

'Amen,' I said, and meant it. 'By the way, the same obituary appears, word for word, on the Class of '78s memorial webpage.' I clicked over to the webpage so they could see what I was talking about. 'It's a really neat website with lots of photos from their Academy days, but other than a blurry photo of Nicholas at bat – he was on the baseball team, apparently – I didn't have much luck.'

'What are you looking for exactly?' Izzy wanted to know.

I shrugged. 'A casual photograph of Nicholas with his arm draped around the guy I'm calling Clark, maybe, who turns out to be his roommate, best friend, possible partner in crime? A gal can dream.' I sighed. 'I can't tell you how many times over the past few days that I've longed for Facebook, but it didn't appear on the college scene until 2004.'

'We might have better luck checking out *Shipmate*. It's online, I believe.'

Mark was referring to the Naval Academy's alumni magazine which was sent out to all alumni, faculty and staff nine or ten times a year. 'It *is* online, Mark, and I logged on with Paul's password to check out the '78 Class Notes sections for every issue from their graduation until

1984. Other than Nicholas's obituary, I didn't see any news that would help.'

'Naval Academy yearbooks?' Jack wondered.

'It's called the *Lucky Bag*,' I told him. 'Nicholas will definitely be in the *Lucky Bag* for 1978, but it's not online yet. Every year from 1894 through 1974 has been digitized, but I've been so busy with the DNA analysis that I haven't had time to walk over to the Academy Library and check out the physical volumes for the years after that.'

'Let me handle it,' Mark said. 'I'm meeting some friends for lunch at the Officers' Club on Tuesday. I'm officiating at their daughter's wedding next April.' He smiled. 'It won't be out of my way. Honest.'

'My hero!' I said, then clicked on another link in my Lewis folder. 'Moving on, I thought you might be interested in seeing the *Evening Capital* from June 7, 1978, which was Nicholas's graduation day. It's kind of fun.' I moused over to the upper right of the masthead: Weather. Rainy.

It *was* a dreary day, according to the front-page article, but the ceremony had been held at the outdoor stadium anyway. In his graduation address, President Jimmy Carter chastised the Soviet Union, urging them to choose either 'confrontation or cooperation.' Meanwhile, also in front page news, singer Anita Bryant announced she was opening a house in Florida where she planned on 'helping homosexuals find deliverance from their lifestyle.' I scrolled slowly forward through the pages so the others could follow along. 'Check this out,' I said when I got to the ads. 'Ground beef is $1.19 a pound, a shirt for Dad on Father's Day will set you back $3.47 at Montgomery Ward, and *Charlie's Angels* is showing on channels two and seven at nine p.m.'

'Those were the good old days,' Jack muttered.

'I looked, but there's no mention of Amy,' I said. 'Hard to believe her murder was already old news.'

'Although I'm enjoying this side trip down memory lane,' Izzy interrupted, 'we need to think about next steps. Jack?'

'Eventually, we'll send Forsythe's photo to Donna Whatshername for a positive ID. Then, turn over the information

Hannah's gathered to the detectives. They'll want to verify the genetic link. Hannah, have you been able to track down Forsythe's wife and daughter?'

I shook my head. 'Not yet. None of the obituaries I shared with you mention the girl's name, or the maiden name of her mother. They just say, "He leaves behind his wife, Lisa, and three-year-old daughter of Camp LeJeune, North Carolina." I haven't been able to find a marriage record for Nicholas and Lisa, either.' Then I was struck by a thought so obvious I couldn't believe I hadn't thought of it before. 'Mark, do you think they were married at the Naval Academy Chapel?'

Back in those days, midshipmen were not allowed to be married and remain students. (And that's still the law.) Consequently, the week following graduation was crammed with back-to-back weddings, one every hour and half hour either in the glorious main chapel – built in 1904 and brightly illuminated, whatever the weather, by Tiffany stained glass windows – or in the smaller, more intimate St Andrew's Chapel on the lower level, not far from the marble crypt where John Paul Jones is buried.

Izzy spoke up first. 'That sounds like your department, Mark.'

Head down, Mark made a note. 'You got it.'

'Nicholas had five older sisters,' I reminded the team. 'They'd be in their seventies now, but most likely still alive. I'll pass their names along.'

'Seventy is the new fifty,' Izzy remarked. 'But, do you think they might comply? Would you sit still for a DNA sample if Nicholas were your brother?'

Would I? I had to think. 'Depends. If I thought he were a dead hero, probably not.' After a moment, I said, 'But, wait a minute! Mark, doesn't the military keep DNA samples of everyone who joins up in order to, you know, help identify combat remains?'

'They do,' Mark said. 'It's called the Armed Forces Repository for Specimen Samples for Identification of Remains, or AFRSSIR.'

'Say that three times fast,' Izzy cut in.

Jack snorted. 'Hah!'

Mark forged on. 'But they didn't start collecting military DNA until 1992.'

'Damn,' I said. 'Long before that, though, didn't they finger-print every recruit? Couldn't they compare the partials left at the scene of the crime with them?'

'Not in a million years,' Jack cut in. 'It's massive, maybe five million records, all told, including every Defense and State Department employee since, well, probably since fingerprinting was invented. It can't be tapped into by law enforcement, anyway. If the prints aren't already in AFIS, the automated database maintained by the FBI, you're out of luck.'

On the screen, Mark was waving to get our attention. 'Lisa Forsythe is a widow. The VA will know where to find her.'

'What if she remarried?' Izzy asked.

'They can track the kid. She'd be getting benefits, up through college anyway.'

'She'd be over thirty now,' I pointed out. 'Maybe married.'

Jack raised a hand. 'Steady, boys and girls. It'll be up to the detectives to run down those leads. Wife, kid, sisters, Academy connections. Not our problem.'

'And if they don't, I sure as hell will,' Izzy said.

Mark surprised me by shrugging. 'Look, you guys. I didn't want to say anything until I was completely prepared, but remember the other day when I said I might be on to something?'

Silence. All of us waiting for him to go on.

'Well, if I'm proven right, this entire discussion is moot.'

'Moot,' I repeated, thinking I'd misheard. 'Moot? I've been working my buns off, Mark. What do you mean, moot?'

'Not exactly, moot,' he said, backpedaling quickly. 'The last week or so, I've been taking a deep dive into the Murder Accountability Project, and I don't think I'm leaping to conclusions when I suggest—'

'Whoa!' I shouted, flapping both hands frantically in front of the camera until I got everyone's attention. 'Help a newbie out, here. What's the Murder Accountability Project?'

'Sorry, Hannah.' To her credit, Izzy looked sheepish. 'I meant to send you those links along with the other files, but *mea culpa*, they got lost in the shuffle when I was rushing to get you on board.'

Mark went on to explain that the Murder Accountability Project was the nation's most complete compilation of case information for homicides, mostly unsolved, going back to 1976. 'You can search on all kinds of data – geography, type of victim, method of killing, timeframe. You can drill down to the age, race, sex and ethnicity of victims, too, as well as the weapon used.'

'Where does the data come from?' I asked.

'The FBI's Uniform Crime and Supplemental Homicide Reports as well as police departments from all over the country,' Jack explained. 'MAP's a big non-profit, but it's solid.'

'OK, I'm listening now,' I said. 'Please go on.'

Mark squirmed a bit in his chair, but soon settled. 'Evidence shows conclusively that Nicholas was present at the cottage at some point during the evening, and that he and Amy had sex. But I've become convinced he didn't kill her. Lately I've been querying the MAP database looking for murders with characteristics similar to Amy's. We now know, thanks to Hannah, that Nicholas died in 1983,' Mark said in a quiet voice. 'But here's the deal. A killer using the same MO is still out there. There's a strong possibility that we're dealing with a serial killer, and since he's been dead for decades, it can't be Nicholas Forsythe.'

FIFTEEN

Rock the Boat (Hues Corporation)

Jack raked a hand over the stubble on his chin. 'Damn. Good work, Mark.'

'It's a theory I've been working on for a couple of weeks, but it wasn't until Hannah conclusively identified Forsythe that I was able to narrow it down to the other guy.'

'Which makes it more important than ever that I get back to work and see if I can identify that other guy,' I said, drawing quote marks in the air with my fingers. 'Clark doesn't have nearly as many DNA matches as Nicholas Forsythe, though, so it might be a slog.'

'A midshipman, too, you think?' Izzy wondered.

I shrugged. 'Hard to say. It's likely, but midshipmen can have civilian friends, too, you know. They aren't hermits.'

'Give me a couple of days to illustrate my case,' Mark said. 'In person or Zoom?'

'Zoom's best for me right now,' I said. When Jack agreed, Izzy promised to set something up. 'Friday? Same time same place?'

After the call, I didn't wait for Izzy to send me links. I Googled Murder Accountability Project and was quickly linked to MurderData.org. Once there, I read that their board of directors is composed of retired law enforcement investigators, including former military police, investigative journalists, forensic psychologists, FBI serial homicide specialists, criminal profilers and other expèrts. I sat back in my chair, impressed with their credentials.

From the 'About' page, I learned that every year in the United States, at least 5,000 killers get away with murder. As a result, MAP estimates that more than 256,000 Americans have perished in unsolved homicides since 1980. The group aims to turn that abysmal clearance rate around. Accordingly, they provide sophisticated online tools that allow the public to explore individual cases, look for occurrences of specific types of homicides, and help identify clusters.

I resisted the strong temptation to delve any deeper. I was already burning the candle at both ends building family trees for anonymous individuals, and the last thing I needed was to be sucked down another rabbit hole. Mark is our MAP expert, I lectured myself firmly. No need for *you* to reinvent the wheel, Hannah. Friday will come soon enough. In the meantime, you have work to do.

As my husband will tell anyone who is willing to listen, once focused on something, Hannah is hard to turn. By Friday, I felt as if I'd made piss-poor progress on Clark's family tree, although I wasn't ready to throw in the towel . . . yet. Clark's closest matches were down in the fourth- to sixth-cousin range with only 1 percent shared DNA. Few had linked family trees and those that did had marked them 'private.' I politely messaged the managers of those private trees, asking permission for access, but hadn't heard anything back. By the time scheduled for Mark's Zoom session on Friday, I was deeply discouraged by my lack of progress and ready for a break.

'How's it going?' Izzy asked when she patched me in at seven twenty-five.

'Don't ask,' I grumped. I shared my frustration about the limited data. 'But, genetic websites are dynamic. Ancestry. com adds two million records every day, or so they claim.' I crossed my fingers and held them up to the camera. 'I'm wearing my lucky socks. Maybe tomorrow will be my lucky day.'

Jack Zoomed in next, reporting that he'd turned everything we knew about Nicholas Forsythe over to his contact on the Anne Arundel County Police cold case squad. 'They were over the moon,' he said with a chuckle. 'Or, as over the moon as seasoned homicide detectives tend to get, which is to say, the officer cracked a smile. He promised to keep me informed.'

When Mark called in, Izzy brought him up to speed on our news, then turned the session over to him.

Mark took a deep breath, then let it out slowly. He shot us a lopsided grin. 'Buckle your seat belts. Here goes.' Head down, he fussed a bit with his keyboard, then looked up and said, 'Naturally, I started with Amy's case. In looking for her killer, I figured it was reasonable to ask myself if there were other similar cases in Maryland. So, let me walk you through it.'

Mark's face vanished and was replaced by the home screen I recognized as the Murder Accountability Project. His mouse darted to the right.

'First, we go over to the *Search Cases* tab.'

The screen dissolved and was replaced by a large, red and gray bar graph with approximately a dozen pull down menus in a column off to the far right.

I leaned forward, squinting, struggling to read the captions. 'Don't worry about this graph,' Mark advised. 'What's important are the pull downs over here.' His mouse moved again, hovering over a bar that resembled a volume control. 'First, I slide the year to 1978,' he said, which explained the purpose of the bar, 'then I go under *State*, unclick *All* and select *Maryland*, go down and select the county et cetera et cetera et cetera. Down a bit further, is where we enter "twenty" under *Victim's Age*, "female" under *Sex*, naturally, and "strangulation" under *Weapons*. It's all pretty self-explanatory.

'When we're finished with all that,' he continued, 'only one case pops up, and it looks like Amy's. To confirm that, I right click on the case, select the download option and call up the details. The *Underlying* data tab tells us that the murder occurred in May of 1978 and that it was reported to the Anne Arundel County Police Department, so we know this is the correct case.'

'Fascinating,' I said, truthfully.

'It is, I have to admit,' Mark said. 'OK, so now I ask myself, were there similar unsolved killings in Maryland at the time of Amy's murder? I go back to the *Search Cases* page and widen my search parameters. Maybe our killer is targeting college women in the eighteen to twenty-one age range, for example. I can add those additional ages to the *Victim's Age* pulldown menu. And then I did this: I widened the years selector from 1978 to the present. Bingo! Now we have six roughly similar cases in Maryland.'

'But, we live in the wider DC, Maryland and Virginia metropolitan area,' Jack pointed out. 'You probably should factor that in.'

'I anticipated that,' Mark told him, 'and then I took it a step even further, asking myself, what if Amy's killer was highly mobile? I go back to the *State* selector and chose *All*.'

Another red and gray bar chart filled the screen. Mark's mouse traced invisible circles on the graph. 'The red represents unsolved cases,' Mark explained. 'Now we are talking around sixty cases. I won't bore you with the details, but with a few mouse clicks, I was able to download all the data concerning these murders and import it into a spreadsheet. After I got that initial list, I began to narrow it down. The Homicide Cold Case Repository is a good place to start. It has direct links to the cold case files of each state, but in many cases, I had enough data to search Google and come up with a match. Then I asked myself, what do these cases have in common?'

Another spreadsheet appeared. 'These are the cases that look most like Amy's,' Mark said as he scrolled to the right, revealing each column on his spreadsheet. 'Around a dozen in all. College age female, red hair, under five feet tall and almost every woman had last been seen at a disco club, rave, or karaoke bar. As you can see, I've sorted the cases by month and year, with the last being the most recent, just over a year ago at the One Note Stand, a karaoke bar in Rockville, Maryland. Roberta Chapman, age nineteen, a sophomore at the University of Maryland. Her body was found in a creek near the golf course in Rock Creek Park.'

'Wow,' Izzy said. 'He's targeting short, college-age red heads?'

'The dude's got issues,' Jack said.

'Yup,' Mark agreed. 'But I'd like to draw your attention to these two columns here.' Mark's mouse ping-ponged between the columns headed *Agency* and *State*. 'What do you notice?'

I leaned closer, touched the screen and traced down the list as I read:

> Annapolis, Maryland
> Newport, Rhode Island
> Norfolk, Virginia
> San Diego, California
> Annapolis, Maryland – again
> Tampa, Florida
> Norfolk, Virginia
> Annapolis, Maryland – again
> Newport, Rhode Island – again
> Montgomery County, Maryland

'Ohmahgawd,' I squeaked. 'Except for that last, they're all navy towns. The guy's definitely in, or was in, the Navy.'

The spreadsheet disappeared to be replaced by Mark's face again, looking serious. 'My bet, he's a SWO.'

'SWO?' Izzy asked.

'Surface Warfare Officer,' Mark explained. 'A ship driver. And if Hannah tracks the guy down before Anne Arundel County does, I'll wager his duty stations will dovetail perfectly with this list.'

'It's definitely a clue,' I said, in absolute awe of what Mark had accomplished. 'Now, all we need is a name. Wish me luck.'

SIXTEEN
Knock on Wood (Amii Stewart)

L ucky in life, lucky in love but as far as Lady Luck herself is concerned, she always seems to be blowing on another gal's dice.

Never win the grand prize in a charity raffle no matter how many tickets I buy.

Forget to take an umbrella? Hello, rain.

And at secret Santa parties, why do I always end up with the Christmas ornament shaped like a dill pickle?

For me, good luck is finding a parking spot in front of our house rather than two blocks away, or not running out of propane in the middle of the last backyard barbeque of the summer.

The day Lady Luck finally showed up, she practically had to shout, jump up and down and wave her arms to get my attention. I'd spent all morning at the GEDmatch website using one of their tools, a sophisticated one-to-one chromosome browser, attempting to determine exactly how some of Clark's DNA matches related to one another. When I ran Clark's DNA 'kit' through the browser, it identified kits in the database that matched his, then graphically mapped the results, highlighting the specific DNA segments the kits shared. Using the browser, I'd been able to triangulate on a common ancestor and link up two of the floating branches I'd built on Clark's family tree, but I still had no direct link to the elusive Clark himself.

No matter which of GEDmatch's 'visualization options' I chose, though, whether by graph, spreadsheet or laid out in twenty-three individual rows like multi-colored Universal Product Codes gone berserk, the analysis required my undivided attention. So, I'd chosen my time carefully – Paul was joining a colleague for lunch – and I'd silenced my phone and the pings of incoming emails.

It was well after my usual lunchtime before I declared a time out. I set my reading glasses down on the table, rotated my aching shoulders, rubbed my eyes, then wandered into the kitchen. I microwaved a plastic container of leftover tuna noodle casserole, grabbed a cold can of Coke and carried them out onto the patio where I stretched out on one of the loungers to enjoy my meal in the dappled shade of a flowering hawthorn tree.

I might have dozed off.

Later, around four thirty while I was watering the houseplants, it suddenly occurred to me that the house had been unusually quiet. No dings, no tweets, no pings. No *ooga-ooga-ooga,* either, which was Paul's special ring tone. I ditched the watering can in the kitchen sink, then went in search of my iPhone, eventually finding it peeking out from beneath a pile of printouts on the dining-room table where I had been working earlier.

Three missed calls: my daughter, the lawn service company and an unfamiliar number with a DC area code.

Two text messages – one reminding me that my prescription at Giant Pharmacy was ready for pickup, and another asking me to text YES if I believed US Supreme Court Justices should be subject to term limits. I texted STOP instead.

And, according to the email icon, I'd missed thirty-two emails.

I sighed, poured myself a glass of chardonnay and migrated to the living room, where I soon became one with the sofa. Using my index finger, I swiped most of the emails into my trash bin. How had I ended up on so many mailing lists? Delete, delete, delete, delete until:

You have received 1 new message from GenTree member CherLannPa.

View your message.

I wasted no time clicking through.

CherLannPa had been a member since December 2021, her message page informed me, and had uploaded three family trees, all marked private, none with more than a handful of members. Her message to me, dated earlier that morning read:

Hello, HAIMaryland. I had my DNA tested, and according to the results I just received, I am closely related to Clark78 on a family tree you manage. The tree is set to private. May I have permission to access it? I am very interested in exploring how we are connected – Cheryl Lannigan.

Closely related? What, exactly, did Cheryl mean by 'close'? The closest match I'd seen for Clark was a third cousin.

If she could see Clark's DNA matches, I knew I would be able to see her matches, too. Clutching my cell phone, I dashed into the dining room and powered up my laptop. The website seemed to take forever to load, but the website and the tree I had created for Clark eventually filled my screen. Holding my breath, I clicked on Clark's *DNA Matches* tab.

CherLannPa's record now topped Clark's list. Her relationship to Clark, with a confidence rating of 'extra-high' was Parent/Child.

In her note to me, Cheryl had apparently chosen to downplay her results, but on Clark's end, the message couldn't have been clearer: *CherLannPa is your daughter.*

When I could breathe again, I texted Mark: *Call me ASAP, plz. Important!*

'What's up, Hannah?' Mark asked about five minutes later.

'The most incredible stroke of luck,' I said. 'I can hardly believe it. *You're* not going to believe it.'

'I believed in Santa Claus until I was ten,' he said. 'Try me.'

I took a deep, steadying breath and let it out slowly. 'Clark has a daughter named Cheryl Lannigan. She just contacted me through the GenTree website. She wants to connect.'

'Holy connoli,' Mark exclaimed.

'Weeks of researching DNA matches no closer than third cousin, and then, voila! A daughter pops up out of the blue. My hands are still shaking.'

Mark laughed. 'Breathe, Hannah! Then go pour yourself a drink. You deserve it.'

I giggled nervously. 'I have a glass of wine around here somewhere. Hold on a minute.'

Once again settled on the sofa, I took a sip and said, 'So,

what do I do now? It's obvious from her message that she doesn't know her father. And clearly, I'm not going to start out by mentioning that he might be a serial killer. Advice, please. You're the guy with the master's degree in psychology.' I paused to take a breath. 'Sorry, I'm babbling. Maybe you should talk to her first.'

'No, no.' He was quick to respond. 'In my experience, woman to woman is better.'

'I'm afraid I'll send her running for the hills.'

'I don't think so. Cheryl, did you say?'

'Yes. Last name Lannigan. I'm guessing from her login that she's from Pennsylvania.'

'OK,' Mark continued. 'I'm assuming Cheryl's in one of two situations. Maybe she received the test kit as a Mother's Day gift and took it on a lark because she was curious about her ethnic origins, wondering whether all the family stories about immigrating to the US during the Irish potato famine were true, for example. Maybe she grew up in a loving family, with a mom and a dad and then, oops! The guy she thinks is her biological father actually isn't.'

'An NPE,' I murmured. 'Not parent expected.'

'Exactly.'

'Or, perhaps she's adopted,' I said, 'and has been searching for her birth family for years.'

'That's where I was going next,' Mark said. 'In either scenario, you have information she's looking for. I doubt she'll head for the hills.'

'Hopefully she has the information *we're* looking for,' I said. 'If Cheryl's biological mother is still alive – fingers crossed – she should be able to name Cheryl's father, unless her pregnancy was the result of stranger rape.' I shivered, thinking about Clark. 'It could have happened after a drunken, one-night stand, of course, or during, you know, the Summer of Love. Turn on, tune in, drop out and all that.'

'That was way back in the sixties, Hannah.'

Thinking about my sister, Ruth, I said. 'Some people never outgrew it.' After a moment, I added, 'As far as Cheryl's biological father is concerned, though, I won't even be able to tell her whether he's alive or dead.'

'If I'm right about Clark being responsible for a string of murders,' Mark pointed out, 'then we know he was still alive around a year ago when that girl's body was found in Rock Creek Park, but I'd keep that theory to myself for now.'

'I'm not a complete idiot, Mark,' I said with a chuckle so he'd know I was teasing. 'But, after responding, "Hello, Cheryl, this is Hannah Ives," I'm kind of at a loss.'

'You have good instincts, Hannah. I'd open soft, don't give too much away, listen to her, feel her out. You'll be fine.'

'Maybe you should come over and hold my hand.'

Mark laughed. 'I haven't known you long, Hannah, but I'm betting there aren't a lot of tough situations you can't handle.'

'Maybe. Dad tells me I was a fiercely independent toddler. My husband accuses me of being strong-willed. It's my superpower, Mark. I use it for good.'

A key turned in the lock and the front door creaked open. 'Speaking of husbands, Paul just got home. We should probably wrap this up.'

'Don't worry about calling the others, Hannah. I'll let Izzy and Jack know.'

'Tell them I won't do anything until tomorrow morning, so if they have any suggestions, let me know. I'm planning to sleep on it. Maybe the right words will come to me in a dream.'

'I'll say a prayer,' Mark said.

'Thanks. Every little bit helps,' I replied, and ended the call.

Paul barely had time to hang his backpack on the coat tree before I ambushed him in the hallway. 'Fifteen minutes,' I said, offering my cheek for a kiss. 'Then I'm taking you out to dinner.'

'Pucker up, babe,' he said, switching gears and giving me a proper kiss on the lips. 'What's the occasion?'

Still standing in the hallway, with my hands lightly resting on his hips, I told Paul about the message I'd received from Cheryl Lannigan.

He beamed down at me. 'Well done, you!'

'I haven't done anything yet. I've been strategizing with Mark Wallis just now. I don't want to screw things up.'

'As if,' Paul said, gently bopping the tip of my nose with his index finger.

'A drink before we go?' I asked.

'I'll have a Guinness when we get to Galway Bay,' he said, guessing (correctly) that I'd be dragging him to our favorite hangout, the Irish pub on Maryland Avenue, half a block up Prince George Street and left around the corner.

'Shepherd's pie for me,' I said. 'Brain food.'

'That's what you said last time, about corned beef and cabbage.'

'Spoiled for choice,' I said. 'Let's go.'

SEVENTEEN
Ask Me (Ecstasy, Passion & Pain)

I spent a restless night, lying awake in the darkened room, watching the oak tree outside the window trace lacy moon shadows on the bedroom wall while I alternately composed and then discarded replies to Cheryl Lannigan.

I gave up at five o'clock. Leaving Paul whiffle-snoring gently, I padded downstairs in my bare feet, punched the buttons that would bring the Keurig to life, and brewed myself a cup of coffee. Sitting at the kitchen table in the dark, I sipped it slowly until dawn's lazy fingers began to paint the sky peach.

I drank my second cup of the day in front of my laptop, staring mindlessly ahead as the screen saver drew technicolor swirls around the screen like a lava lamp. Finally, because I could see no reason not to, I logged onto GenTree, navigated to the tree settings menu and asked GenTree to send CherLannPa an invitation to view Clark's tree, including living persons, who are usually blocked. Clark's tree was hardly ready for prime time, resembling as it did a jigsaw puzzle of floating branches in desperate search of the missing piece that would connect them. Perhaps, if I considered it alongside Cheryl's trees, I would be able to fill in some blanks.

What had Paul suggested at the restaurant the previous evening? The server had just set a bowl of warm bread pudding, slathered in Bird's vanilla custard, on the table between us with two spoons. Paul had picked up one of the spoons and dug in, but paused before taking a bite to say, 'Why not approach it this way? You're both crashing around in the dark. You both have a mystery that needs solving, questions that need answering. Why not suggest you join forces, help each other out?'

I was mulling over that strategy when I bent over the keyboard and wrote:

Dear Cheryl,
Thank you for reaching out. Although it is far from complete, you should be able to search Clark78's family tree now. I will be happy to talk with you, but it might be better if we took our discussions private. Please feel free to email me or call. My direct contact information is below.
Best wishes, Hannah Ives.

Four hours later, just as I was climbing out of the bathtub, my cell phone rang. I toweled off quickly, slipped into my bathrobe, and accepted the call.

It was a woman's voice, quivering with emotion. 'Hi. This is Cheryl Lannigan. Hope I haven't gotten you at a bad time.'

'No, not at all,' I lied, eager to put her at ease. 'Um, I just finished unloading the dishwasher. I'm glad you called.'

Cheryl wasted no time getting to the point. 'Is that his name, then, my father? Clark? Like Clark Kent?'

'I don't know his name,' I admitted as I lowered the lid on the toilet and sat down on it. 'I had to call him something, so I named him Clark, after the explorer.' Her silence went on for so long that I wondered if she knew which explorer I was talking about.

'If you don't know who he is, then how . . .?' She gasped. 'Oh my God, he's dead, isn't he? I've seen those TV shows! You're trying to identify a dead body from his DNA, right? Found murdered in a ditch off an old country road or something. Oh my God! I'm too late!' She began to sob.

I raised my voice, hoping she'd hear me over the weeping. 'No, no, no! Cheryl, listen to me! It's not like that at all. Listen. To. Me!'

Oh, shit, I thought. *You really handled that well, Hannah.*

I must have gotten through because the sniffling quickly subsided. 'Just who are you?' she asked once she had calmed down, but in a voice tinged with suspicion.

'I'm a genetic genealogy researcher,' I explained. 'Some

people call us search angels because we're volunteers who help people analyze their DNA results and track down their biological family.'

My answer seemed to satisfy her. 'So, he's definitely my father, this Clark78 guy?'

'DNA doesn't lie.'

'Wow, just wow,' she whispered. 'This is so unreal.'

'Tell me about yourself,' I said, keeping my voice low, non-threatening, smooth as a late-night radio DJ. If I could get her talking about herself, maybe she'd forget to wonder about how I fit into her birth father's picture.

'You already know my name,' she began. 'They figure I was born around June thirtieth, 1977, but can't say for sure. I was dumped outside a fire station near Harrisburg, Pennsylvania when I was just a couple of hours old.'

'Did they ever track down your mom?' I inquired gently, keeping my fingers crossed.

'No. They tried, for sure. Articles in the paper. Announcements on the evening news. Flyers with my baby picture stapled to telephone poles.' She paused for a moment, then said, 'They've got Safe Haven Laws these days so it's OK to leave a baby you don't want at a hospital or police station, but back then . . .' A deep sigh. 'Back then, it would have been a crime, so I get it that my mother never stepped forward.

'They called me Baby June,' she said after a pause for breath, her voice brighter now. 'I was dressed in a yellow onesie, with a white knit cap on my head, and all bundled up in a flannel Winnie the Pooh blanket. Thanks to my foster mother, I still have them.'

'So, you were adopted?'

'Eventually, yes. Joe Lannigan, the fireman who found me? He had to turn me over to Child Welfare, of course, but after a while, he and his wife Patty became my foster parents. Adopted me when I was three. Best. Parents. Ever,' she said, emphasizing each word. 'That's why I never . . . well, never mind. They've both passed away now, so I thought why not do the test.

'I looked at his tree,' she said, suddenly shifting gears. 'No offense, but it's kind of spotty.'

'I know. Not up to my usual standard, but then there's so little data to work with.'

'Can I make a confession?' she asked in a girlish whisper.

'Yes, of course. Fire away.'

'When I took the test? I was mostly searching for my birth mother. She could have had an abortion, right, but she didn't. Instead, she decided to go through with the pregnancy. She carried me around inside her for nine months, and there's gotta be a lot of love in that, right? She's the one who gave me up, and I know it must have been hard, but I'd really like to know why. My biological father?' I could almost hear the shrug in her voice. 'He's no better than an anonymous sperm donor as far as I'm concerned. I really hadn't given him much thought at all, so when that match to my father popped up, and not my mother . . . Pow! Hit me square between the eyes.'

'I can imagine,' I said.

'Up until then, it was mostly gobbledegook, my results.'

'Sometimes the data can be confusing, even for a pro,' I admitted.

'You can say that again. A lot of my matches didn't make much sense, but I think it's because I didn't really know what I was looking at. What's the difference between second cousins and first cousins once removed, I ask you? And who cares?'

'I'd be willing to take a look at your results, if you like,' I said. 'What do they say? Two heads are better than one?'

'Ha! Especially if one head knows what it's doing. And that sure isn't me!'

'Do you trust me?' I asked.

'What? Of course. You're the genetic genie or whatever, not me. You can't possibly mess up my family tree any worse than I have. Centimorgans? Endogamy? Give me a break. You might as well be speaking Serbo-Croatian. So, what do you need me to do?'

'Go to your DNA results tab and set me up as a collaborator on your account. If you can't figure out how to do that, just email me your account name and password, and I'll take care of it.'

'So, you're volunteering to be my search angel?'

'That's what I do. Keeps me off the streets and out of trouble.'

'That's super kind of you, Hannah,' she said. And then, with the same note of suspicion creeping into her voice again, 'So, I'm still wondering about this. If you don't know my father, how did you get your hands on his DNA?'

Dang, I thought, *time to lace up your tap shoes and start dancing.*

I took a moment to organize my thoughts, then cleared my throat and tried to explain it in terms Cheryl would understand, but without lying to her or setting off any alarm bells. 'As I said earlier, I work as a forensic genetic genealogist with a group of like-minded volunteers. Way back in 1978, there was a party at a summer house in Annapolis and a girl named Amy died. DNA was collected at the scene, and your father's DNA was among them. Only a handful of people know what actually went on in that house that night, but most of them are now dead. Amy's mother is still alive, though, and we're hoping to get closure for her. Your father, if we can locate him, might be able to make that happen.'

'Are you thinking my father was responsible for that girl's death?'

'I really don't know, Cheryl. He wasn't the only person present that night, and we're still trying to figure out what happened. Obviously it would help if we could talk to him.'

'I hate that word, closure,' she muttered. 'Such bullshit. There is no such thing, you know. You can never close out the hurt entirely.'

'You must miss them terribly,' I said, sensing who was on her mind. 'Your adoptive parents.'

'Mom and Pops were the best,' she said simply.

Silence grew in the cyberspace that stretched between my phone and hers. Cheryl was the first to break it. 'Do you think my father knew about me?'

'Impossible to say, Cheryl, but when I track your father down, it's one of the questions I plan to ask him.'

'I hope you find them,' she said quietly. 'They're all I have left.'

EIGHTEEN

Heaven Must Be Missing an Angel
(Tavares)

L
ess than an hour after our conversation ended, Cheryl
came through.

I accepted the invitation to collaborate on her DNA
account, logged on to make sure the permissions were
working correctly, and was about to dive in when she texted:

*Check out my Facebook page! More about me than you'll
ever want to know!!*

Eager to put a face on the woman I'd so recently been
talking to, I tapped the Facebook icon on my phone and
accepted the friend invitation she'd sent.

Cheryl June Lannigan was in her mid-forties, but could
easily have passed for someone a decade younger. She
had fair, unblemished skin, blonde hair cut in a stylish
chin-length bob and green eyes peeking out from under
expertly shagged bangs. For her profile picture, she'd worn a
navy-blue suit with a pink blouse, and I wondered if she'd
uploaded a professional headshot. Did she sell real estate?
Work for the government? Teach?

According to her Facebook profile, Cheryl lived in Oakmont,
Pennsylvania, a suburb on the Allegheny River just north-
east of Pittsburgh, and worked as a librarian in nearby
Monroeville. She had 398 friends with whom she enjoyed
kayaking, attending book signings at a place called Mystery
Lovers Bookshop, and partying at sports bars where she
drank draft beer and rooted for the Steelers, who were having
a so-so season and could use all the encouragement they
could get. With a smaller group of girlfriends, she'd taken
several Royal Caribbean cruises and one, much longer cruise
to the Greek Isles with the luxury Azamara Line. The rest of

her life seemed to revolve around Holy Family Parish, Saint Irenaeus Catholic Church in particular.

Cheryl listed herself as single. Had she ever been married? I wondered.

A baby picture for Throwback Thursday showed a chubby, laughing three-year-old dressed up for Halloween like a bumble bee. Who wouldn't fall in love with this kid?

Scrolling back in time through her posts, I found a photograph of Cheryl's adoptive parents, the Lannigans. Sitting side by side, Patty Lannigan is tilting her head toward Joe's shoulder and both are grinning at the camera over an enormous sheet cake iced with red and white roses and 'Happy Fiftieth Anniversary to Joe and Patty!' Patty's permed, iron-gray hair looks beauty-parlor fresh while whatever hair remained on Joe's head is covered by a baseball cap embroidered with a big, yellow 'P'. Joe is wearing that same baseball cap – a Pirates fan till the end, it seems – in another photo Cheryl posted on Father's Day two years later. 'Miss you tons, Pops!'

According to the US Phone and Address Directory I consulted next, Cheryl had lived at the same Highland Park address for almost twenty years. Using Google Street View, I strolled by a turreted, extensively remodeled Victorian pile that had been subdivided into four apartments. A peek inside one of the apartments via Zillow revealed elegant staircases, dark wood paneling, varnished pine floors, stained glass transom windows and fireplaces galore. I could be happy living there.

I closed the Zillow app, thinking that after a rocky start, Cheryl had made a good life for herself. Would what we were about to do turn her comfortable, settled life upside down?

Cheryl had told me where she'd been abandoned as an infant, so I decided to check area newspapers for details. It wasn't hard to find: the story dominated the news for days as the fruitless search for Baby June's parents went on. An early article featured a color photograph of Baby June, wrapped in a Pooh blanket, looking like most newborns – not pink, round and chubby-cheeked, but grumpy, red-faced and puffy-eyed.

Harrisburg Chronicle
July 1, 1977

A baby girl swaddled in a blanket with her umbilical cord still attached was abandoned at a fire station outside Harrisburg and police are looking for her parents. Captain Joseph Lannigan said he discovered the baby early yesterday morning in a duffle bag left just outside the firehouse doors and called the police. Temperatures were in the mid-eighties that day.

'I picked her up and the blanket kind of fell away, and I could see that she still had the cord attached,' Captain Lannigan told WGAL-TV. 'This adorable, hours-old newborn was left abandoned and alone,' a Harrisburg police spokesman said. 'We need help locating the parents to get them the assistance they need. Mom, if you're hearing this, please call.'

The baby is doing well after undergoing evaluations at a local hospital, police said. Authorities say they have received an influx of adoption requests for the child they have nicknamed 'Baby June', but said they are not involved in the adoption process.

'Baby June' has been turned over to Child Welfare Services and will be placed into foster care until her family can be identified.

This is the second newborn found abandoned in recent weeks . . .

I quit reading. The first infant had been found in the woods, wrapped in a plastic garbage bag. He hadn't been as lucky as Baby June.

I fumbled on the tabletop for the tissue I use to clean my reading glasses and dabbed at my eyes. I wasn't crying, was I? No, no. Pollen season. Must be my allergies acting up.

As I tucked the tissue into my pocket it occurred to me that there was no mention in the article of Baby June wearing a yellow onesie, and in the photograph, the infant had been hatless. Had the Lannigans embellished Cheryl's story to make it feel a little more warm and fuzzy for the baby girl who had been thrown away?

Now that I had full permission to access Cheryl's account, I logged on. Cheryl had started three trees, but abandoned each early on. Only one, pitiful six-person tree was linked to her DNA results. She had named the tree Baby June.

Swallowing hard, I grabbed for the tissue again.

When I brought up Baby June's DNA matches a few minutes later, though, I had to smile. Cheryl had several strong, second cousin matches on her mother's side – a mere three generations back. I'd have to check, but even if those cousins hadn't linked their DNA results to family trees, they might be able to tell us about their great-grandparents if we simply wrote and asked.

To Cheryl's untrained eye, the proliferation of matches, mostly on her maternal side, with the variety of account names, centimorgan counts, percentages and predicted relationships – half 1C1R? 2xGGniece? – must have been overwhelming. I could tell by the colored dots tagging some of her matches that she'd attempted to organize the results using the Leeds Method, but she'd apparently started with the higher-ranking cousins rather than the lower, made mistakes and given up in frustration.

No way to straighten the mess out; I'd have to start from scratch. I scrolled up, clicked the edit icon on her first match, deleted the colored dot and set to work.

After four long days, three carry-out dinners and missing out on the last high school band concert of the year – grandson Timmy played clarinet, badly – I zeroed in on the two sets of grandparents Cheryl and her second cousins had in common. Their grandparents had been brothers, George and Henry Bigelow respectively, sons of Matthew and Isabel Bigelow of Hagerstown, Maryland.

Isabel had lived to be 101, bless her, and, as is often the case, it was her obituary in the *Daily Mail* of September 1996 that turned out to be my Rosetta Stone. It listed her surviving children, George and Phyllis, and the son, Henry, who had predeceased her. George and Phyllis eventually turned out to be dead ends (and dead by now, too), but Henry Bigelow's 1980 obituary led directly to his son.

Frederick Reed Bigelow, 72, local businessman and long-time owner of Bigelow Pharmacy on West Franklin Street passed away peacefully at home on Tuesday, February 8 surrounded by his loving family, after a long battle with lung cancer. He is survived by his children, Steve, Ellen (Peter) Haller, and Laurie (Matt) Nixon. He will be missed dearly by his seven grandchildren. A requiem mass will be said on Saturday, February 19 at 11:00 a.m. at St Joseph's Catholic Church in Hagerstown with burial following at Rose Hill Cemetery. Funeral arrangements are being handled by the Taylor-Smith Funeral Home. In lieu of flowers, donations may be made to Hospice of Washington County.

If Cheryl's birth mom were psychic, she might have sensed my net closing in.

After crawling along the branches of Cheryl's newly expanded family tree, after shaking every leaf to eliminate other possibilities, I knew Cheryl's biological mother had to be one of two sisters, either Ellen or Laurie Bigelow.

NINETEEN
Hasta Mañana (ABBA)

'So, how's it going, sweetheart?'

Paul had eased through the dining-room door so quietly that he scared me half to death. I pounded my chest with the flat of my hand, trying to jump start my heart. 'Give a gal a little warning, huh?'

He laid his hands on my shoulders and kissed the top of my head. 'Sorry, sweetie, but seriously. How's it going?'

I tilted my notebook in his direction. 'I've narrowed it down to one of two sisters. Now it's a matter of figuring out which sister was in the right place at the right time.'

Paul eased the notebook out of my hands but didn't look at it. 'How about saving the big reveal until later? It's been three days, and you've hardly budged from this chair.'

'Not true,' I insisted. 'I've visited the bathroom at least twice.' I snatched the notebook back. 'But, I'm so close!'

He squeezed my shoulders affectionately. 'And good for you, but all work and no play . . . you know what they say.'

'Don't you have any meetings to go to?' I said, hoping to get him out of my hair, at least temporarily. Midshipmen were off for the summer, but there always seemed to be a departmental meeting or professional development seminar that required his attendance.

'It's Saturday, Hannah. Nobody meets on Saturdays in the summer.'

I managed a grin. 'Oh, right. I've been so involved that I've even lost track of what day it is.'

'What'd I tell you.' Paul seized my hand, pulled me to my feet and turned me around to face him. He gently removed my reading glasses and set them on the dining table. 'And you haven't been getting enough sleep. Your eyes are red.'

'I know, but . . .'

'Let me take you away from all this,' he said.

'But . . .'

'No buts. Let's go stay at the cottage for a week or two.'

Paul was referring to Our Song, the 250-year-old cottage we'd purchased about five years before near Elizabethtown on Maryland's eastern shore. At the beginning of May, we'd spent a weekend at the cottage, opening it up for the season, but had been waiting for a proper visit until the academic year was over and Paul would be responsibility-free.

'No more tutorials? No meetings?' I inquired.

'I had a manuscript consultation set up for next week, but I cancelled.' He stroked my cheek with his thumb. 'It wasn't that time critical. I think we both need to get away. Like now.'

'We'll need groceries,' I said.

Paul grinned. 'Doesn't Acme have an app for that? We'll order ahead. Use Drive Up and Go.'

'The internet's kind of slow,' I complained.

'It's not *that* slow,' Paul said reasonably. 'If I can stream Netflix, it's robust enough for Google.'

I felt myself weakening. I had a closet full of casual clothes and a duplicate set of toiletries at the cottage, so other than my electronics, I wouldn't even need to pack.

Paul continued to plead his case. 'No distractions.'

'Other than the geese,' I said, smiling as I remembered how they flocked noisily over the river, adjusted their wings and coasted to a landing before waddling into the buffet of eel grass and spartina our marshland provided.

I didn't want to admit it, but my butt had fallen asleep and my knees needed oiling. I'd been staring at my laptop screen for so long that my eyes ached. My *brain* ached.

Besides, I was fresh out of objections. I stood on tiptoes and gave Paul a peck on the cheek. 'You're right,' I said. 'Amy's been waiting for more than forty years. I don't think she'd mind if I took a little break.'

Paul grinned and checked his watch. 'If we leave now, we'll get there in time to catch the sunset.'

I wrapped my arms around his neck, stared up into his

dark, persuasive eyes. 'You pack the wine,' I said. 'I'll go get my coat.'

'You promised me a sunset,' I pouted. We were standing on our deck overlooking the Chiconnesick River, watching dark clouds pile up along the horizon.

Paul gestured with his wine glass, one finger raised, pointing west. 'There's a bit of sun poking out over there. See?'

'Close,' I said, unimpressed with a sliver of crimson that vanished as quickly as it had appeared. 'Close, but definitely no cigar.'

We sipped our wine in silence for a while, except for the soothing *ribbit-ribbit-ribbit* of a frog chorus and cicadas *chee-chee-cheeing* in the trees.

'Rain's on the way,' I said, shivering.

He wrapped an arm around me, drawing me close. 'Need help putting the groceries away?'

'Done and dusted,' I said. 'When do you want to eat?'

'Not just yet. I'm enjoying the view, and the company,' he said, his head bent close to mine.

It was too cool to dine on the deck, so when our wine glasses were empty, we moved into the kitchen. Our grocery order had included two Italian subs which I'd laid out on the tablecloth, along with an unopened bag of potato chips and a jar of dill pickles.

'A feast,' Paul said as he unwrapped his sandwich.

'Been slaving away in the kitchen all day,' I quipped as I sat down at the table and ripped open the potato chips. 'Dig in.'

'Go on to bed, Hannah,' Paul said a bit later, after we'd polished off a pint of rum raisin ice cream. 'I'll do the clean-up.'

Other than trash, clean-up consisted of two wine glasses and two spoons, but I didn't complain. I kissed him on the cheek and wished him a good evening, then wandered off to the master bedroom suite.

Did I undress? Put on a nightshirt? Wash my face? Brush my teeth? Evidence suggests I did, but I don't recall. All I know for sure is that I slipped under the covers and slept until

I was awakened by the sun, full on my face, and the aroma of fresh coffee wafting in from the kitchen.

Clearly, Paul was already up. Still feeling sluggish, I drifted out in my nightshirt to join him.

'Slept like the proverbial log,' I reported.

Paul grinned. 'Sawing logs, too,' he said.

'You're kidding.'

'I am not.' He demonstrated with a loud, pig-like snort.

'Don't be a meanie,' I said good-naturedly.

'I brought your stuff in from the car. Put it in the office,' he said, gesturing with his coffee cup. Our office was on the main floor, adjacent to the laundry room, in a modest wing on the opposite side of the living room from the master suite.

'Thank you,' I told him and, carrying my coffee, I moseyed off to dress.

Around nine o'clock, freshly showered and clad in jeans and a T-shirt, I sat down at the desk and started to organize my workspace, hoping I wouldn't be distracted by the scenery. Outside the office windows, leaves shimmered like emeralds with droplets of overnight rain and a trio of acrobatic squirrels raced up the trunk of our stateliest oak and made successful, death-defying leaps into the branches of a tulip poplar just beyond.

Reluctantly, I left them to their antics and busied myself with the power adapters and charging cables. 'Don't we have a power strip somewhere?' I yelled in Paul's general direction.

'Top drawer!' he yelled back.

Even though we'd had the cottage rewired since the reign of George the Third when it was built, there never seemed to be enough electrical outlets. I found the power strip where he said it would be and had everything plugged in, turned on and charging when Paul brought me a fresh cup of coffee. He set it down by my elbow. 'Eeny, meeny, miney, moe, which will it be first, Ellen or Laurie?'

'Ellen, I think. She's closer in age to Amy. Might possibly have been her friend, with you-know-who in common.'

'Clark?'

'That's the one.' Coffee cup in hand, I grinned up at my husband. 'Don't you have chores to do?'

'Are you referring to the hedges, by any chance?'

'I am.'

Eventually, with the dull, intermittent surging of the electric hedge trimmer as background music, I opened up my laptop and got down to work.

Neither sister had a Facebook page, but both were high-achieving women whose names popped up readily on Google and in newspaper database searches.

There was nothing in Ellen Bigelow Haller's resume that inspired anything but unqualified awe. She had graduated from Swathmore, a highly ranked liberal arts college in Pennsylvania, the same year as Amy would have graduated from St John's, then went on to attend medical school at Vanderbilt University in Nashville, Tennessee. Sometime during her residency in dermatology at Parkland Hospital in Dallas, Texas, she met and married Peter Haller, an oral and maxillofacial surgeon. Although Swathmore was only a two-hour drive from the Naval Academy in Annapolis, I couldn't imagine any logical scenario where Ellen and Clark might have met. The schools played sports in different divisions, and Ellen didn't seem like the type whose idea of a good time would be clambering aboard buses in the dead of winter with a couple of hundred other girls to attend tea dances run like cattle calls at the Naval Academy. There seemed to be no gap in her college or graduate school records that would have allowed for a full-term pregnancy, and being in the medical field, she surely would have had ready access to resources to deal discreetly with any unwanted pregnancy.

In late 2012, Dr Peter Haller was deployed with Médecins Sans Frontières to a hospital in Nigeria where he headed up a multidisciplinary team treating noma, a rapidly progressive, polymicrobial, sometimes gangrenous infection of the mouth. According to a feature article in *Texas Monthly* about this medical power couple, Peter and his wife Ellen had three grown children, two grandchildren and another one on the way.

I drew a line through Ellen and moved on to Laurie.

Seconds after I typed Laurie's name into Google, I sat back, impressed. Laurie worked as a biostatistician with Astra-Zeneca in Wilmington, Delaware. Not high enough on the corporate ladder to merit a puffed-up profile on the Big Pharma giant's corporate webpage, but important enough to have been interviewed by the *Wall Street Journal* when the clinical trial of an antipsychotic drug went tragically wrong.

Laurie and her husband, Matt Nixon, were movers and shakers in New Castle County social circles. According to a slick, full-color article in the Life section of *The News Journal*, Matt had recently retired from his position as an executive vice president of M&T Bank and was planning to devote some time to raising funds for a new oncology wing at the Nemours Children's Hospital near the couple's winter home in Lake Nona, Florida. Meanwhile, according to *Out&About Magazine*, the Nixons had donated a Nissan Leaf, five-door, battery-electric vehicle to the previous year's Delaware Military Support charity auction. The smiling couple was pictured standing by the driver's side door of the bright red vehicle. Matt, rail-thin and sporting a shock of snow-white hair, combed straight back, was shaking hands with a representative of the military support group wearing a Vietnam Veteran ball cap. Standing next to the vet, dressed in a navy-blue suit and sensible heels . . . my heart beat a quick *rat-a-tat-tat.*

Fair, faultless skin. Bright green eyes. Take away the tortoiseshell claw that swept her blonde hair up and away from her face rather than letting it curl softly around her cheeks . . . if I didn't know any better, I could be looking at a photograph of Cheryl Lannigan.

Case closed?

The final sentence of the article read: *Mrs Nixon, a 1980 graduate of the US Naval Academy, is a senior executive with Astra-Zeneca.*

Counting backwards, I did the math. Laurie would have entered the Academy in 1976.

I bent over my keyboard and started typing.

In October of 1975, the US Congress passed Public Law 94-106 requiring all military service academies to admit women. Being one of the first women to attend the US Naval Academy was a huge deal. The group was small and select – only eighty-one women met the criteria. So, when eighteen-year-old Laurie Bigelow from St Maria Goretti Catholic High School in Hagerstown, Maryland was sworn into the Plebe Class on July 6, 1976, it made all the local papers.

A year later, in September of 1977, Third Classman Bigelow had been interviewed by the *New York Times* as part of an article, 'Women at 4 Service Academies Viewed as Equal to Men Cadets' in which she was quoted as saying, 'It's all about ability, you know, not gender.' *You go, girl*, I thought.

Case definitely closed.

Laurie Bigelow Nixon had to be Cheryl Lannigan's mother.

TWENTY
Contact (Edwin Starr)

Paul and I were enjoying egg salad sandwiches on the deck trying to talk over the roar of the lawn mower that Rusty Heberling, our caretaker's son, was driving at warp speed around the property.

'So, what's your next step, Hannah?' Paul yelled.

'Talk to Laurie,' I shouted back.

'What if she doesn't want to talk to you?'

'I'll never know unless I try,' I said.

'Or denies everything.'

'Midshipmen don't lie, cheat or steal,' I said, quoting the Naval Academy's honor code. 'I'm an optimist, I guess.'

I tossed Paul an orange and started peeling one for myself. Rusty had ridden on to the field adjoining the old cemetery, so we could finally speak without cupping our hands around our mouths like mini megaphones. 'First step, though, is to let Izzy and the gang know what I've been up to.'

'How about the daughter, then. Cheryl? Are you going to tell her you found her mother?'

'I'll need to talk to Laurie first. After so many years, it's possible she doesn't want to be found.' As we talked, I separated my orange into segments and lined them up on the arm of my Adirondack chair. 'But I guess I'll cross that bridge when I come to it. As soon as I finish lunch, I plan to give Laurie a call.'

'Just like that?' Paul snapped his fingers.

'Well, maybe not quite as easily as that. She's an executive at Astra-Zeneca in Wilmington, so I'll try to reach her there first. Wouldn't be fair to ambush her at home. Her husband, Matt, is already retired, but I'm thinking she's still a bit young to hang up the job.'

I slipped a section of orange into my mouth and chewed

it thoughtfully. 'My stomach is in knots, Paul. What if I screw this up? I'd be letting so many people down. Izzy, Jack, Mark, for sure, because they seem to trust me, but mostly I'll be failing Amy and all those other girls who didn't need to die.'

Paul laid a hand on my knee and squeezed it affectionately. 'First of all, you won't screw it up. And second of all, even if Laurie Nixon stonewalls you, Jack will turn the information you've gathered over to the police. I don't know about you, but I'd rather have a nice, quiet discussion with Hannah Ives about something that happened in my reckless youth rather than be grilled by a battle-scarred homicide cop under a bank of ten-thousand-watt klieg lights.'

That made me laugh. 'Thanks for the pep talk, Professor Ives. Now, let me alone while I finish my orange. I need time to think.'

Paul swept the orange peels onto our empty plates and headed back into the house. 'Call me if you need anything,' he tossed over his shoulder. 'I'll be taking the hedge clippers to that silly topiary.'

'That silly topiary' was a swan that had come with the house. Right now it looked less like a swan and more like a camel, collapsed from heat stroke on the desert sand. 'Better you than me,' I said.

It was early in the work week, a Tuesday. I couldn't be sure what time Laurie usually took her lunch, so I waited until after two to make the call. Astra-Zeneca had at least three contact numbers listed on their webpage, so I tried the 800 numbers first before hitting the jackpot with a local 302 number that was answered by a real, live switchboard operator.

'My name is Hannah Ives and I'd like to speak to Laurie Nixon, please.'

After a pause, presumably to check a directory, she said, 'Just a moment, and I'll put you through.'

Whew! I sighed with relief. At least Laurie still worked there. My heart fluttered like butterfly wings as I realized I might soon be speaking to her.

Alas, the next person to pick up the line was definitely not Laurie. 'Ms Nixon's office, this is Prashant. How many I assist you?' A young man, I thought, speaking in melodic Indian-accented English.

I repeated what I'd told the operator. 'My name is Hannah Ives and I'd like to speak with Laurie Nixon, please.'

'Is Ms Nixon expecting your call?'

'She is not, but I have some important information for her.'

'Ms Nixon has a busy schedule today. May I tell her what is the nature of your call, please?'

I paused for a few seconds, wondering what key word to use that would get Laurie's attention. 'Please tell her it's about Baby June.'

'Baby June,' he repeated. I suspected he was writing information down on one of those pink 'while you were out' telephone message pads. 'And your call back number, please?'

I recited my cell phone number for Prashant. 'But I'd really like to speak with her today, if she's available. It won't take long.'

After a short pause, Prashant said, 'Just one moment, please,' and soft jazz music replaced his voice on the line.

I waited while Miles Davis segued into Kenny G, who stopped abruptly, his soprano sax strangled in mid-solo.

'This is Laurie Nixon. Hannah, did you say your name was?' Her voice sounded deep and gravelly. I wondered if she was recovering from a cold. Perhaps she smoked.

'That's right, Hannah Ives. I'm a genetic genealogy researcher and I was hired by a woman named Cheryl June Lannigan to help find her birth parents.'

Laurie was silent for so long that I feared she had ended the call. Then she sighed deeply, sniffed and said, 'I've been expecting this call for more than forty years.'

'Is there some place we can talk face-to-face?' I asked.

'Not here, not at my office. Would you be free tomorrow for lunch, around one? I gather from the Maryland area code that you live close by.'

'I'm even closer than that. My husband and I have a cottage down in Tilghman County. It'll take me about an hour to reach you.'

'Ah, you'll be coming north on 301, then, merging into I95. Take the Concord Pike exit onto 202. You'll pass right by our headquarters, but if you continue up 202 there'll be a number of strip malls on the right. Let's meet at Panera. It's just past the Sherman Williams Paint Place. If you get to the Methodist Church, you've gone too far.'

'I'm sure I can find it, or my GPS can.'

'Tell me something. Who knows about this?' Laurie asked in a quiet, raspy voice.

'Nobody yet. After we talk, perhaps I'll have some direction, but right now, what I discovered is just between you and me.'

'Thank you for that.' She sighed, sounding relieved. 'I'll need time to prepare my family.'

'Of course,' I said. 'You have my phone number if you need to reach me.'

'Until tomorrow at one, then,' she said, and ended the call.

TWENTY-ONE
Shame (Evelyn 'Champagne' King)

The following day, I was up early, rummaging through the cottage closet, looking for something more appropriate for meeting with a big-wig female executive than the cargo pants and sleeveless shirts I usually wear for gardening. Until I pulled it out from behind a clutch of Paul's Hawaiian shirts, I'd forgotten about the floral Chicos jacket I'd worn to an art gallery opening several years before, draped on a hanger over a tangerine top and a pair of slim, black jeans. With black slip-on flats, it would do nicely.

When it was time to go, I plugged Panera's address into Waze which informed me that if I left immediately, I'd arrive at twelve forty-two. Thinking a bit of a buffer would be a prudent thing, I started the car and headed out.

By the time Route 301 merged into I95, however, the traffic had been so forgiving that Waze had revised my arrival time to twelve-thirty. I'd have to pass the Astra-Zeneca headquarters in any case, so with a few minutes to spare, I decided to swing by. I turned off Powder Mill Road onto Astra-Zeneca Drive, and began circling the sprawling, multi-winged, four-story brick and glass complex. I wondered what it would be like to claw my way to the top, as Laurie Nixon had done, in a corporation so huge it had 121 locations in sixty-one countries.

Following signs to the Visitor Parking, I made a loop around the circle at the Visitors' entrance, pausing for a moment to admire a tall, twisty, flame-like sculpture, which I realized was some artist's stainless-steel representation of the Astra-Zeneca logo. What was I doing there, anyway? Was I hoping to catch sight of Laurie Nixon leaving the building? Foolish, I suppose. Rather than use the same entrance as the riff-raff, company executives probably had a separate parking lot and a dedicated entrance out back.

After my little detour, I circled out and headed north on Concord Pike. Panera was easy to find. I pulled into the parking lot and slotted my car into a space in front of the paint store.

Laurie was already there, waiting just inside Panera's door.

Laurie was at least half a head taller than me, big-boned and solid, but without an ounce of fat. I needn't have worried about a dress code. She must have taken the day off, because she was dressed in gray Lululemon joggers, a blue jean jacket worn open over a baggy white T-shirt and Adidas running shoes. Her pale hair was tied back with a purple scrunchie into a low ponytail. I walked directly up to her and extended my hand. 'Laurie, I'm Hannah.'

Her hand swallowed mine, her grip was firm. She didn't smile. 'How did you . . .?' she began.

'You look just like her,' I said.

Laurie's eyes glistened. A single tear escaped, but she swiped it away with the back of her hand. 'I've already ordered,' she told me. 'I've saved us a booth at the back, just around the corner from the beverage machines.'

'Thanks,' I said, 'I'll get lunch and join you in a couple of minutes.'

Although I wasn't hungry – jangled nerves dampen my appetite – I ordered one of Panera's Duos, a cup of French onion soup and half a turkey-avocado sandwich on wholewheat bread. At the beverage machine, I filled my glass with ice and pink lemonade, stuck a plastic straw through the plastic lid.

I found Laurie easily, slid my tray across the table opposite hers and sat down. 'What are you having?' I asked, just to break the ice.

'Corn chowder, but I'm not really hungry.' Using two fingers, she pushed the half-eaten bowl aside, then set her spoon down. She'd purchased a drink, too, a smoothie, green and nasty-looking, but undoubtedly healthy.

'Me, neither,' I said. 'We can ask for take home boxes, I suppose.'

At that, she managed a smile. 'First things first, though. How did you find me?'

'After her adoptive parents died, Cheryl took a DNA test,' I explained, 'She uploaded the results to all the major genealogy databases. Quite a few second- and third-cousin matches popped up, and she tried to make sense out of them, but when she couldn't, she contacted me. I'm what they call a search angel.'

'Sweet,' Laurie said in a voice so gruff and flat I couldn't tell whether it was praise or pan. She leaned forward with her forearms resting on the table. 'But that doesn't really answer my question, does it? How did you find *me*?'

'It's a bit complicated, but your niece, Ellen's daughter, had her DNA tested and so did two of your Uncle George's grand-kids. That, plus miscellaneous third and fourth cousins that descended from a brother on your great-grandmother, Isabel's side.' I shrugged. 'After that, it took math, logic, research and a good deal of experimentation with probabilities in order to narrow it down.' I paused, gave her a wan smile. 'I can't find my dining table because of all the spreadsheets.'

When she didn't respond, I continued. 'Eventually, I figured out that Cheryl's mother had to be either you or your sister Ellen. After researching both of your backgrounds, it was you who seemed to be in the right place at the right time.'

She raised an eyebrow. 'And that would be . . .?'

'The United States Naval Academy, Annapolis, Maryland, early October, 1976.'

It had been a long time since I'd watched a strong woman crumble. In the booth across from me, Laurie Nixon appeared to deflate, head bowed, shoulders slumped, arms dangling loose at her sides. By the way her shoulders trembled, I knew she was crying.

I took a bite of sandwich, ate a spoonful or two of soup, waited her out.

Eventually, she raised her head, grabbed a wad of napkins off her tray and wiped her eyes. 'Sorry,' she said, then used one of the napkins to blow her nose. 'It all flooded back on me just then.'

'Bad or sad?' I asked.

'A bit of both,' she said. 'They hated us, you know.'

'Who?' I asked, although I could guess.

'The men. They turned their backs on us whenever we walked by. I could take shunning, but one night at dinner, it got physical. My platoon leader shook a finger in my face, screamed at me and swore he would make it his mission to see to it that I was gone before he graduated. I had to stand there mute, all braced up with his spit drying on my face. Sonofabitch.'

'Why did they hate women so much?'

She shrugged. 'Back in those days, women weren't allowed to serve in combat roles, so some of the guys, and even the professors, worried that we were taking spots away from men who *could* fight.' She twirled her beverage straw thoughtfully for a moment, then said, 'Do you remember James Webb?'

'The NASA space telescope guy?'

She snorted. 'Not that James Webb, the other one. Naval Academy grad, Marine in Vietnam, was a senator from Virginia when they passed the bill that allowed women into the service academies. He didn't vote for it, natch. At the beginning of my first class year he wrote a screed for the *Washingtonian* titled "Women Can't Fight", in which he claimed that women were "corrupting" the military. It was pure, unadulterated poison. A couple of years later, Ronald Reagan appointed Webb Secretary of the Navy, so whatcha gonna do? I served my five and got out.'

'If it was so horrible at the Academy, why did you stay?'

She straightened a bit, rotated her shoulders and settled back more comfortably against the upholstery. 'My parents were spending a bundle trying to keep Ellen in Swathmore. I aced the SATs in math, so when the guidance counselor suggested I might have a shot for a free education at the Naval Academy, it seemed like a no brainer. The harassment seemed like a small price to pay.

'Besides, I was too damn stubborn. I tried to see it for what it was, a bunch of macho bullshit. The Academy had been all male for over a hundred-and-thirty years and they really didn't want girls joining their private club. The class just ahead of us was particularly beastly. They had banners made up saying LCWB.' She snorted. 'Last class with balls.'

She closed her eyes for a second, then opened them slowly. 'Do you know about the Herndon climb?'

'My husband's taught at the Academy for over twenty years,' I told her. 'So, yeah.'

Herndon is a granite obelisk about twenty-one feet high named after Commander William Lewis Herndon who went down with his ship off the coast of North Carolina during a hurricane in 1857. Every May, the monument gets slathered with Crisco and a 'dixie cup' hat – required wearing for plebes – is superglued to the top. In a raucous ceremony that officially marks the end of their lives as lowly plebes, they scrabble up the greased monument and replace the dixie cup with an upperclassman's hat.

I wasn't sure where this discussion was taking us, but Laurie knew why I had come to see her, so I decided to let her get there by her own route, and in her own time. My job was to keep the conversation going. 'When we first came to the Academy,' I told her, 'I tried to go to everything – the dutiful faculty wife and all that – but I have to confess that the Herndon climb made me extremely uncomfortable.' I paused, trying to come up with the right word. 'It seemed so . . . feral.'

'Barbaric,' she said, nodding in agreement. 'My plebe year, the men had T-shirts made that said NGOH: no girls on Herndon. And they meant it, too. After they got the human pyramid going, my roommate tried to climb on, but they yanked her down. Kitty had been a cheerleader in high school. She could have reached the top in two seconds flat, but, no, they yanked her down. Took those macho assholes two and a half hours to get that cap down, which was a piss-poor record, by the way. Serves them right.'

She tapped tented fingers against her lips. 'We were so outnumbered, us girls, that opposition seemed fruitless. Eighty-one women, four thousand men, that's, what? Two percent of the brigade? Usually there's safety in numbers, but they scattered us all around Bancroft Hall. I was in a company with a few other women, but some of the companies had no women at all. Thank God for the bathrooms. It was the only place I could find peace.'

Laurie began to pick at the napkin bunched up in her hand. 'Travis caught me at a weak moment.'

'Travis?'

'The baby's father.'

Travis who? I wanted to shout, but it was more important to keep my mouth shut and let her talk.

'Someone put a dead rat in my mailbox, and I just lost it. I'd been crying in the bathroom for about fifteen minutes when I decided that was a complete waste of time, so I went for a long walk along the sea wall.' She paused. 'Gazing at the water is really calming, don't you think?'

I had to agree.

'Anyway, that's where Travis found me, sitting on a bench by Triton Light. He was out for a jog, stopped, asked me if I was OK, was there anything he could do. He was a second classman, but I knew him because he was my squad leader. He was the only upperclassman to treat me nicely after that whole, hot, horrible summer. So, we talked for a little while, then went for a walk around by the new Sailing Center. One thing led to another . . .' Her voice trailed off, then a slight smile animated her face. 'It was in one of the 44s,' she confided. 'We could have snuck aboard *Intrepid*, or *Vigilant* or even *Dauntless*, I suppose, but the boat was named *Flirt*. Isn't that hysterical? Sister Mary Aurelie would have been scandalized. She taught us that unmarried sex was a fast-track route to Hell. But after that evening with Travis, I had news for Sister Mary A. Sex can be great!'

Then, as now, upperclassmen dating plebes is strictly forbidden. 'Pretty risky,' I chided. 'If someone found out about the relationship, you both could have been expelled.'

She waved my concerns away. 'It was one and done,' she said. 'Ships that pass in the night, if you will. Travis and I never spoke of it again, and after first semester was over, I probably saw him only once or twice across the yard.'

'And then . . .' I prodded.

'It was four months before I suspected I was pregnant,' Laurie said. 'With all the physical activity and the stress and all, my period had gone all whack-a-doodle. No morning sick-ness. No heartburn. No bloating. Nothing. And you probably know about Severn River Hip Disease,' she said, drawing quote marks in the air with her fingers.

'The Freshman Fifteen,' I said, 'Naval Academy style. What a four-thousand-calorie a day diet will do to you if you're not careful.'

'Truth,' she said. 'I was a big girl anyway – played soccer in high school – but it wasn't until February rolled around that I knew I was in a shitload of trouble.' She grimaced. 'We didn't refer to February as the Dark Ages for nothing. I'm not sure what the rules are now, but back then, I had only two options.' She ticked them off on her fingers. 'One, I could have an abortion, but that wasn't going to happen.' She crossed herself. 'Roman Catholic, you know. Hail Mary, full of grace, blessed art thou among women and all that, amen. Second, I could resign. I figured if they were going to kick me out anyway, I might as well get as many academic credits under my belt as possible before they tied a rocket to my tail.'

'So you never told Travis, what's-his-name?'

'Palmer. Travis Palmer.' She shook her head. 'Paternity was a dismissal offense, too. As I said, Travis had been nice to me, so why ruin his life?'

Travis Palmer. Travis Palmer. Travis Palmer. I repeated the name silently. *Palm trees in Traverse City.* No way I was going to forget it.

I forced myself to refocus and asked, 'What happened to him, do you know?'

'He wanted to fly, but I hear he got disqualified. I think he went SWO.' She shrugged. 'I don't keep up. Don't read *Shipmate.* Never attended a reunion.'

I remembered with absolute clarity the final months of my pregnancy with Emily. My mother joked that I looked like an olive on a toothpick. (Gee thanks, Mom.) No way I could have hidden my condition, even if I'd wanted to.

I leaned closer over the table, lowered my voice. 'But, Laurie,' I said, 'how on earth did you pull it off?'

'I think I told you that the Academy was almost totally unprepared to deal with us. After Congress changed the law, they had less than a year to get ready, and other than the bathrooms . . .' She shrugged. 'Take uniforms. Our dress uniforms were the same as they issued to women in the fleet: a skirt, stockings and heels. We were expected to march and drill in skirts, wearing three-inch heels, carrying a rifle. There were so many injuries, that the navy decided to fix the problem by simply sawing the heels off the shoes. You can imagine how well that worked.'

'Reminds me of that famous quote. Like Ginger Rogers, you had to dance as well as Fred Astaire, except do it backwards and in high heels.'

Laurie grinned, aimed an index finger at me and said, 'Exactly!'

'I'm surprised you weren't crippled for life,' I said, a bit puzzled about where this discussion of uniforms was going.

'Me, too, but to their credit, the officers in charge were just winging it. They rushed us in so fast that our working uniforms had to be adapted from what they issued to the men. Nothing fit right. Except for the white works,' she added. 'Drawstring bell bottoms, and because I had more bust than a male midshipman, the tunic was quite roomy. It was like walking around all day in your pajamas.'

I had inherited two pairs of those drawstring bell bottoms from a mid we had sponsored, so I knew what she was talking about. And if I had been pregnant . . . suddenly, I got it.

'I'm going to show you a picture.' Laurie reached for her cell phone and tapped a few keys before turning the screen in my direction. Posing next to a pillar in the Zimmerman bandstand was Midshipman Bigelow, dressed in the working uniform known as blue alpha: a short-sleeved black shirt belted into a pair of black trousers, shiny black shoes. 'This is me, taken around Easter. Do I look pregnant to you?'

I stared at the photo for a long time. 'You look well-fed and healthy, but no, not the least bit pregnant.' I looked up, caught her eye. 'Are you sure this photo was taken at Easter?'

'April tenth, 1977. I looked it up. And check out the tulips.'

There was no arguing about the tulips.

'Our dress uniforms had jackets, thank goodness, but

squeezing into the working uniform was a bit more of a challenge. If anybody noticed, though, they never let on.'

She reached out for her phone, so I handed it back. 'I'm five foot ten, so I was allowed to weigh up to one hundred and seventy-seven pounds. I never went over one hundred and fifty, even toward the end.'

The end. The inevitable baby. That's what I didn't understand. Midshipmen are in the Navy. A few weeks of leave, maybe, but they don't get summers off. At the end of plebe year, third-class mids like Laurie would have been sent on a summer cruise, a 'day in the life' kind of thing, serving on a surface ship or a submarine.

'But, what about your youngster cruise?' I asked.

Laurie grimaced, making me wonder if I'd hit a nerve. 'Women weren't allowed on combat ships until 1994 and we couldn't serve on subs until 2010. Twenty effing ten! Jeesh! And if you think guys at the Naval Academy were upset about women trying to crash their party, you should have heard the complaints from men in the fleet. Even their wives were outraged.' Laurie screwed her face into a pout and whined, "I don't think it's fair that they take our husbands away from us for months at a time and then put other women with them." Boo effing hoo. Quite simply, there weren't enough slots for everyone.' She stirred a straw around in her smoothie and took a leisurely sip. 'I actually considered dropping out of the Academy because of that, the limited career paths that were available to women, I mean, but I decided to gut it out. And in the end, it worked out great.'

'How so?' I asked.

Laurie smiled, a bit wistfully, I thought. 'The Navy didn't know what to do with me after graduation, so they parked me in a doctoral program at George Washington University. In biostatistics,' she clarified. '*Et voilà!* So, here I am.

'I envy the women who join up today,' she added after a moment. 'There isn't any job they can't do.'

'I read that a woman has just qualified to be a SEAL,' I said, 'and SEAL training is brutal.'

'Bravo zulu!' Laurie said, raising her drink. 'I'm grateful, really. I don't think I would have made a very good sailor.'

'Why's that?'

She leaned forward, lowered her voice. 'I get seasick.'

'So, what *did* you do that summer?' I asked, trying to steer her back on track.

'Long story short, I spent part of my third class summer shuffling papers around the big Navy Support depot in Mechanicsburg, Pennsylvania. They didn't know me, I didn't know them, and we both were happy with the arrangement. After Ellen went off to Vanderbilt, I inherited her old VW Bug. It was a lifesaver that summer. I was just heading off for three weeks of leave when I went into labor.'

I didn't know much about Laurie's family, but I was willing to bet she wasn't planning on spending her leave at home that summer. 'You must have known the baby would be coming soon. What was your plan?'

'Plan? What plan? I didn't have a plan. I was in total denial. I rented a cottage on the Jersey shore – it wasn't as posh then as it is now – but, I never made it there. The baby was born in the bathtub of a motel somewhere along state route 15,' she said. 'The rest you know.'

We sat in silence for a long time after that, me picking at my sandwich, Laurie sipping her smoothie and, seemingly embarrassed by what she'd just disclosed, looking everywhere but at me. She was the first to break the silence. 'So, where the hell do we go from here?'

'What do you want me to tell your daughter?' I asked gently.

'As I said when you called yesterday, I've been expecting this news for more than forty years, but I've never been brave enough to confide in my family. I still need time to work it out. Please, go ahead and tell her my name and as much of my story as you think she can handle, but mostly, tell her how much I loved her. I'm deeply ashamed of what I did, but I was young, incredibly stupid, and scared stiff. Someday, I hope she'll forgive me.'

I reached over my soup, now stone cold and congealing, to squeeze her hand. 'You can tell her that yourself, Laurie.' I picked up my cell phone and opened my contacts. 'I'm sharing Cheryl's contact information via AirDrop. Use it when you're ready.'

Laurie picked up her iPhone, tapped the screen and accepted the file. 'Thank you, Hannah. Two weeks, no more. Tell her I'll call.'

For Cheryl's sake, I hoped it was a promise her mother would keep. It might be hard to make up for lost time, I thought, but there was no reason Laurie couldn't try.

TWENTY-TWO
It's Raining Men (The Weather Girls)

Travis Palmer, class of 1978. Sum total of the information I had.

Before passing the good news on to the Sleuths, I wanted to dig up some background information on the guy. Was he still alive, for example? Seemed as good a place as any to start.

After leaving Panera, I sat in my car for a while giving Professor Google a workout, so it was closing in on five-thirty before I got back to the cottage. 'Hey, honey, I'm home!' I sang out.

'So I noticed,' Paul replied from the kitchen where I found him looking adorable wearing the ruffled, 1940s vintage apron Emily had given me one Christmas. He dumped the contents of a Caesar salad kit into a blue glass bowl and flashed me a grin. 'Mac and cheese is in the oven.'

'Smells divine.' I hugged him from behind. 'I'm pretty sure I would marry you all over again, if only for your mac and cheese.'

Paul followed the recipe on the back of the Mueller's box, the same as my mother always did. With the exception of Mom's meatloaf with mashed potatoes and gravy, it was the best comfort food ever.

'From the look on your face, I gather your visit was a success,' he said.

I snitched a crouton from the top of the salad and popped it into my mouth. 'Cheryl Lannigan's father is a 1978 Naval Academy grad named Travis Palmer.'

'Good job, Hannah!'

I bowed modestly. 'Thank you.'

'Have you told the gang?'

'Not yet. Laurie hadn't kept up with Travis, or with any of

her classmates, actually. I know zero, zip, nada about Travis Palmer, except what I just told you.'

'You'll be able to find him in the *Lucky Bag*, at least,' Paul reminded me.

'I'm going to check with Mark to see if he's made it over to the library yet. Once we have yearbook photos of the two guys, we'll need to run them by the bartender, Donna Crowe. Izzy has her contact information.'

Paul opened the refrigerator and slotted the salad bowl into a narrow space on the top shelf between the half and half and a tub of vanilla yogurt. He emerged holding a bottle of chardonnay. He filled two wine glasses that were waiting on the counter and held one out to me.

'You're reading my mind,' I said, reaching for the glass.

'Let's go sit on the deck,' he said, turning to lead the way. 'You can tell me about your day.'

On my way past the pantry, I snagged a bag of pretzel sticks. 'Right behind you,' I said.

'Cheryl's the image of her mother,' I told him once we'd gotten settled in our chairs. 'Wouldn't need a DNA test to confirm that relationship.'

I summarized my conversation with Laurie, sharing everything I had learned about the circumstances surrounding her baby's clandestine conception and birth. When I ran out of steam, Paul asked, 'How did she seem, then, the mother?'

I thought for a moment before replying. 'She broke down once, but overall? Cool, professional and somewhat emotionally detached. I'm no psychiatrist, but I think she's still in denial about the baby. On an intellectual level, she knows what happened, but . . .' I fumbled for the right words. 'I think she may feel a bit like an observer, as if it happened to somebody else.'

Paul wagged his head. 'I fail to understand how a woman can carry a pregnancy to full term and yet nobody notices.'

I tore open the bag of pretzels and offered it to Paul. 'It's called cryptic pregnancy, and it's more common than you might think. One in every four-hundred-and-seventy-five pregnancies, according to WebMD. And in one out of two thousand five hundred cases, a woman doesn't realize she's carrying a baby until she actually goes into labor.'

Paul nibbled thoughtfully on the end of a pretzel stick. 'Sounds like something you'd read in a supermarket tabloid: "Unsuspecting Woman Gets Surprise of a Lifetime!"'

'The Learning Channel aired a whole series on cryptic pregnancies, Paul. It ran for four seasons.'

'The so-called Learning Channel?' Paul snorted. 'The network that gave birth to mindless reality shows like *Extreme Cougar Wives*, *Dr Pimple Popper* and *Little Honey Boo Boo*? *That* Learning Channel?'

'*Cake Boss* was kind of fun.'

Playfully, Paul tossed the stub of his pretzel in my direction. It ricocheted off my shoulder and shattered into a thousand crumbs on the deck where the squirrels would enjoy it in the morning. 'I still don't get it.'

I brushed salt off my lap and tried to explain. 'That's because you're remembering short, fat, lumbering me. *Moi*, the woman who couldn't hoist herself out of a bean bag chair without the aid of a forklift. Laurie's tall, big-boned and super athletic. Tall women with tight abs often carry their baby up and behind their ribcage where it hardly shows. Laurie showed me a picture of herself at seven months and I swear, you absolutely could not tell, and I was looking for it.'

Paul leaned sideways until his temple was touching mine. 'Never argue with a woman about female bodily functions.'

'That is wise advice, Professor Ives. Advice I wish you would share with certain spineless politicians.'

Paul laughed, pressed his hands flat on his thighs and levered himself into standing position. 'On that note, I think there's some mac and cheese calling for my attention.'

'Call me when it's ready,' I said. 'In the meantime, I'm going to sit here and commune with Mother Nature.'

While Paul put the finishing touches on dinner, I sipped my wine and watched a mother duck lead her ducklings across the lawn. At the river's edge, they hesitated until, one by one, reassured by her quacking, they waddled close and tumbled into the water after her. Mothers should protect their children, I thought sourly, not stuff them in duffle bags and leave them for strangers to care for. Cheryl asked me to find her mother, and I had, but I couldn't write the end of their story. That was up to them.

After dinner, back in the office, I nibbled one of the ginger cookies Paul had provided for dessert and got back to work.

First, I wrote a long email to Cheryl summarizing my conversation with her mother. I urged her to be patient and wait to be called, but gave her Laurie's contact information in case that call was too long in coming. Was I taking sides? You bet. After my meeting with her mother, ninety percent of my sympathies lay with Cheryl.

That done, I went looking for Travis Palmer. After twenty fruitless minutes, I was beginning to think he'd been beamed down from Planet Gallifrey like Doctor Who.

On Facebook, the name was fairly common. I found an outfielder for the Pittsburg Pirates, a high school football coach, a marine surveyor, a cameraman, an actor on the long-running reality show *American Pickers* which follows a team as they scour the US looking for hidden gems in basements, junkyards, garages and barns, and also meet quirky characters like the goofy Travis Palmer in Topeka, Kansas pictured wearing a colander on his head. That Travis Palmer was a proponent of Pastafarianism, a spoof religion whose prophet is the Flying Spaghetti Monster. 'I was touched by his noodly appendance,' he posted. 'R'amen.'

None of those Travis Palmers had profiles that seemed to fit the guy I was looking for.

'A middle name would certainly help,' I grumped aloud.

Paul must have overheard. He stuck his head through the doorway. 'Why are you knocking yourself out?'

I glanced up over the top of my reading glasses. 'I thought you were watching the Orioles play Cleveland.'

'They're getting trounced,' he said as he entered the office.

'To answer your question, I don't like being thwarted.'

'That's a lovely word, thwarted. Has good mouth-feel.'

'So does "chortle," but I don't feel much like laughing right now. There are simply too many Travis Palmers in the world.'

I scowled. 'And if there's any justice in that world at all, I hope there will soon be one less.'

I took off my glasses and rubbed my tired eyes. 'But you're right. No sense knocking myself out when Mark Wallis should be able to track the guy down through his Navy contacts.'

'Exactly.'

I smiled at my husband, put my glasses back on, bent over the keyboard and began typing. 'Let me text the group, and then I'll call it a day.'

I wrote: *Cheryl's father is Travis Palmer, USNA '78. No other info.*

I didn't even have time to shut down my laptop before the accolades came rolling in. Clapping hands emoji. A big thumbs up. Bravo zulu, that last one from Mark.

I texted again. Mark. *Can you get the Lucky Bag photos?* He texted back. *On it.*

One more text: *Izzy, I know you're slammed. Send contact info for Donna Crowe and I'll take it from there.*

Izzy sent a heart followed by a big thumbs up.

Night all. I closed with a happy face and a long string of Zs. Then I powered off my laptop and went to bed.

TWENTY-THREE
Knowing Me, Knowing You (ABBA)

M ark Wallis wasted no time getting back to me. He must have been waiting on the doorstep when the library opened for summer hours at seven-thirty because the yearbook photos pinged into my mailbox at nine o'clock.

Palmer born in Gainesville, FL. 10-2-57. Going for OMPF.
He'd signed off with a fingers crossed emoji,

OMPF? I did a quick lookup. Official Military Personnel File.

If access to military personnel records was as closely guarded as my personal medical information under HIPAA, I figured Mark would need a SWAT team to gain access to them. Nevertheless, he'd served in the Navy for decades and had friends in high (very high!) places, so maybe his optimism wasn't misplaced.

Feeling excited, like I was about to cross an important threshold, I downloaded the images to my desktop, moused over the first JPEG and clicked.

Nicholas Edward Forsythe I recognized, of course. His *Lucky Bag* photo had been used in an announcement of his graduation, the one the Public Affairs Office had released to his hometown paper. Same dark curls, an errant comma hovering over his brow. Same astonishing blue eyes. Tragic that he died so young.

In stark, yin-yang contrast to his friend, Travis Shillingford Palmer looked so relentlessly Scandinavian you'd wonder if he'd just skied in from Denmark to invite you over for *smørrebrød* and schnapps. His straight, white-blond hair was parted on the left and swept right, combed low over his forehead. His right eyebrow was mischievously quirked; arched any higher and it would have disappeared under the fringe. Pale sideburns, evenly trimmed, as per regulation, ended level with the middle ear. Clearly, Cheryl's blonde genes weren't all inherited from her mother.

I considered Travis's photo dispassionately. Of course women would fall for this guy. A mother would swoon if her daughter dragged him home for Thanksgiving; she'd serve him an extra slice of pumpkin pie. A dad would whip the tarp off the '64 Mustang he pampered in the garage, hand over the car keys and invite him to take it out for a spin.

No wonder he could get away with murder.

Armed with Palmer's full name and birth date, I decided to try my searches again.

Yes, he had been born in Gainesville in October of 1957, and according to a public records search, he still lived in Florida.

Florida is among the states whose voter registration information is readily available online. With my heart doing flip-flops in my chest, I clicked my way over to the voter database section of MyFlorida.com, entered Palmer's full name and birth date, verified that I was not a robot by selecting pictures of fire hydrants, and finally, while holding my breath, I clicked 'submit'.

According to his voter registration record, Palmer lived in a condo on Bulkhead Road in Green Cove Springs, a village in Clay County not far from Jacksonville, and had been registered to vote there since 1991. I noted he voted Democratic. Well, that was one thing in his favor.

I Googled his address which, from the name – Bulkhead Road – I expected to be a luxury, waterfront condo. Sadly, the number I'd assumed was an apartment number turned out to belong to a private mailbox maintained by St Brendan's Isle, a mail forwarding service popular with people on the move, like cruisers, RVers, long-haul truckers, expats, doctors, nurses, and military personnel.

That really narrowed it down, I thought sourly. Travis S. Palmer could be living, quite literally, anywhere in the world.

Donna Crowe, on the other hand, lived in Mesa, a city just south of Scottsdale, Arizona. According to Izzy, Donna designed exhibits for the i.d.e.a. Museum there, an interactive art museum for kids of all ages. Before reaching out to the former bartender, I created a folder on my desktop labeled 'MugShots' and moved Travis and Nicholas's yearbook photos into it. Then, I logged on to the Nimitz Library website, located the most recent *Lucky Bag* they had digitized – 1974 – and scrolled through the pages, selecting four additional midshipman photos, more or less at random, to add to the lineup. Then I labeled the images Mid1 through Mid6. Had I watched too many episodes of *Law and Order*? Probably, but it seemed the proper way to go about it.

Using the email address Izzy had supplied, I emailed Donna, introduced myself, explained my mission, asked her to suggest a good time for a Facetime call, attached the MugShot folder and sent it off. With nothing left to do but wait, I set my phone aside, put on my water shoes and dragged the kayak down to the dock.

Fog still lay heavy on the water when I set out, but by the time I reached the Chesapeake Bay, the sun had begun to burn through the haze. I turned the kayak around and paddled back, pleased to see that the bald eagles we had discovered the previous spring were still nesting in the dead, bleached-white branches of one of the tall trees along the bank. Ospreys were nesting, too, on the green channel marker at the head of the creek. It was late June, and the chicks would be hatching soon.

When I returned to the cottage, I found Paul in the kitchen, looming over the toaster.

I hung my windbreaker on a hook just inside the back door and said, 'Does it toast any faster if you threaten it?'

Paul laughed. 'Shall I put a slice in for you?'

'Yes, please.'

Paul obliged. 'Your phone has been pinging.'

'Oh, good,' I said. 'Maybe it's that bartender out in Arizona.' I waited until my slice popped up, then slathered it with butter and added a generous sprinkle of cinnamon sugar. Munching happily, I headed to the office to check my messages.

Any time after noon, Donna had texted. *OMG is this for real?*

Noon. Arizona was on Mountain Standard Time, but most of the state, I knew, didn't observe Daylight Savings Time.

Were we two hours ahead on the east coast or three? It was nearly noon where I sat, so just to be on the safe side, I grabbed a tissue out of the box I keep on the desk, wiped butter off my hands and texted back: *OK. How about one? I'll call you.*

During the summer months, east coast time is three hours ahead of Arizona. Just so you know.

Three minutes before four, I sat down at my desk, powered up my laptop and placed the call.

Donna picked up right away. 'I sure hope I can help,' she said.

Donna took my call in a room piled high with colored blocks. A giant red Crayola crayon stood to her right and a dragon constructed from Lego blocks spread its magnificent wings on a table behind her.

I wasn't surprised she worked in a museum. She looked like the arty type. Her salt-and-pepper hair was scrunched into a lumpy, off-center ponytail and she stared at my image through a pair of oversized eyeglasses with cherry-red frames. No make-up, but she'd made up for the lack of facial adornment by going overboard on the body jewelry side: two piercings in the right ear, a gold cuff on the left and a modest diamond stud decorating her left nostril.

'You got the photos?' I asked.

'I did,' she said. 'I printed them out on the printer we use at the museum and had a really good look.'

'What can you tell me?'

I noticed that Donna had spread the six photos out on the table in front of her. First, she held up the photo of Nicholas so I could see it. 'This guy, Mid4, is definitely the guy I saw dancing with Amy.' She tapped the image. 'Those eyes. Sweet Baby Jesus, you could drown in those eyes.' Almost reluctantly, she set the photo down, rested her forearms on the table and leaned closer to the camera. 'He was quite a dancer, too. The hip action, holy cow! I remember thinking, damn, too bad I had to work tonight.' She shrugged. 'Story of my life. Always a bridesmaid never a bride.'

As I watched, she bent over and began sliding the photos

around. 'This guy here, Mid2, looked familiar, but then I realized it was because he was a regular at Doots. Name's Eli something. But he's a bit older. Maybe a company officer or teacher? And I'm pretty sure I didn't see him that night.

'These two guys, three and five,' she continued, 'I've definitely never seen them before, but these two . . .' She selected the photographs I'd labeled Mid1 and Mid6, both blonds, held one photo in each hand and turned them to face the camera. 'I went back and forth about these two. You gotta admit that what with the uniforms, short hair and all, they're kind of cookie cutter, right? But then I realized . . .' She discarded the photo labeled Mid1, pushed the photo of Mid6 closer to the camera and jiggled it for emphasis. 'I'm pretty sure this is the hippie who spent most of the night hanging around the juke box. He was really, really blond, like this dude, but it was actually the hair that threw me off for a minute. The guy that night at Doots had a long, blond ponytail sticking out of a hole in the back of his ball cap. You know what I mean?'

I said I did.

'Totally fake, of course. Soooo . . .' she said, drawing out the 'O' while she searched for something on the table. 'So, I printed another copy and, well, tell me what you think.'

Donna had taken the photograph of Mid6 and, using crayons or colored pencils, had dressed him up in a blue ball cap with a long, blond ponytail flipped casually over his shoulder.

'I think you're a talented artist,' I said.

She smiled modestly. 'This is him. Definitely.'

It was Mid6. Travis Shillingford Palmer.

TWENTY-FOUR

Ain't No Stopping Us Now
(McFadden & Whitehead)

*H*oly cannoli, I think I know this guy! Mark Wallis texted. *Maintaining radio silence. Digging deep.*
A few hours later, Izzy texted back. *Working w/Mark on serious phone banking. Stand by till further notice.*

Jack, in the meantime, had passed Donna's positive identification of Travis Palmer on to the local police, but our project was on hold there, too. New evidence was welcome, of course it was and thank you, but the detective pointed out that just because Mrs Nixon identified Midshipman Palmer as Ms Lannigan's biological father didn't mean the baby couldn't have been fathered by somebody else. And just because Midshipman Palmer had been fingered by Ms Crowe as having been present in Doots' Bar the night of the murder didn't mean he actually went partying with Ms Madison at her father's cottage, or that he had anything to do with her murder. Even a first-year law student would chop testimony like that into mincemeat. In short, unless we frog-marched Travis Palmer into the police station and held him down while they took a swab, their hands were tied.

Although seething with fury that our (my!) witnesses were being impeached – Laurie Bigelow, promiscuous? No way! – I had to admit the cops had a point. We needed to lay hands on Travis Palmer himself, but where the hell was he?

Other Travis Palmers continued to pop up on the internet – a new one had been born just three weeks ago in Henderson, Kentucky – but ours remained a phantom. While 'standing by' as Izzy had requested, I'd hop online from time to time, hoping against hope, but aside from that private mailbox in Green Cove Springs, Florida, the man remained a mystery. No marriage announcements. No obituaries. No Facebook, Twitter or Instagram accounts. Hadn't been arrested or run for public office, the two not being mutually exclusive. Hadn't written an outraged letter to the editor of any major US newspaper. Even the Naval Academy Alumni Association had lost touch with the guy, listing him among their lost sheep.

The US Navy would have known where he was, of course, at least up until his retirement, so rather than spinning my wheels, I decided to exercise some self-control and wait to see what Mark and Izzy were up to.

Besides, Paul and his hedge clippers had made a mess of that topiary – from swan to camel to what might be described as a turtle if you squinted at it with your head turned sideways. I had remedial pruning to do.

Paul and I had been back in Annapolis for over a week when Izzy called sounding excited. 'Face to face at Barnes and Noble tomorrow at two?' she asked.

I agreed. 'What's up?'

'For that,' she said mysteriously, 'you'll just have to wait.'

'Izzy!' I squawked. 'That's twenty-four hours away! How will I be able to sleep tonight?'

She laughed. 'Just pulling your chain. It took a while, but Mark and I have mapped out Palmer's entire career. He was in the navy for twenty-nine years, can you believe it? Retired as a commander. And I have to tell you, the guy's a genius at staying under the radar.'

'Tell me about it,' I said. 'I was beginning to think we'd made him up.'

Izzy chuckled. 'No, he's very real. And Mark was right. The guy was an SWO.'

'When Mark texted, he said he thought he knew Palmer?'

'Right. Turns out he ran into him a couple of times up in Newport. Didn't ring a bell until he saw the sketch with the ball cap.'

'What a small world,' I said. 'And how . . .?'

'Keep your panties on,' Izzy cut in cheerfully. 'Tomorrow all will be revealed.'

*   *   *

When I arrived at Barnes and Noble – ten minutes early, I should like to point out – Mark was already there, presiding over a table for six toward the front of the store. Izzy and Jack showed up together shortly thereafter and, once we were all seated with assorted coffee drinks at hand, Mark passed us each a printout. Centered across the top of the printout, in bold capital letters, read: *Commander Travis Shillingford Palmer, US Navy (Retired)*. And centered on the line under that: *Timeline*.

'What, no PowerPoint slides?' I complained, only half seriously.

'I talked Mark out of it,' Izzy said with a grin.

I scanned the list: Date, Assignment, Location, followed by a sentence or two of explanation. I realized at once that Mark had been right all those weeks ago when he noticed the correlation between unsolved murders of young women and what might be duty stations of a geographically mobile surface warfare officer.

I didn't want to be a Debbie Downer, but I knew that Navy ships had hundreds, in the case of aircraft carriers, thousands of crew. You could analyze the career of most any SWO and find similar correlations, but I decided not to point this out. Instead, I said, 'Mark, I know you were going for the OMPFs and that they're guarded like Fort Knox, so how—'

Mark raised a hand, cutting me off. 'Not everything is locked up in a filing cabinet in St Louis, Hannah. Sometimes you go low tech. It was easy to identify Palmer's Academy roommates. Turns out I served with one of them on the *San Jacinto*, a guided missile cruiser out of Norfolk. A good kid, raised as a Quaker. When the Middle East started heating up, he started having serious doubts about whether he could launch a nuclear missile or take another person's life. We saw a lot of each other, and stayed in touch after he left the Navy. I don't want to use his real name, so let's call him Jim.'

'Mark started with that roommate, Jim, and branched out from there,' Izzy explained. 'Tracking down officers and shipmates and getting the skinny. Sometimes I'd interview them.' She shot Mark a crooked smile. 'I have no idea how some of them might have gained the impression that I was writing a puff piece for *Baltimore Magazine*, do you?'

Mark grinned. 'Not a clue.'

Jack waved the printout like a flag to get Mark's attention. 'Can we get on with it? I'm hoping there's more to this effort than what's printed on this page.'

'Grab a pen,' Izzy said. 'You'll want to take notes. Mark really gets into the head of this guy.'

'OK,' Mark began. 'This is what we discovered. Travis graduates in June 1978 somewhere near the bottom of his class, so any prayer he has of going to flight school is out. He's also not cut out to be a Marine, too many physical fitness requirements. Two of his roommates remember hearing him complain *ad nauseum* about the PRTs.'

Jack glanced up from the printout. 'Physical readiness tests, I'm guessing. What are the requirements?'

'Sixty-five curl-ups, forty-five push-ups and run a mile and a half in ten-and-a-half minutes,' Mark said, ticking them off on his fingers.

Jack whistled, long and low. 'That leaves me out.'

Mark laughed. 'Anyway, the only ships remaining when he goes to ship selection night are minesweepers and aircraft carriers. Minesweepers are small, so he knew he'd be one of just a handful of officers, and might actually have to work, so he picks the USS *Eisenhower*, an aircraft carrier out of Norfolk which has just emerged after a long period in the shipyard.'

'He doesn't report to the *Eisenhower* right away, though,' Izzy said. 'The Navy keeps him in Annapolis for seven months working as a temporary ensign in the Seamanship Department.'

'TAD,' I cut in, being familiar with the term. 'Temporary additional duty. They must not have been ready for him on the ship.'

'So, he's stuck working at the Academy . . .' Jack prompted.

'Hardly working, according to the roommate,' Mark added. 'Mostly hanging out in bars in town and drinking heavily.

'In February of '79,' Mark continued, 'Travis and this roommate, also an SWO, get sent up to Newport, Rhode Island

for SWO School. Hates it. Really hates it. It's brutally cold
in the winter, especially when tooting around Narraganset Bay
learning how to drive the old YPs.'

'Yard patrol boats,' I added for Izzy's benefit. 'About eighty
feet long, like an old-fashioned cabin cruiser if you like your
cabin cruisers painted gun-metal gray with big white numbers
on the hull.'

'By the time September rolls around,' Mark rattled on, 'he's
eager to report to Norfolk and finally get onboard the
Eisenhower. The ship's tempo is slow and much to his liking.
The carrier would put out to sea for a day or two to work on
qualifications but mostly he's left alone. A shipmate told us
that the job that took up most of Travis's time was making
sure all the soda machines on board remained filled.'

Jack set the paper down on the table and stabbed at it with
his pen. 'Taxpayers fork over a couple of hundred thou to
educate a naval officer and the Navy has him schlepping sodas?
What a great return on investment.'

Mark ignored him. 'Anyway, Travis spends three and a half
years on the Mighty Ike, earning his SWO qualifications and
is happy to be promoted to lieutenant junior grade during its
deployment to Naples, except that means he has to buy all the
officers in the wardroom a drink for his wetting down party.
It could have been a party in Naples where the liquor is cheap,
but oh no, the promotion had to come through while the ship
was in Corfu, a resort island in Greece at the height of the
tourist season.'

'Bummer,' Jack chortled.

'In any case,' Izzy went on, 'when the ship gets back to the
States, he's happy to stay aboard where he knows all the ropes
and can keep a low profile.'

I raised my hand to interrupt. 'If he's spending all that time
living aboard ship, does that indicate he's not married?'

'As far as we can tell, Travis never married, at least not
while he was still in the Navy,' Izzy said.

'Moving on now to the summer of '82, he's promoted again,
this time to full lieutenant. Finally, he's making good money
and, because he's so senior, he's able to pass the bullshit jobs
on to junior officers. He's been on the Ike for a long time,

though, so when he hears it's going to be deployed again to the Med, he decides to request a transfer so that more junior officers will have "a chance to excel."' Mark drew quote marks in the air with his fingers.

'Generous of him,' Jack grumped.

'The next three years, he's stuck in a desk job with the 2d Fleet in Norfolk. It's a big staff with a lot of junior officers sucking up to him, so he's able to hide out most of the time, doing the minimum, but he realizes that if he wants to be promoted again, he'll need to get back on a ship.'

'So here's the thing,' Izzy cut in. 'Mark tells me it's really unusual for a junior SWO like Travis to volunteer for a carrier, especially for a second tour.'

Mark nodded. 'Izzy's right, but there's method to his madness. This particular carrier will be in drydock and won't be going anywhere. By now, he's nine years out of the Academy, and he's done well enough to get promoted to lieutenant commander. If he can stick it out, get on another ship and get promoted to commander, the Navy would allow him to go on and serve a full twenty-eight years.'

'And after twenty-eight years,' Izzy added, 'you can retire with a really good pension.'

'Right,' Mark said. 'So, in August of '87, Travis reports for duty aboard the *Bunker Hill*, a big guided missile cruiser out of San Diego. He's a lieutenant commander, so he qualifies for several high-profile jobs like chief engineer or navigator, but in either one of those jobs, he'd be held accountable if the engines break down or if the ship goes off course or, God forbid, somebody runs it aground.'

Next to me, Jack stirred. 'Running your ship aground is a hanging offense.'

Mark chuckled. 'Definitely not career-enhancing. Anyway, so what does he do? At the Naval Academy he liked weapons, and the weapon's officer position is open. It's high enough profile to give him access to the skipper who loves to talk about weapons and knows intricate details about all of them.'

'But there's a catch,' Izzy said. 'The ship is ordered to prepare for deployment to Yokuska, Japan. Travis is back to square one. He knows he'll either have to become the navigator or the chief engineer, so he works out a deal to go back to the Naval Academy and teach.'

'He hates teaching, but he loves Annapolis,' Mark went on. 'He sticks it out for two years, but when Operation Desert Shield begins in the fall of '90, he realizes that the Naval Academy is a backwater that has impeded his promotion to commander. So, he volunteers for an individual augmentation position on the staff of Central Command in Tampa, Florida.'

I raised my hand. 'What does individual augmentation mean, exactly?'

'It's temporary duty,' Mark explained. 'You're on loan to another command. Central Command is part of the Department of Defense. It serves as the administrative headquarters for all US military affairs in twenty countries in the Middle East, Southwest Asia, Northeast Africa and the Arabian Gulf and draws the personnel it needs from the operating forces of each of the military services. Coordinates with our allies, too.'

Izzy consulted her printout. 'Travis spends six months in Tampa, starting in the spring of '91, where he's able to watch the war from afar. At one point, he takes a thirty-day trip to a forward headquarters in Saudi Arabia which qualifies him for combat pay. And when he returns to the Naval Academy it's as a combat veteran with a new medal to pin on his chest.'

'Sweet work if you can get it,' Jack mumbled.

Mark picked up where Izzy left off. 'Travis spends the next couple of years back at 2d Fleet in Norfolk where he does well enough to finally earn that coveted promotion to Commander. Starting in '95, he's back at the Academy, but he's not happy about his options. He doesn't want to be a battalion officer because he'd be responsible for several hundred midshipmen who will almost certainly do the same dumb-ass things he did as a midshipman. The only subject he's qualified to teach is Seamanship, but remember how much he hates the YPs? I can't figure out exactly how, but he manages to wrangle an active duty spot on the staff of the Naval Academy Athletic Association. He's responsible for a few facilities and for interacting between coaches and officers in Bancroft Hall, but mostly, he just hides out for three years.'

'He's been in for twenty years by now and is eligible to

retire,' Izzy said, 'but he doesn't. He heads up to Newport as deputy director of the Leadership School, basically an administrative paper pusher.'

Mark looks at me. 'And that's where I connected with the guy. I was teaching an eight-week course at the Chaplain's School and kept running into him at the gym. One thing that always bothered me, though, particularly now that I look back on it. A lot of foreign naval officers attend the Command and Staff College in Newport and they often bring their families with them, families that sometimes include exotically beautiful wives. Whenever I ran into Travis at the Officers' Club, he seemed to be paying more attention to the wives than to the guys he was drinking with.'

'Maintaining good foreign relations, I suppose,' Jack said with a grin.

I felt a sudden chill that wasn't coming from the air conditioner. 'Please don't tell me any of those foreign wives were assaulted.'

Mark shook his head. 'I doubt it. Too risky, and Travis, as we have seen, is risk-adverse.

'Anyway, in 2004,' Mark went on, 'the Navy calls for individual augmentees for staffs in Iraq. So, just like he did during Desert Shield, he sees a chance to feather his bed. He volunteers and serves as part of the Iraqi Forces Command. The guy in charge over there is a four-star general with a big staff, so as a Navy commander, Travis knows he'll serve in some out-of-the-way position, which suits him to a T. It's not particularly risky, either. Headquarters is in a luxury palace in Baghdad, and because the palace also serves as the US Embassy, there's a shitload of security. There's also a vibrant bar scene surrounding the enormous swimming pool behind the embassy which gives him lots of social action.'

'Wait a minute,' I said. 'Bar? I thought you weren't allowed to drink in Iraq.'

'Technically true,' Mark said. 'General Order 1 prohibits alcohol consumption by military members, but civilian workers on staff have no such restrictions. He develops friends on the civilian side, and because he's relatively obscure, he can violate the order whenever he feels like it, which is often.' Mark looked up. 'Know what his shipmates used to call him?' Without waiting for a reply, Mark said, 'Vegas.'

'That brings us up to 2005,' Izzy said. 'In July, he returns to the War College as a war hero with a chest of medals to prove it.'

Thinking about the ultimate sacrifice that Nicholas Forsythe had made in Beirut, referring to Travis Palmer as a hero seemed like a sick joke. 'Even if he weren't a murderer,' I muttered, 'I just know I'd hate this guy.'

'He must have been pushing fifty by then,' Jack commented. Despite looking bored during most of Mark's presentation, he'd obviously been keeping up.

'Almost,' Mark agreed. 'He spends a couple more years in Newport teaching Navy staffs how to staff or something, but when he reaches mandatory retirement age, the war is still going on, so they allow him to stay on duty until June of 2008, twenty-nine years to the day after his USNA graduation.'

'And after that?'

'We don't know. One of his colleagues from his time at the War College said he talked about buying a fixer-upper on the water somewhere down south, but the guy doubted it would happen because Travis wasn't exactly a do-it-yourself kind of guy.'

Izzy laid the document she'd been reading from flat on the table, but kept her hand resting on top. 'So, there you have it, boys and girls. The portrait of a serial killer.'

With her free hand, she reached for a second printout – one I recognized as the list Mark had compiled earlier of unsolved murders similar to Amy's – and slid it across the tabletop until it sat edge to edge with the first. 'Put these two lists together, and maybe we can catch the sonofabitch.'

'Do we think Travis committed crimes while he was stationed abroad?' I asked.

'Too smart for that, from what I've learned here today,' Jack said, 'but I have contacts at the FBI. We'll see.' He stacked one printout on top of the other, tapped the edges together and slid them into a briefcase that was resting on the floor next to his feet.

'So, what's next?' I asked.

Mark opened his mouth to say something, but Izzy beat him to it. 'We don't give up until we find him.'

'Swell,' I said. 'We're doing all the hard work while the cops seem to be sitting on their hands.'

Jack bent down, picked up his briefcase and got to his feet. 'I'm planning to swing by their headquarters in Millersville. Maybe, armed with this, we can light a fire under them. Get things moving in a positive direction.'

I hope so, I thought. I couldn't speak for the other members of my team, but I was fresh out of ideas.

But Izzy wasn't. She looked up from the website she'd been consulting on her cell phone. 'I'm going to follow up on the Roberta Chapman case,' she said, referring to the young redhead who had been found murdered the previous year in Rock Creek Park. 'It's recent enough that witnesses may still be around who can tell us something.'

'I tried to pry some information on that out of my contacts in Montgomery County,' Jack grumped, 'but her case is still active. They're not willing to let amateurs play around in their sandbox just yet.'

Izzy waved a hand. 'Enter Isabel Randall, girl reporter. Perhaps it's time for a follow-up story on the investigation.' She turned to me. 'Fancy a night out on the town, Hannah?'

'Depends on when and where,' I said.

'Tonight. That sports bar over in Rockville where she was last seen. The One Note Stand? It's Tuesday, and according to their Facebook page, karaoke starts at nine.'

I grinned. 'Short notice and a bit past my bedtime, but, sure. Why not?'

TWENTY-FIVE
Last Night a DJ Saved My Life (Indeep)

Paul was scrubbing the remains of dinner out of the cast iron skillet when I presented myself in the kitchen for inspection. 'How do I look?'

He turned away from the sink, looked me up and down and asked, 'How are you supposed to look?'

'I don't know,' I said. 'I've never been to a karaoke bar before.'

For my expedition with Izzy, I'd chosen to wear a loose-fitting floral top over black jeans. I'd washed my hair and fluffed it out with curling mousse. I'd gone a little heavier than usual with the eye makeup. Gold hoop earrings dangled from my ears.

'You look hot to me, babe, but I'm betting it'll be so dark you could walk in wearing pajamas and nobody'd notice.'

Izzy had texted that she was waiting for me on the street outside, so I gave Paul a kiss, told him I'd be back 'whenever,' and headed out to meet her.

According to Waze, One Note Stand was out on Rockville Pike, just past the 'Y' intersection with Viers Mill Road. Traffic on the beltway was light, so it took us only forty minutes to get there. Judging by the number of cars in the parking lot, the joint was jumping.

Paul had been right. Visibility inside the One Note Stand was limited. A bar made of dark wood stretched along the far wall, illuminated almost entirely by the glow of more wall-mounted television screens than the control center at CNN. Every barstool appeared to be occupied. The bartender, a blonde-haired woman wearing a bright yellow, cold-shoulder blouse, hustled behind it, efficiently drawing beer for her customers from a bank of six taps.

Karaoke night was in full swing. A crowd of customers –

some wearing neon glow sticks as necklaces or halos – had
formed a semi-circle around the stage where a young man
clutching a microphone was belting out an off-key rendition
of 'Billie Jean' that would have killed Michael Jackson if
the pop icon hadn't already been dead. A disco ball rotated
slowly overhead, sending multicolored shards of light swimming, like minnows, over the audience.

'Follow me,' Izzy said breezily as she headed toward the
bar. By the time I'd elbowed through the crowd and caught
up with her, she'd managed to charm a barstool out from
under a chivalrous gent wearing a Stetson. Perched on the
stool, she rested her elbows on the stainless steel countertop
and waited until she caught the bartender's attention.

'What'll it be?' the bartender asked.

'A scotch on the rocks for me, and . . .' She turned to me
standing behind and to her right.

'Mojito,' I said.

'And a Mojito for my friend. Thanks.'

When our drinks arrived a few minutes later, Izzy quickly
slid her ID across the countertop and said, 'I'm a reporter for
WBNF in Baltimore, and I'm doing a follow-up story on the
murder of Roberta Chapman.'

The bartender frowned and shook her head. 'Horrible, simply
horrible. I hate to think that any customer of mine could be
a killer. The world's gone all to hell, if you ask me.'

Izzy pushed the ice around in her drink with the plastic
swizzle stick. 'Were you here that night?'

'No, but the DJ was.' She gestured with a bar rag in the
direction of the stage where the Michael Jackson wannabee
had been replaced by a woman who was waving the microphone in the air like a baton and massacring 'Let It Go.'
'His name's Dan. This set should be over in around five
minutes. You can talk to him then.'

'Anyone else?' Izzy asked.

'Sarah, the girl who waited on them, but she's off tonight.'

'Thanks,' Izzy said.

Carrying our drinks, Izzy and I joined a college-aged couple
sitting at a table as close to the stage as we could get. Dan,
the DJ, turned out to be a skin-headed dude decorated with

tats. Wearing black jeans, a leather vest and big, black boots, he looked like he'd be more comfortable riding a Harley than a swivel chair in front of an audio mixer sound board.

Up on the stage, demonstrating his musical chops, a middle-aged guy dressed in chinos and a white polo shirt began crooning a mellow, easy-on-the-ears rendition of 'My Way.'

'That's a welcome change,' I muttered to nobody in particular.

After listening for a while, the young woman sharing our table centered her beer on a coaster and said, 'He's good, isn't he? That's Father Dave. He's a regular.'

'Father?' I asked as the singer launched into the fifth and final verse.

'He's a priest at St Mary's,' she informed me. 'Just down the street.'

'Ah,' I said, sipping my mojito. 'Well, he's almost as good as Ol' Blue Eyes.'

'Who?' she asked.

'Frank Sinatra. He made the song famous, but it was written by Paul Anka.'

I could tell from her puzzled expression that she didn't know who Paul Anka was either. Damn, I was getting old.

Next to me, the girl shrugged. 'Whatever. I just love the message, though. Nothing is more important than living on your own terms,' she continued. 'Super advice, don't you think?'

I had to agree that it was.

Back on stage, Father Dave wrapped up. Bowing modestly, he accepted the applause from the crowd, but waved off their cries of encore. Before leaving the stage, he slipped the microphone into a stand adjacent to the monitor. I suspected he knew 'My Way' by heart and hadn't needed to refer to the subtitles that had scrolled by on the monitor's oversized screen.

The DJ began fiddling with knobs and toggles. 'This is our cue,' Izzy said, rising quickly to her feet. To our tablemates, she said, 'Watch our drinks, will you?'

Izzy zeroed in on DJ Dan like a laser beam. 'Excuse me?'

Dan glanced up from his console. 'Yes?'

Izzy went through her usual song-and-dance routine about doing a follow-up story on Roberta's murder for WBNF. 'We understand you were here that night.'

Dan nodded. 'Yeah. Goddam shame. Such a pretty redhead. Couldn't help but notice the way the strobes reflected off her hair. They were sitting at that high top over there.' He aimed a beefy finger at a small section of pedestal tables not far from where the two college kids sat watching our drinks grow warm.

'They?' I prodded.

'It wasn't as busy as it is tonight. I remember that she came in alone. He joined her about half-way through the second set. Tall dude. He had to fold his legs under the stool like pretzels, and even then, his knees stuck out.'

'Did it look like a pickup, or do you think she knew the guy?'

Dan scratched the stubble on his chin. 'Hard to say. But, they seemed friendly enough. He was buying the drinks, anyway. Knew what she wanted.'

'Which was . . .?' I asked.

'White wine. No idea what kind. Not my area of expertise,' he said, reaching for the bottle of Heineken that sat sweating on the stage next to his chair.

Izzy's hand plunged into her handbag and came out with a fistful of photographs. 'May I show you a few photos? Ask you if you recognize anybody?'

He took a sip of beer. 'Sure.'

Izzy handed the whole pack – about six photos in all – over to DJ Dan and watched as he leafed through them. 'This is her,' he said wistfully, holding up a photo of Roberta Chapman that Izzy had retrieved from the newspaper's archives. Photos of the other two women – who Izzy chose at random from a recent Goucher College yearbook – he set aside. 'And this is definitely the guy she was with that night.' The DJ was indicating a photograph of Travis Palmer that Mark had dug up from a 2005 US Naval War College newsletter. 'Older now, of course, but same sissy hair. Maybe he's got a hairdresser or something, like one of those talking heads on *Fox News*?' He rubbed a hand over his own bald pate. 'Not that I'm jealous or anything.'

I had to laugh, picturing a stiffly-coifed Travis Palmer perched on a sofa with two other 'air personalities' dishing out conservative headlines for *Fox & Friends* viewers every morning. It would, of course, make him easier to find.

'Have the Montgomery County Police been in touch with you recently?' I asked.

Dan nodded. 'Yeah. About two weeks ago, then came back to talk to me and to Sarah, the woman who served Roberta and the guy that night.' He shrugged. 'There wasn't much more to tell them, but at least they haven't forgotten about her. So, do you think he did it? The guy in the picture?'

'It's possible,' Izzy told him.

'Someone needs to nail the sonofabitch,' he said, handing the photos back.

Izzy tucked them into her handbag. 'Thanks. I'm sure the police are on top of it. But, if you think of anything else, here's my card.'

'Sure thing.' The DJ studied Izzy's card, then eased it into the back pocket of his jeans. 'Nice talking to you ladies, but I better get busy. Next set starts in five.' He smiled. 'And keep up the good work.'

We thanked Dan for his help and returned to our drinks, which Izzy decided were too warm for human consumption. She headed back to the bar.

My frugal Puritan genes wouldn't allow me to waste a single drop of my perfectly delicious, admittedly warm, cocktail, so I drained my glass while Izzy was away arranging to replace it with a fresh one. The line at the bar must have been long, because she returned to her seat empty-handed. We sat through a pathetic rendition of 'Ring of Fire' sung by a middle-aged lawyer-type who had probably hadn't been born in 1963 when Johnny Cash sent the song soaring to the top of the charts. After the last 'ring of fire' died away, our young tablemates excused themselves and said they were heading back to their dorms.

Eventually, another mojito appeared on the table. 'Anything else, ladies?' our server inquired.

'Nothing for me,' Izzy said, tapping her chest with her thumb. 'Designated driver.'

I sipped the mojito appreciatively while a George Michael wannabee skillfully channeled the pop star's soulful vocal style for 'Faith,' throwing everything he had into the climactic 'Baby!' He even wrapped up with a cute ass wiggle, just as George had in the video.

A pair of sisters, identically dressed in retro bell-bottom trousers and peasant blouses, stormed the stage next, leading the audience in a raucous call and response version of 'Love Shack.' As far as I could tell, the chorus consisted entirely of a whole lot of bang, bang, banging on the door, oh babes, and the title words, Love Shack, repeated until everyone either gave up, or fell face first into their nachos, exhausted.

After a third, ill-considered mojito, pressed upon me by Izzy who insisted that I had worked hard and deserved it, I determined it was time to class up the joint with Patsy Cline's country music standard, 'Crazy.' Grinning broadly, Dan escorted me onto the stage and pressed a microphone into my hand. I'm proud to say that I followed the captions flawlessly while nailing the ascending and descending intervals and Patsy's signature vocal catches every time. Just to be a show-off, I held the note on the final 'you' until I felt my face turn blue from lack of oxygen, then fell back, gasping, to bask in the applause of my audience which was, while enthusiastic, not quite up to the decibel level earned by Father Dave.

I was extremely grateful there were no calls for an encore.

TWENTY-SIX
I've Been Waiting for You (ABBA)

T hanks to the sun, my day started painfully early. I scrabbled for my phone on the bedside table, squinted at it through blurry eyes and, after noting the time, saw that a series of text messages from Cheryl topped the screen.

> *Thank you, thank you, thank you!!!*
> *I met my birth mom yesterday!!!*
> *I have 2 sisters!!!*
> *See my FB page!!!*

I plumped up my pillow, stuffed it behind my back and sat up straight. It took a few minutes to locate Cheryl's Facebook page, but it was certainly worth the effort.

Laurie and Cheryl, smiling, looking like the mother and daughter act they were always meant to be.

Cheryl, flanked by two women, arms draped around one another, beaming. They could have been mistaken for triplets, not identical, but close.

A photo of the whole group, wreathed in smiles, taken in front of the greenhouse at Winterthur Gardens, the former estate of Henry Francis duPont.

The women seated around a table for four at the Cottage Tea Room, presumably taken by their server.

I was grinning over a photo captioned 'Girls going goofy on the Garden Tram' when Paul wandered into the bedroom carrying a mug of coffee and a bottle of aspirin. He handed them to me. 'After last night's escapade, I figured you could use the aspirin. But maybe no. You look quite happy.'

'Good news,' I said, accepting the coffee and handing him the phone. 'Cheryl met her birth family yesterday, and it appears to be the start of good things to come.'

'Girls going goofy?' he asked as he sat down on the foot of the bed.

'Scroll up,' I suggested.

'I wonder how her husband took the news,' Paul said after a moment.

I reached for my phone. 'How would *you*?'

'A good question, but let me think about an answer.' He stared at me, unblinking, for what seemed like a long time before saying, 'The child out of wedlock I'm sure I could deal with. Her abandonment at a fire station, not so much.' Paul laid his hand on the blanket covering my leg and gave it a gentle squeeze. 'But you know what? It's not the child's fault. It's never the child's fault, so that would be my starting point.'

'I love you, Paul Everett Ives.'

'It's a good thing, because I'm crazy about you, too,' he said.

Paul got to his feet. 'You don't have any children I don't know about, do you?'

By way of answer, I grabbed a pillow and threw it at his head.

He caught it, laughing, and tossed it back.

'By the way,' he said after a moment, 'I've got the password you were looking for yesterday. It's not one I use very often, so I had to look it up.' He eased a couple of fingers into the back pocket of his jeans, pulled out a slip of paper and handed it to me.

'NAWTFMTWOTMI1969?' I read. 'You've got to be kidding me.'

Paul shrugged. 'Easy to remember. It's the first letters of "Neil Armstrong was the first man to walk on the moon in 1969".'

'Easy for you, maybe.' I looked up from the slip of paper. 'But, if it's so easy to remember, why did you have to look it up?'

'I have more than one password, Hannah, don't you?'

Of course I did. Everybody did. I had four whole typewritten pages of passwords hidden in an encrypted file on my laptop. Ridiculous.

'By the way, what did you need it for, anyway?' Paul asked.

'I haven't checked the Naval Academy Alumni Association website for a while. I keep hoping that somebody will update Travis Palmer's contact information. He's one of their lost sheep.'

'How about that other guy, then, Nicholas whatshisname.'

'Nicholas Forsythe, but he's been dead since 1983, Paul. You know that.'

'Of course, I know that, but the Alumni Association likes to keep track of widows and widowers, too.'

I stared at him, dumbfounded. 'They do?'

'Of course they do. No stone unturned when it comes to begging for dollars. Palmer and Forsythe were friends, right? So, maybe Forsythe's widow knows where Palmer's got to.'

I threw back the covers and hopped out of bed. Without bothering to get dressed, I rushed past my husband – stopping only to plant an appreciative kiss on the forehead – streaked downstairs like a comet through the living room and into the dining room. I powered up my laptop. When Google came up, I quickly logged on to the Naval Academy Alumni Association's webpage and, using the username and password Paul had provided, clicked on the Alumni Directory.

When I typed in Nicholas's information, there she was, plain as day: Lisa Forsythe, with a mailing address in New Bern, North Carolina, and a telephone number.

I leaned back in my chair and shouted, 'Paul, come here!'

When he appeared, I pointed at my laptop and said, 'You are a genius.'

He bowed slightly at the waist. 'Thank you.'

'I hope the information's recent,' I said.

'You won't know if you don't try.'

'What time is it?' I asked.

Paul checked his watch. 'Time to get dressed and eat some breakfast before you start out on the wrong foot by getting some unsuspecting stranger out of bed.'

I had to laugh. 'Why do you always have to be right?'

I dressed, ate a carton of black cherry yogurt with granola sprinkled on top, loaded the dishwasher, then puttered around the house tidying up things that didn't really need tidying up until ten o'clock rolled around.

Then I made the call.

I nearly fell over when someone answered on the second ring, using the same formal greeting style I'd been taught as a military brat: 'Forsythe residence, Lisa speaking.'

So, I thought. She probably hasn't remarried.

'Hello,' I said. 'My name is Hannah Ives and I'm calling from Annapolis, Maryland. Do you have a minute to talk?'

'If you're calling for money, I already gave,' she said, sounding about as cheerful as I do when telemarketers hawking time shares interrupt our dinner.

'No, no,' I said, fearing she might hang up on me. 'I'm trying to get in touch with an old Naval Academy classmate of your husband's—'

She didn't wait for me to finish. 'Who are you looking for?'

'A guy named Travis S. Palmer. They were both class of '78.'

Icy silence filled the ethersphere between us. Then she said, 'They weren't exactly friends.'

'You knew him, then?' I asked, feeling hopeful.

'Not really. I only met him once, and it wasn't exactly a pleasant experience.'

'Can you tell me about it?' I asked, keeping my voice even and trying not to sound too needy.

'Who did you say you were?' Lisa asked, her voice oozing suspicion.

I decided to tell the truth, partially, at least. 'I'm a genealogist working with a team of investigators on an unsolved murder from 1978. Travis's DNA was found at the scene.'

Lisa snorted. 'Well, that doesn't surprise me.'

'The guy seems to be eluding all efforts to locate him,' I continued. 'After he retired from the Navy, it's like he dropped off the face of the earth.'

'Good riddance, if you ask me,' Lisa replied.

'What can you tell me about him?' I nudged gently.

'It was around 1981, our first year at LeJeune. Nick and I were living off base in a tiny rancher that my parents owned – base housing sucked in those days – when Travis called. I told him Nick was at work, so he left his name and said he'd call back, but he wouldn't tell me what he wanted. A couple of weeks later, Travis called while Nick was home. I answered the phone, but when I told Nick who was on the line, he refused to take the call. After I hung up, I asked my husband why, but all he told me was the guy was bad news.

'So, one day around dinner time, Travis just shows up on our doorstep.'

'Tall guy? Really blond?' I asked, just to make sure we were on the same page.

'A bleached, surfer-dude type? Yeah, that's him. Anyway, Nick took him around to the backyard. I was curious, so I peeked out the dining-room window and it was clear from the body language that they were having it out about something. Eventually, Travis stalked off and Nick came back inside. He was pretty rattled.'

'Any idea what happened to Travis?'

'I don't know and I don't care. After he left that day, Nick shut himself up in the study and drank a whole bottle of Scotch.' She paused to take a deep breath. 'Just so you know, Nick hardly ever drank. Just a beer or two with the guys on the weekends, you know, so I figure whatever Travis told him, it had to be something disturbing.

'Nick was totally out of it,' she continued. 'He kept mumbling about Las Vegas and driving somebody's car and how he didn't know, and the bastard lied.' She paused, 'Please excuse my language, but that's exactly what Nick said. None of it made any sense, not to me at least.' She paused. 'But what really freaked me out was Nick started quoting scripture. You know that Bible verse about justice rolling down like an ever-flowing stream?'

I said that it sounded familiar.

'Well, that *really* didn't make any sense, still doesn't. Nick and I went to church regularly and all, but he wasn't a Bible thumper, if you know what I mean.' She took a deep breath, then let it out slowly. 'Anyway, I gave him a couple of aspirin, made him drink a glass of water and helped him into bed.'

'Next day he was rock solid,' she continued. 'Really calm, like he'd made up his mind to do something. About a month after that, the Marine Corps sent him back to Beirut and, well, you probably know how that turned out.'

'What do you think Nick had made up his mind to do?'

'I reminded him that there were people on base who specialized in working with PTSD, so he agreed to make an appointment at the Naval Medical Center here. They started him on one-to-one talk therapy, and it really seemed to be helping, at least the nightmares grew less frequent.'

'Nightmares?'

'Oh my God, they were awful, Hannah. He'd moan and toss and finally scream himself awake. The sheets would be drenched with sweat. All I could do was wrap my arms around him, rub his back, and try to calm him down.' She paused. 'He told me he thought he might have killed somebody.'

'Had he?' I asked, realizing almost as soon as the words tumbled out of my mouth that it was a dumb question.

'He was a Marine stationed in Lebanon, for heaven's sake. He couldn't tell me anything about his assignments, of course, so in spite of his gentle nature, he was a lean, mean, killing machine. Who knows what the Marines might have called upon him to do.

'One night,' she continued, 'he confessed that the killing wasn't in Lebanon; it was when he was at the Naval Academy. Nick told me he remembered going out on the town with Travis. They'd turned up at a disco bar where Nick really hit it off with some local girl and was invited back to her house where they pretty much emptied the liquor cabinet. It was hard for him, but after the therapist advised him to come clean he admitted to me that one thing had led to another and he and the girl had had consensual sex, but then he blacked out. Next morning when he came to, he realized he'd lost eight hours. Had no idea where he'd been or what he'd done.'

'Who was the girl? Did he say?'

'He said he couldn't remember. A total blank. Anyway, I tried to reason with him. I pointed out that if he had killed someone in Annapolis, particularly a young woman, wouldn't it have been in all the newspapers? He would have heard about it, seen her picture on TV.'

'Not necessarily,' I pointed out. 'The murder that we're trying to solve took place in 1978, less than a week before Nick graduated. Nobody had cell phones in those days. If there was any TV at all, it would have been in the wardroom. And unless mids went to read them in Nimitz Library, there were no newspapers lying around, either.'

I thought back to the news coverage of Amy's murder. The first stories hadn't mentioned the victim's name, and her full obituary hadn't been published in the *Washington Post* until a full week after her death. By that time, Nick would have been grunting and sweating and getting muddy with the Marines in combat training down in Quantico, Virginia. Unless Amy's death had made the national news, it's likely he'd never heard about it.

Travis Palmer, however, had remained in Annapolis for seven months after graduation, assigned to the Seamanship department.

I shared this information with Lisa.

'Now I'm getting scared,' she said. 'Do you think Nick murdered that girl during a drunken blackout?'

'No, I don't. But he was definitely a witness, Lisa.' I took a deep breath, let it out and forged on. 'Nick's DNA was found at the scene, too.'

'Oh, God,' she said.

Somebody, I knew, had to have dragged Amy's body down to the river and dumped it in. Somebody had to drive Amy's car back into town afterwards and get rid of any prints. Travis was tall, strong, athletic. He could have accomplished those tasks on his own, of course, while Nick lay passed out in the passenger seat of Amy's TR6. Nick would have been none the wiser.

'Lisa,' I asked as a thought suddenly occurred to me. 'What size shoe did your husband wear?'

'10½ B. Why?'

'Well, if I remember the police report correctly, the shoe prints found near the pier where they think her body entered the water were a size 12C.'

'Not Nick, then,' Lisa said breathily, sounding relieved.

'Not Nick.'

After a moment of silence, I asked, 'Lisa, do you think Nick continued his therapy once he got back to Beirut?'

'It was hit or miss,' she said, 'but, yes. In one of his last letters to me, he told me that his memory was coming back, almost like a series of flashbacks.'

'I was wondering. Did Nick keep a diary?'

The question made Lisa laugh. 'I don't think so. He wasn't much of a writer.' She paused and grew silent for so long I thought we'd lost the connection. 'Look, can I call you back tomorrow? I just thought of something.'

I gave her my contact information. 'I'll be home all day, so feel free to call anytime.'

'Thanks, Hannah. Until tomorrow then.'

The following day, about an hour before lunchtime, Lisa called back, via Facetime. I'd been on proverbial pins and needles waiting for her call, so I picked up right away.

'Hi,' I said, as Lisa's face materialized on the screen. 'I'm afraid you haven't gotten me looking my best.'

I was wearing the clothes I usually wear for puttering around the house waiting for important phone calls – jeans and a T-shirt. The shirt I'd chosen that day was a Christmas gift from my granddaughter, Chloe: black, imprinted with white letters that said: *I'm a Grandmother. What's Your Superpower?*

Lisa Forsythe must have been in her mid-forties. Anyone would describe her as a beauty, with dark hair and fair Irish skin which stood out in sharp contrast to the vibrant crimson of her scoop neck shirt. 'I'm sorry I put you off yesterday,' she began, 'but I had to go look for something.'

Curiosity was killing me, but I stayed quiet, waiting for her to go on.

'Do you know what they do with the personal possessions of soldiers who die in combat?' she asked.

'I don't, not exactly. But I'm assuming they return them to the next of kin.'

Lisa nodded, her dark curls bobbing. 'After they round them up, they send them to a distribution center. Everything gets washed and neatly folded, then packed into a plastic foot-locker. Because of the explosion, Nick's footlocker had only one uniform, a tattered jacket . . .' Here her voice caught. She took a deep breath, swallowed hard, and went on. 'His wedding ring and watch were cleaned and stored in little drawstring pouches. They placed them right on top, along with his personal Bible.'

My eyes began to tear up just thinking about it.

Lisa sighed. 'When the footlocker came, I really couldn't deal with it, so I slid it under my bed. Heather and I had moved in with my parents by then, and the box stayed with Mom and Dad until yesterday when I drove over to their house to fetch it.

'What were you looking for in the box, Lisa?'

On her side of the screen, Lisa held up a Bible. Its leather binding had once been black, but now the edges were singed brown and curled. 'I really didn't know, but after our conversation, I figured it was time to face up to reality and sort through his things.'

Lisa opened the Bible about halfway, and pulled out what looked like a sheet of notebook paper folded into quarters. 'This might have been part of Nick's therapy,' she said. 'He's written it out by hand, but it's a rough draft, full of mistakes and corrections, so I don't think he actually mailed it to anyone.'

As I watched, Lisa unfolded the page and held it up to the camera. The writing appeared to be in pencil and covered both sides of the lined paper.

'What does it say?' I asked.

'It's a confession, kind of,' she said, 'but it makes it clear, to me at least, that Nick didn't murder anybody. Travis did. I'm going to take pictures of it with my iPhone and send it to you.

'Do you know where I found the letter?' Lisa asked me suddenly. 'In the Book of Amos. Nick had circled Amos 5:24: *But let judgment run down as waters, and righteousness as a mighty stream.*'

'Justice for Amy must have been weighing heavily on his mind,' I said. 'Thank you for trusting me with this information. But please keep the original safe. I have a feeling the police will be interested in having a look.'

'It breaks my heart, Hannah. Just a few months later, and he would have been coming home.'

'I know, and I'm so, so sorry. It must have been small comfort to you to know he died a hero.'

'It was something for Heather to hang on to, so that's good. She had just turned three when her daddy died. Other than a picture on the mantel, she hardly knew him. She went to the Naval Academy like her father, though. Did anyone tell you that? Class of 2003. She's flying helicopters for the Navy now. He would have been so proud.'

After a quiet moment, she added, 'Know what else I found in the box? A turkey handprint she'd made for her daddy in pre-school.'

'You never remarried, Lisa?' I asked gently.

Lisa snorted. 'No way. Nick was the love of my life. He'd just arrived at LeJeune when I met him. One of his buddies talked him into coming to a church supper at First Presbyterian. The uniform was sexy as hell, you know, but one look into his eyes, and I was a goner.'

'I've seen pictures,' I said. 'He was dashingly handsome.'

'Heather has Nick's eyes,' Lisa said dreamily.

'Watch out world,' I said.

Less than ten minutes later, two images pinged into my Messages folder. Lisa had named them Nick1 and Nick2. I saved both images to my Photos, then brought each of them up on the screen in turn.

To whom it may concern,

On May 27, 1978, I met a girl named Amy at Doots Bar. We hit it off, and she invited me to continue the party at her father's vacation home somewhere outside Annapolis. Amy was driving, so I don't know exactly where the house was. ~~Vegas~~ Midshipman Travis Palmer showed up at Doots, too, and decided to ride along with us. ~~Vegas~~ Travis was a guy I knew but not very well. The first time I had contact with him, he ~~wanted~~ was offering to sell me and some of the other ball players an advance copy of the EN400~~, Principles of Ship Performance~~ exam. It's an engineering course you have to pass to graduate. ~~We~~

~~call it Boats~~. He said he'd picked ~~it~~ the exam out of the trash at the print shop. I told him to ~~go to hell~~ pound sand. I should have reported him, but I didn't want to get my teammates in trouble. ~~He seemed okay with that.~~

At Amy's house, we had a ~~shitload~~ lot to drink and I think maybe Travis spiked the drinks. Amy and I had consensual sex in front of the fireplace, and that's the last thing I remember until waking up in Amy's TR6 the next morning. I kinda remember Travis handing me a rag and ~~ordering~~ asking me to help ~~him~~ wipe down the inside of the car.

I think the therapy is working. It's scary. I have flashbacks. I hear Amy calling for help. One thing I know for sure was that Amy was alive after we had sex. I didn't even know she had died. ~~I thought we had some fun and gone our separate ways.~~ When the pieces started coming together, I tracked Travis down in Norfolk and called him on it. Travis ~~says~~ claims that Amy must have been killed by an intruder after we left the house, but ~~I called bullshit~~ if that was true, how did her car get back into town? He ~~said he'd~~ threatened to claim that I killed Amy during sex gone bad. I told him that if he lied about that, I'd blow the whistle on him over the stolen Boats exam and mess up his cushy career big time. He kept calling my house, bothering Lisa . . .

And there it ended.

I forwarded the images to the Sleuths, along with a summary of my conversation with Lisa.

A confession? Of sorts. But one thing was sure. Nick had come back from the dead and was pointing an accusing finger directly at Travis. Now, where the hell was he? I was about to find out.

TWENTY-SEVEN
Maniac (Michael Sembello)

A dreary Monday morning in Annapolis. Because of the heat, though, I welcomed the gentle rain, and so did our backyard garden.

While the thirsty rhododendrons and droopy Japanese maples drank their fill, I sat at the kitchen table nursing my second cup of coffee, feeling smug because I'd solved that day's Wordle in three tries. Flushed with victory, I switched over to check my progress on Words With Friends. The previous evening, I'd been three points away from beating Susan Clifford – a rare occurrence – but this morning she played GNAW on a triple word square and cleaned my clock. Maybe my brain needed a holiday.

Enough of that, I decided. I stood up, plugged the cell phone into a wall charger, inverted my coffee cup over a peg in the dishwasher, and trotted down to the basement to toss some laundry in the dryer.

I didn't check my email again for almost an hour. As usual, it was mostly junk: ads from politicians I'd previously donated to, special offers from stores where I shopped, a reminder from Volvo that our car was overdue for servicing. I got notices from colleges I'd attended, too. Oberlin College Alumni sponsored private tours and lectures which I was often able to work into my schedule, and the University of Maryland Alumni Association sent out regular 'Monday Roundup' e-blasts that were so go-go sports (yay Terrapins!) and job board-centric that I usually gave them a pass. I hadn't been back to the University of Maryland campus since I got my master's degree, so the Monday Roundup calendar rarely interested me.

That morning, as usual, I scrolled through the Roundup quickly. Just as I was about to swipe the e-blast into oblivion, a name flashed by – Travis S. Palmer, Commander, US Navy (Ret.) – then vanished.

I gulped. Had the name bled over from another iPhone application? From Notes, perhaps, or Messages? Was Palmer weighing so heavily on my brain that my eyes were playing tricks on me?

I flicked my finger down the screen, moving upward through the announcements, scrolling back to the beginning of the posting. And there it was. I was not going insane. Travis Palmer was slated to give a series of three lectures at the Robert H Smith School of Business on the University of Maryland's College Park campus. Coincidence? Serendipity? Whatever, I'd take it. A button was provided for 'Read More,' so I clicked it as instructed and there he was.

Travis had aged well in the years since graduation. Pushing sixty-five, his hair was whiter now, but abundant, still swept casually across his forehead. His brow was more deeply lined, the crow's feet bracketing his blue eyes more prominent, but the biggest change was the mustache which crawled across his upper lip like a bushy white caterpillar. For his head shot, he'd opted to dress in civilian clothes, what looked like a navy-blue sharks skin suit. A pin the size of a quarter decorated his lapel, but even though I tried to enlarge the image, I couldn't make out the insignia. A tie with blue and gold stripes, what else, completed the look.

According to his bio, Palmer had spent the years since his retirement from the Navy doing consulting work for Amentum, formerly known as Dyn Corp, an international private security firm headquartered in Gaithersburg, Maryland. Amentum boasted 34,000 employees in 105 countries and fifty states. He was far too senior to be a soldier for hire, I thought. Covert operations, then? No wonder we couldn't find him.

I texted the Sleuths: *Travis Palmer to deliver a series of lectures at UofM. Works for Amentum. The lost has been found.*

Izzy wasted no time calling me back. 'Hannah, what the hell?'

I explained about the university's Monday Roundup and confessed to having nearly missed the announcement. 'It sounds pretty deadly, though. "Integrating Commercial and

Military Technologies for National Strength: An Agenda for Change".'

Izzy illustrated her opinion with a snore. 'Sorry,' she said after a pause. 'I know it's not funny.'

'And get this,' I said, reading from the listing on my cell phone. 'They describe Travis as a decorated war veteran.'

'Excuse me while I barf,' Izzy said. 'That's an insult to all *real* war veterans. Are you going to go?'

'Of course I'm going to go, but I certainly don't plan to confront him. I have to confess that after all this time chasing a phantom, I just want to lay eyes on the guy. Make sure he's for real.'

'You're not going to do this alone, Hannah. When did you say it was?'

'He's actually giving three lectures over the course of a month, but the first one is this afternoon at three, and I'd really like to be there.'

'I'll have to check . . .' Izzy began. After a pause, she added, 'I'll let the Manor know that something's come up and to tell Mother I won't be in today. Not that it'll matter. She gives me grief for not visiting when I've been there for an hour and just getting back from the bathroom.'

Izzy was coming from Severna Park, so we agreed to meet at the CVS on Riva Road and drive in together from there. The drug store was open twenty-four/seven, so I figured we weren't likely to get towed.

I parked, started a new game of Words with Friends – fifty-five points, take *that* Susan Clifford! – and had started to delete messages from my junk mail folder when Izzy pulled up beside me in a silver Hyundai Elantra. She tapped her horn.

I grabbed my handbag, locked my car and climbed into hers. 'I hope you don't mind driving,' I said as I fastened my seatbelt. 'I didn't realize until I got here that I was so low on gas.'

'No problem.' Izzy checked the rear-view mirror and began backing out of the parking space. 'As long as you know where we're going.'

'I haven't been on campus for years, but I checked the

campus map before leaving the house, and there's a parking garage near the business school we can probably get into.'

Forty minutes later, half an hour before Palmer was scheduled to begin his talk, we pulled into the Mowat Lane Garage and began winding our way up inside, finally finding a spot on the fourth level.

On the drive over, we'd discussed our plan. The lecture began at three and was supposed to last an hour, with a thirty-minute period at the end for questions and answers. We would attend the lecture, we decided, but sit out of the way in the back. Afterwards, one or both of us would follow him to his car and get the make, model and license plate number.

'How do we know what door he'll come out of?' Izzy had wondered.

'Except for emergency exits, I think there's only one door,' I said. 'And it's the closest one to the parking lot, so it shouldn't be hard.'

'We don't want Travis to think we're stalking him,' Izzy said.

'But we are,' I said as we crossed the street and approached the building. 'Let's hope he doesn't notice.'

'Why's it called Van Munching Hall?' Izzy asked as we made our way along the brick sidewalk that led up to the entrance.

'The money came from a guy who was heir to a beer fortune. They christened the building by smashing a bottle of Heineken on the façade.'

That made her laugh.

We climbed the double flight of stairs together, pulled open one of the double glass doors and found ourselves in an area like the vestibule of a bank, back when banks looked like banks and not glass and steel lean-tos attached to ATM machines. An atrium design split the building down the middle. The floors were made of highly polished stone, wooden panels in abundance lined the walls where comfortable seating, including couches with laptop tables on swivels, were heavily in use by students.

In the appropriately named Center for Global Business we asked for and received directions to the lecture hall where

Travis Palmer would be speaking. When we got there, we found the door closed, but we opened it and wandered in to find a technician – not Palmer – testing the microphone. 'Facilities have improved a lot since my student days,' I whispered to Izzy as we stood at the back of the room admiring the double projection screens that hung from the ceiling. A bank of whiteboards spread across the entire length of the wall just below the screens. The technician fired up a laptop on the podium and the first slide of a power point presentation filled the screen: *Integrating Commercial and Military Technologies for National Strength: An Agenda for Change.*

'Something tells me we're in the right place,' I said.

Izzy nudged me with her elbow. 'What was your first clue?'

Izzy and I took seats toward the back, but as the classroom started to fill up, I began to doubt the wisdom of our plan. Students in a variety of sizes, shapes, sexes and ethnicities to-ed and fro-ed around us, but one thing they had in common was age: none appeared to be over thirty-five.

In the seat next to me, Izzy squirmed uncomfortably. I figured she noticed, too.

Two elderly ladies stuck out in this sea of youth like zits on a prom night.

I leaned toward Izzy and whispered, 'Change of plans. Meet me in the hallway.'

'What's up?' she asked when we were settled into one of the sofas, the cushions still warm from the previous occupants.

'Even if we sit in the back, Palmer's going to notice us, and once we're noticed, we lose all flexibility. We know where he's going to be for the next hour and a half, so I think we should hang out here. Wait for him to finish and follow him outside when he's done.'

'What? And miss the lecture?' Izzy gasped in mock horror. 'And I was planning to take notes.'

'Tragic, I know, but try to bear up. Besides, there's always Rudy's,' I said, pointing at the entrance to the café just off the lobby. 'We can grab a bite to eat and still have plenty of time before Travis finishes speaking.'

We took turns going for food so we wouldn't lose our seats on the sofa. I nibbled on my chicken sandwich and nursed my cappuccino, but Palmer still had a half hour to go by the time we'd finished our lunch.

'Tell you what,' Izzy said as she gathered up our trash. 'You stay here, but I'm going to wait outside just in case he comes out one of the emergency doors. There's that big clock tower on the side of the building. I can see both Van Munching and the parking garage from there.'

Divide and conquer, that was the plan, but at least I would be the one with the air conditioning.

I had caught up with my email and won three games of Words with Friends when students began to stream out of the lecture hall. Ten minutes early, by my estimation. Apparently they'd run out of questions.

I texted Izzy: *The eagle has landed.*

Five minutes later, Travis Palmer himself emerged, standing a head taller than the two East Asian students who accompanied him. As Palmer entered the atrium, flanked by the pair, they began peppering him with questions to which Palmer offered rapid-fire responses. I could almost hear him thinking, *What did you think the Q&A period was for, dudes?*

Swinging his briefcase, Palmer made a beeline for the door, but the young men didn't take the hint. One pushed the door wide and held it open until Palmer passed through, followed by his friend. Palmer couldn't shake them. Halfway down the flight of steps they caught up with him again and the conversation continued.

I followed at a safe distance, so I couldn't overhear what they were saying even if I'd wanted to.

Eventually, Travis shook both the young men's hands and sent them on their way. Then he hustled down the sidewalk in the direction of the parking lot.

Izzy was on the case.

Keeping my distance, I watched her loiter near a trash bin until Travis disappeared into the parking garage. She followed close behind, casually fingering her car keys. We had no idea where Palmer had parked, of course, so I knew she'd have to follow him all the way to his car.

I waited nervously, counting the seconds, hoping she wouldn't be spotted.

Cars began to stream out of the garage – a compact, two SUVs, a BMW, a Jeep – and then, Izzy's little silver Hyundai. Izzy saw me waiting on the sidewalk and pulled up to the curb. 'Going my way, sailor?'

'Very funny,' I said as I climbed into the passenger seat.

'It's that BMW,' she reported, pointing up ahead. 'White. Florida plate BYB I40.'

I could see the BMW then, idling behind an SUV, waiting for its chance to ease into the traffic circle and turn right on Campus Drive.

As we joined the queue, Izzy shot me a wicked grin. 'Shall we tail him?'

Wearing an equally wicked grin, I nodded. 'What's the worst that will happen? We lose him?'

By some miracle, we were able to keep Palmer's BMW in sight all the way north on US Route 1 and follow him as he merged onto the Capitol Beltway. But, just north of the Route 50 interchange, the worst happened. Izzy's Hyundai got sandwiched between two tractor trailers and by the time she was able to pull out into the passing lane, we'd lost him.

'Not as good as you see on TV,' Izzy said while pounding on her steering wheel in frustration.

'Mission a success, though,' I said. 'Tell me you wrote the plate number down.'

Izzy tapped her cell phone where it sat upright in the cup holder. 'Oh, ye of little faith. Check out my photos.'

I plucked the phone out of its holder. 'Password?' I asked.

She reached over and pressed her thumb on the home button. 'When you find it, email it to Jack.'

Florida plates are white and green. An orange – what else? – sits dead center, separating the two halves of the plate number. Izzy had captured the image perfectly.

'Compelling composition,' I said. 'Unique color and lighting.'

'I'll be sure to put that on my résumé,' she said. 'Quigley will be impressed.'

TWENTY-EIGHT
S.O.S. (ABBA)

Two weeks passed before I heard from Izzy again.

'Hannah, it's me, Izzy.' I didn't know where she was calling from, but she wasn't alone. She had to raise her voice to be heard over the crowd noise in the background.

'Hi, Izzy, what's up?'

'You'll scold me,' she said, sounding uncharacteristically subdued.

'Why would I do that?'

'Broke protocol, but I couldn't help it.'

'What the hell are you talking about?'

'I'm at College Park. Went to Travis Palmer's lecture. Got tired of waiting for the police to do something with all the information we've sent them, so I figured it'd be OK to check it out on my own. This one was called . . . Just a minute.' Paper crackled. 'It's a mouthful. "The Positive Impact of US Navy Staff and Logistics Processes on Corporate Profits in the Twenty-first Century."'

'Sounds deadly.'

'Hitting myself over the head with a hammer would have been preferable. I absolutely cannot wait for lecture three. But, here's the thing. After the lecture was over, I kind of hung around, hoping maybe to talk to him.'

'Izzy! You're the one who lectures us about not going real life, and yet . . .' I sputtered, thoroughly exasperated. If I had gone real life when I first learned the monster's name from Laurie Nixon, Travis Palmer would be trussed up in a rural barn, experiencing, à la *The Mikado*, something humorous, but lingering, with either boiling oil or melted lead.

'I know, I know,' she continued sounding not the least bit contrite. 'But the police seem to be moving so glacially! Even the license plate search was a bust. Jack said it just led back to that damn private mailbox in Green Cove Springs. It makes me spitting mad! There's Travis, free as a bird, surrounded by fawning acolytes, a couple of whom, may I point out, are young women in their early twenties. It's my fantasy to walk up to him, skewer him with my eyes and say, "I know who you are and I know what you did."'

'Too much like a B movie,' I offered. 'And a good way to get *yourself* killed.'

'Don't worry, I came to my senses. But it did cross my mind that if he thought someone was on to him, he wouldn't dare kill again.'

'He could also catch a plane to Morocco or Indonesia or some place with no extradition treaty with the US. Then there'd be no justice for Amy or for any of his other victims.'

'I realize that, Hannah. It's just . . .' Her voice trailed off.

'So, you didn't blow your cover. That's good. Where are you now?'

'At Stamp, the Student Union, down in the food court. I'm nursing an iced latte and keeping an eye on them.'

'On who?'

'Palmer and one of the students who came to his lecture. He walked her over here after his talk and now they're sitting at a table together, eating chicken strips and waffle fries. I'm freaking out here, Hannah. She's short, and her hair is auburn.'

'Shit,' I said.

'Oh, hell. She just reached for a fry and he did, too, and their hands met sort of accidently-on-purpose. I'll call you back.' And Izzy ended the call.

Sensing that Izzy may have been about to turn real life into an action movie, I texted: *Don't do anything stupid! I'm on my way.*

There's gotta be a law. When you're in a hurry, the Washington Beltway turns into a parking lot. After two years of commuting to College Park from Annapolis while working on my MLS, I had learned a few tricks, so when Waze informed me of the backup, I peeled off Route 50 as soon as I could and wound my way west on Route 193, avoiding the beltway altogether.

Parking can be a bear on the University of Maryland campus, even if you understand the signs, a color-coded combination of letters and numbers, with lines of miniscule print that describe hours and exceptions that would take a PhD in cryptology wielding a magnifying glass to decipher. Some lots, I knew, were free after four p.m., but I took no chances and parked in the Union Lane Parking garage, the public parking facility directly across the street from the Stamp Student Union. A few minutes later, I barged through the double glass doors at the main entrance and headed straight down the staircase to the food court opposite the bookstore on the lower level.

They'd remodeled the food court extensively since my graduate student days, but the smell was still the same, a combination of fried chicken, hamburger grease, coffee, and unwashed bodies, fresh from workouts.

The dining area was long and narrow, furnished with molded plastic chairs in neon yellow pulled up to square, dark gray tables that were easy to move and reconfigure. McDonalds was gone, but otherwise, all the usual suspects were represented: Subway, Chick-fil-a, Saladworks and Qdoba, among other concessions, all tucked away neatly under overhanging galleries supported by massive pillars, painted yellow to match the chairs.

It was coming up on dinnertime, so the place was crowded. I strolled up and down the food court, checking the tables, scanning the customers waiting in line for their turn to place orders. I checked the lounge area and the hallway outside the bookstore, too. No sign of Travis Palmer and the young woman Izzy had described. No sign of Izzy, either.

Suddenly, my phone began to play the marimba – Izzy's ring tone. I backed myself into a corner near the UPS store and took the call. 'Where the hell are you?'

'Stairwell,' she panted. 'Past the elevators and the restrooms, on the north-east side of the building.'

'Are you—' I began, but Izzy abruptly ended the call.

Wishing she'd been a bit more specific, I raced out through the food court in what I guessed was a northerly direction. The Hoff Theater occupied the entire north-west side of the building,

so I hung a right at the off-campus housing office, hurried past
the elevator bank and made a beeline for the Exit sign. As I
clambered down the stairwell, I called out her name. 'Izzy!'

'Down here,' she replied in a perfectly normal tone of voice.

I found my friend sitting in an untidy heap at the bottom
of the flight of service stairs.

I rushed over, extending my hand to help her up. 'Are
you OK?'

She waved me off. 'Just give me a minute to catch my
breath.' She scooted away from me, dragging her butt
along the concrete floor until she could rest her back against
the wall.

I crouched next to her. 'What happened?'

'Travis effing Palmer, the bastard.'

'Did he push you?'

'No. I was following him downstairs like the idiot I am,
and I tripped. He went that-a-way,' she added, pointing
toward the nearby loading dock, its door yawning open as a
pair of truckers in gray uniforms unloaded cardboard boxes
labeled Sysco.

'Shall I go after . . .' I began.

'No need,' she interrupted. 'Before I came in here this
afternoon, I stuck a GPS tracker on the guy's BMW.'

'You didn't!'

'It's amazing what you can buy over the internet,' Izzy said.
'Thirty-nine ninety-five at Target.com.'

'How do you make sure he doesn't find it?' I asked, feeling
confident that anything purchased at Target for thirty-
nine ninety-five would be worth, well, about thirty-nine
ninety-five.

'It's magnetic,' she explained. 'I stuck it to the metal frame
under the driver's side where he'll never see it. We won't
lose him like we did the last time.'

I had to admit that Travis Palmer didn't seem like the
type who would risk dirtying his freshly pressed chinos by
crawling around under a car checking it for bugs.

'How about the girl you said he was with? What happened
to her?'

Izzy smiled. 'Oh, I don't think she'll be spending much

time in future with Commander Travis Palmer, US Navy, retired.'

I was relieved to hear that. 'How can you be so sure?' I prompted.

Izzy shifted her position, winced and began kneading her thigh.

'Are you *sure* you're OK?'

'Don't worry, I'm fine.' She flapped a dismissive hand.

'What the hell were you thinking, Izzy?' I sputtered. 'You're the one who lectures about not going real life, and yet . . .'

'Relax, Hannah. Take a pill. I can explain. As I started to say, after I talked with you, I kind of eased over, keeping a pillar between myself and their table, so I was in a good position to see but not be seen. She was gushing over this fab book she was reading called *Shoe Dog* by the founder of Nike that, like totally, totally changed her life, and the next thing you know, he's suggesting they continue their conversation over a drink down at Looney's and I thought, *whoop-whoop-whoop*, no way, not on my watch.'

Looney's Pub was a popular sports bar, just up the road from the university. If I'd been in Izzy's position, I'd have gone all Jessica Fletcher on Palmer, too.

'So, I popped around the corner, pretended we'd met before and asked how his poor wife, Lorraine was doing after the cancer surgery and chemo and all. He sputtered and claimed I must be mistaking him for someone else, yadda yadda yadda. Oh, Hannah, it was a beautiful sight to see him squirm. The girl, her name is Lacey, by the way, gathered up her things and slunk away.' Izzy swiped her hands back and forth. 'Mission accomplished, at least in that department.'

She began patting around on the concrete floor. 'Now, where's my damn phone?'

I pointed. 'It's in your breast pocket.'

Izzy patted the pocket of her shirt, flushed, then eased the phone into her hand. She tapped the screen and handed the phone over to me. 'The gizmo I put on Palmer's car is tied to an app.'

According to the map on Izzy's phone, Travis Palmer's car, represented by a blue sedan, was heading west on the

Washington beltway, just passing the Mormon Temple at Connecticut Avenue.

'So, if they ever get around to picking him up, they'll know where to find him.' She flashed me a wicked grin. 'And the battery is guaranteed for two years.'

I sat down on the bottom step, adjusting my position as the cold of the concrete seeped through my khakis. 'It's frustrating, I know, waiting for the cops to get their act together. Jack assures me that at least three of the jurisdictions claim to be retesting their case DNA, but he says we have to be patient. It's not *CSI Miami*. They have backlogs, budget restraints, other priorities.'

If Izzy was listening to me, she showed no sign of it. Her eyes scanned the stairwell, then came to rest on a spot behind me. She flicked her index finger in that direction. 'Over there. My backpack? Could you hand it to me, please?'

I scooped the bag up by one of the straps and passed it over. She rummaged inside for a moment, then withdrew a green plastic bag with a paw print on it. I used a similar brand of bag whenever I walked Coco, to scoop up her poop. The handles of the bag were neatly tied over an object inside.

'What's that?' I asked.

'Exhibit A,' she said. 'A certain popular chocolate-flavored beverage.' She untied the handles of the bag without touching the contents to reveal an empty, twelve-ounce beverage bottle with a bright yellow label. 'Needs to be tested. I'll get that to Jack ASAP.'

'Yoohoo?' I scoffed. 'Palmer drinks Yoohoo?'

'There's no accounting for taste,' she said.

'Talk about off label use,' I commented, as I watched Izzy retie the pooper scooper bag over the bottle Palmer had drunk from.

'Hey, it's what I had.'

Izzy tucked the bottle bearing both Palmer's DNA and fingerprints into her backpack, while I wondered if there'd be legal issues over chain of custody. I decided it'd be prudent not to mention it.

She held out her hand. 'Help me up?'

On her feet at last, she dusted off her jeans. When she bent down to pick up her backpack, I noticed that she'd split a seam from zipper to crotch, exposing a half-moon of pale pink underwear. This, I decided to mention.

'Damn! I just bought these jeans!'

I slipped out of the hoodie I was wearing and tied it around her waist by the sleeves. 'Just don't bend over,' I advised.

As we made our way to the elevators, Izzy clung to my arm, limping slightly. 'You're coming home with me,' I insisted. 'We'll come back for your car in the morning.'

'No, no, I'm fine. Besides, I have to visit Mother in the morning.'

'Are you sure?'

'Positive,' she said, misunderstanding my question. 'They're wanting to move her to the memory care unit. I predict World War Three.'

I walked Izzy out of the Stamp and all the way back to her car. By the time we reached the lot behind the field house where she'd parked it, she was walking without a limp and had let go of my arm.

'Where's your car?' I asked.

Izzy dug a fistful of keys out of the zippered pouch on her backpack, fumbled with it until she isolated the key fob, then aimed. I heard a *beep* and the lights on a silver Elantra two rows over began to flash. When we reached it, I opened the driver's side door and held it open for her. 'Are you sure . . .?' I asked again.

She patted my arm. 'I'm fine, Hannah. Nothing that a nice, hot bubble bath and a good night's sleep won't cure.' She tossed her backpack across the console onto the front passenger seat. 'I'll check in with everyone in the morning.'

I pointed at the backpack. 'How about the Yoohoo?'

'I'll drop that off with Jack in the morning on my way to the nursing home.' Izzy lived on Evergreen Road in Severna Park and Jack somewhere up in Glen Burnie, so that made sense to me.

'Izzy?'

'What?'

'Just so you know. If I'd been in your shoes, I'd have done

the same thing. No, on second thought, I might have picked up a chair and clobbered the sonofabitch with it.'

She extended her arms and folded me into them. 'Ouch!' she said, followed by, 'If it scared him off, it was totally worth it.'

'Take it easy,' I said, offering her my arm again as she slid into the driver's seat. I closed the car door gently, waited while she started the ignition and didn't head back to my own car until her taillights disappeared around the corner of Fieldhouse Drive.

TWENTY-NINE
Don't Leave Me This Way
(Thelma Houston)

One week after Izzy's adventure, Jack called a meeting. I showed up at the Harbour Center early. I needed to exchange a pair of jeans that I'd bought online at Chicos for the next size down, then I planned to stop at Fresh Market for a garlic-rosemary chicken. Paul had requested one for dinner.

Ten minutes before the meeting was scheduled to begin, I lugged my groceries out of the market and headed for my car. I had popped the trunk and was tucking the cool bag containing the butter and half and half under Coco's quilted car blanket when I heard raised voices.

Two rows over, Izzy was standing outside her car, having an argument with Jack. She waved wildly to emphasize some point, while he stood stock still, arms folded, solid and unmovable as a pillar. I couldn't hear what they were quarreling about.

By the time I got over to Barnes and Noble, they had already gone inside. I found everyone sitting at our usual table; Izzy looking flushed, Jack stonily silent, and Mark full of good cheer that was shortly going to be quashed.

Mark waved me over. 'Good to see you, Hannah.'

'Hi all,' I said.

'We've lost him,' Jack huffed, scowling.

'Lost who?' I asked as I pulled out a chair and sat down.

'Travis Palmer, who else?'

'What do you mean "lost?"' Mark wanted to know.

'According to the tracker that Izzy installed, Palmer's car has been sitting in long-term parking at Dulles for over a week.'

'So? Maybe Amentum sent him off on assignment,' I said, adding my two cents to the discussion. 'Or he's taking a vacation.'

'He could also have rented a car and driven to Kansas,' Jack grumped. 'Ditched the rental and paid cash for a second-hand clunker and headed off to Las Vegas.'

'Golly, Jack,' I said. 'You should write for television.'

'You can't know that he's on the lam,' Mark said reasonably. 'Has anybody checked with the airlines? Canvassed the car rental agencies?'

'Need a warrant for that,' Jack said.

'And may I point out,' I said, 'if it weren't for Izzy, you wouldn't even *know* that his car had been sitting at Dulles for a week.'

'And the cops wouldn't have a Yoohoo bottle with his DNA and fingerprints all over it,' Mark added.

Jack raised a hand. 'You're right. Sorry, I guess I'm just in a bad mood this morning.'

'Look,' I chimed in, 'nothing Izzy did should have set off any alarm bells. She was just some crazy bitch who mistook Palmer for somebody else, right?'

Izzy rested her forearms on the table. 'I've been thinking back over what I said to Palmer, word for word, and I'm not sorry. I did what I felt I had to do, and now maybe there's a young redhead in College Park who will never know what a close call she had.'

'Still,' Jack said, climbing back onto the complaint wagon, 'since we have no idea where he lives, it would have been helpful to collar him at his last lecture.'

'There's still one lecture to go,' I pointed out reasonably.

'Unless he's on the run,' Jack said.

Thinking about the incriminating bottle of Yoohoo, I asked, 'What are the police telling you about how their investigation is going?'

Jack straightened his back. 'Carmichael says they're digging out the evidence on the Madison case and taking a fresh look. Back in the day, they hadn't developed the superglue fuming technique, so they're hoping to turn up a better set of prints. If they can match them to the prints on the Yoohoo bottle, it'll be golden.'

'I remember from the case evidence report that they collected quite a few highball glasses and liquor bottles at the scene,' I said. 'If they held on to them, I'm thinking there's reason for optimism.'

'They held on to them,' Jack said. 'High marks for that.'

'How long does that kind of testing take?' Mark wanted to know.

'With the speed they're going, till Christmas,' Jack said sourly.

THIRTY
Got To Give It Up (Marvin Gaye)

I couldn't figure out where the sound was coming from at first. While I'd been snoozing on the sofa, my cell phone had slipped between the cushions and seemed to be bleating for help. By the time I dug it out, the call had gone to message, but I could see that it came from Izzy, so I dialed her right back.

'Hannah,' she said, sounding breathless. 'Palmer's on the move again.'

That news made me sit up straight. 'Are you sure? Maybe they've just decided to tow away his car?'

'Not unless the impound lot is in southern Maryland. I've been following the signal, and he's moving south around the beltway. He's just gone over the Woodrow Wilson Bridge.'

'Does Jack know?'

'Yes, I'm with him now.'

'Any clue where Palmer's headed?'

'Of course not, but it looks like somewhere in Maryland.'

'Where are you now?' I asked.

'In the car with Jack, heading your way.'

'Look, there's not much anyone can do until he reaches where he's going.' I paused for a moment. 'Unless Jack has one of those strobe lights he can slap on the top of his car.'

'Jack says very funny.'

'Look, and this is a serious question. I know Jack's no longer a cop, but can't he make a citizen's arrest?'

Izzy must have had me on speakerphone, because Jack bellowed, 'Only if he wants to screw up the case.'

'OK, so I guess there's not much to do until we find out where he's going. Why not wait here at my house until we're sure.'

I guess Jack approved of the plan because I heard him say,

'Tell her to fire up the coffee pot. We'll be there in about twenty minutes.'

In the end, there was no time for coffee.

Izzy pounded on my front door and when I opened it, she pointed to the street and said, 'Jack's waiting. C'mon.'

I grabbed my hoodie off the hook on the hall tree and followed her. As I approached the SUV, the side door powered open. I climbed up and slid into the seat. I was still fastening my seatbelt when Izzy leaned around the bucket seat and said, 'Jack apologized for jumping to conclusions. Obviously I did not run the guy out of town.'

'So, what's the plan?' I asked as Jack steered the SUV down Maryland Avenue towards the traffic light on King George.

'Verify that it's him,' Jack said.

'And then what?'

'Let the cops know where to find him once the warrant comes through.'

'Honestly, Jack, I feel like we've been doing all the heavy lifting here. What more do they need? They've got Palmer's DNA and his fingerprints. They've got evidence that he was in the right place at the right time for at least six of the murders . . .' I shut my mouth in frustration.

Jack glanced into the rear-view mirror and caught my eye. 'But now, they've got a positive ID. A victim who survived an attack picked Palmer out of a photo lineup just this morning.'

I flopped back in my seat. 'Finally!'

Izzy turned in her seat to grin at me. 'I wanted to tell you right away, but Jack wanted to see the expression on your face.'

'Which case was it, do you know?'

'Alibi's Bar and Grill up in Pasadena. About five years ago? She was a flight attendant from Southwest, at home visiting her family.'

'So, tell me there's a warrant out for his arrest,' I said.

'When I checked with Carmichael this morning, they said it was in the works,' Jack reported as he breezed through the yellow light at King George and College.

'What does "in the works" mean, exactly.'

'The DA's filed an affidavit with the judge, and if the judge determines that there's probable cause, they'll issue the warrant.'

'Gosh, how long does that take?'

'They do it all electronically these days, so it could be any minute.'

We didn't speak for a while, sitting quietly with our own thoughts, as we drove south on Solomon's Island Road, gradually closing the gap between us and the blue icon on Izzy's app that represented Palmer's BMW. At the Central Avenue intersection, Jack followed, turning left. Five minutes later, we were proceeding at a leisurely pace down Muddy Creek Road, a pleasant, two-lane highway that paralleled the Chesapeake Bay coastline.

'He's stopped in Churchton,' Izzy reported. 'At Christopher's Fine Foods, it says here, so his house probably isn't far away.'

By the time Muddy Creek merged with Shady Side Road, Palmer was on the move again, heading south on State Route 256 towards Deale. We followed him left on Franklin Manor Road and straight down Battee into a modest, residential community called Cape Ann.

We were only five minutes behind, when Travis's icon approached the T-intersection at Shore Drive and Harbor Way and came to a stop. As we eased into the neighborhood, Jack approached at a snail's pace down Harbor Way, parking his SUV just around the corner from Shore Drive where we could keep an eye both on the house and Travis's car.

Travis lived in a modest raised rancher on a corner lot facing Broadwater Creek. Apparently, he hadn't been home for some time; grass stood high in the back yard and the shrubs around the foundation of the house badly needed pruning. A garden shed, its siding in much better repair than the siding on the house, occupied one corner of the yard.

A light blue hard-side suitcase sat on the driveway next to the open trunk of the BMW. The front door opened, and a tall, blond man emerged from the house and stepped down off the porch to retrieve it.

'That's him,' Izzy whispered.

'Confirmed,' I said.

'He's coming at least, and not going,' Jack said, reaching for his phone.

Travis slammed the trunk shut with one hand, then trundled the roller bag up the sidewalk, hefted it up the steps and dragged it the rest of the way into the house.

Suddenly, as if he'd been summoned, a teenage boy riding a John Deere mower whipped around the corner of Shore Drive and began mowing the lawn.

At the same moment, Jack's phone peeped. I was surprised he could hear it over the roar of the tractor. Jack checked his messages, then set his phone back down on the console. 'Southern district is on their way,' he reported. 'We're to stay put.'

'Where are they coming from?' I asked.

'Edgewater,' he said.

The Edgewater police station was next to the post office, at least twenty minutes away.

'What if he makes a run for it?' Izzy wanted to know.

'You've watched too many cop shows, Izzy,' Jack said, patting her hand where it rested on the console. He let it linger there for what seemed like a moment too long.

Were Jack and Izzy . . .? I wondered. *None of your business, Hannah.*

'How long does it take to mow such a small lawn?' I asked over the roar of the tractor. It was taking forever for the kid to get the job done, but eventually he parked the tractor on the street in front of the house, hopped off the seat and knocked on the door. Travis appeared, wallet in hand, and handed the kid a few bills. The kid counted them, saluted smartly, then left, driving the tractor at high speed back the way he had come.

Something moved in the range of my peripheral vision. I turned my head toward the house, and there it was again. A curtain twitched, drew fully aside and a face peered out. It was the face of a young woman. I couldn't see her hair, but I was betting on red.

Suddenly, I knew what had bothered me about the suitcase in the driveway. It had been light blue. Travis Palmer's suitcases would be black, or a sedate gray. That suitcase had belonged to a woman.

'Jack! There's a woman in there with him! She just looked out of the kitchen window.'

'Shit! Just what we need is a hostage situation.'

'She must be there willingly, Jack. The front door stood wide open when he came out to fetch her suitcase, and he didn't look nervous at all when he paid off the kid with the mower.'

'I don't mean now, Hannah, I mean later when they come to arrest him, which should be in . . .' He checked his watch. 'About fifteen minutes.'

'Any reason to think that he's armed?' I asked.

'I don't know, Hannah, but he was in the military, for Christ's sake. He knows how to shoot. He could have a whole arsenal in the house for all we know.'

'I have a plan,' I said. 'And it's not dangerous at all.'

'Hannah, are you out of your mind?'

'No, no, I think this will work. I can get him out of the house, and while I'm doing that, you can run in and grab the girl.'

As I unhooked my seatbelt, Izzy reached back and grabbed my arm. 'You can't . . .'

I shook it off. 'Well, you can't go! You're the crazy food court lady.'

Before anyone could change my mind, I opened the door, slid out of the seat. I pounded the driver's side window lightly with a balled fist until Jack rolled the window down. 'Watch out for me!' I said, and headed for the house.

Behind me, I heard his car door click open.

The front porch and the steps leading up to it had been constructed of wooden decking stained dark brown. The salt air had aged the planks and here and there they'd begun to splinter. The front door was built of sturdier oak, with an oval of glass etched with a great blue heron. Holding my cell phone in my hand to the picture I'd pre-selected, I knocked on the door.

Through the glass, I could see the dark outline of someone approaching. By his height, it had to be Palmer.

I was trying to keep my breathing even when the door opened wide. 'Yes?' he said pleasantly.

'Oh, hi,' I said airily, stepping back a bit to put some distance between us. 'I'm your neighbor down the road over there.' I waved vaguely. 'I'm really, really sorry to bother you, but I think my cat is trapped in your garden shed.' I thrust my iPhone close to his face so he could admire the picture of Trish and Peter's cat, the one I use as my screen-saver. 'His name is Hobie. He's a Lynx Point. I was trying to lure him out through that hole in the back that I'm sure you've been meaning to get fixed,' I rattled on, 'but then the lawnmower came roaring by and scared Hobie half to death, and now he won't come when I call. Do you think you could have a look?'

Travis's mustache twitched and a grin lit up his face. By way of answer, he stretched his arm out to a hall table and scooped a fistful of keys out of a basket. 'Tansy,' he called over his shoulder, 'I'm just going to help this lady find her cat.'

The woman he'd called Tansy stepped out into the hallway from a room I took to be the kitchen. Tall and slim, she was wearing white shorts and a pink T-shirt and held a large salad bowl in her hands. The salad bowl was getting a good work over with a blue and white dish towel. She might have been as young as thirty or as old as forty, and her hair was a mass of rusty ringlets. Please, please, I prayed silently, let this woman be Travis's daughter and not his girlfriend.

'Just back from vacation?' I inquired casually, indicating the suitcases that sat just inside the door.

Tansy smiled. 'St Pete. Dad booked a VRBO down there,' she said, pronouncing the name *ver-bow*. 'I could have stayed forever, but he had to get back for some stupid lecture.' She turned away, calling over her shoulder, 'Good luck finding your cat.'

Feeling somewhat relieved that she'd called the guy 'Dad', I stepped away from the door and started across the porch.

Travis followed.

We trooped down the stairs, with me in the lead, and walked around the house into the backyard. I could see Jack's SUV out of the corner of my eye. The garden shed I'd spotted earlier, tucked into a back corner of the lot, was about eight by ten square feet, resting at each corner on pilings made of two stacked cinder blocks. As we approached, I started calling for my poor, lost cat, 'Hobie, Hobie, it's OK, you can come out now. The bad lawnmower man is gone.'

'I think he got in back here,' I told Travis as I led him around the back of the shed where we would be completely out of view of the house and of the SUV. 'Hobie! Come out! I have a treat for you!'

Unfortunately, there didn't appear to be a hole in the back of the shed, not even one big enough for a mouse to pass through, let alone a fully grown cat. I knelt on the grass and stuck my hand under the shed near one of the pilings. 'He might have crawled in from under,' I suggested, glancing up at Travis where he loomed over me.

'We can see,' he said. He extended his hand, I took it (with reluctance!), holding on while he pulled me to my feet. Together, we ambled around to the front of the shed where the double, barn-style doors had been secured with a padlock. Travis began thumbing through the keys, looking for the one that would fit the lock, and I took the opportunity to steal a glance toward the SUV. The doors remained closed. Half a block up the street, a light-colored Ford Explorer sat idling. Had we driven past it on our way in? I couldn't remember.

With a twist of his wrist and a quiet, 'There ya go!' Travis undid the lock, hooked the shackle over one of the hasps, then pulled both doors toward us.

You could have held a party in that shed, eaten straight off the clean-swept floor. A shiny, new stainless steel barbeque grill sat in one corner. Next to it, several bags of grass seed and one of fertilizer were stored upright in a large, plastic tub. A long, narrow workbench stood to my left, over which hung a pegboard where each tool had its place – an outline painted in white made sure of that.

'Hobie, Hobie, Hobie,' I yodeled, stooping to look under the bench and behind the grass seed, staring up into the rafters. I spread my arms, manufactured an exasperated sigh, turned to Travis and said, 'Definitely not here! I'm wondering if he got himself out while I was standing on the porch talking to you. He's probably sitting on my porch right now wondering where I am. No treats for you, Mr Hobie cat!'

The only thing standing between me and the door leading out of the shed was Travis Palmer, serial killer. My heart began to pound, but I dredged a smile up from somewhere and managed to paste it on my face. 'I am *so* sorry that I bothered you,' I said as I scurried around him and out the door.

'That's perfectly all right,' Travis said as he relocked the shed.

'Well, bye,' I called as I made my way across the grass and onto the street, heading away from the house and the SUV but drawing ever closer to the Explorer. 'Maybe we'll see you and your daughter at the Crab Fest?' I called back over my shoulder.

'Maybe you will,' he said. 'And I hope you find your cat.'

After I was clear of the yard, the Explorer began rolling quietly down the hill; no lights, no sirens. From behind a large oak tree, I watched it all go down.

On his way back to the house, Travis paused to snap some dead branches off a sad-looking forsythia bush. The detectives, two of them in plain blue suits and one in uniform, simply walked across the lawn, presented their badges, and confronted him there. The casual observer would have thought they were having a pleasant conversation – he'd reported a stolen car perhaps, or his shed had been broken into. But before long, Travis turned his back, linked his hands behind him, and waited patiently while they slipped on the handcuffs.

Immediately after they whisked Travis away in the Explorer, a white van from the Evidence Collection Unit arrived; soon they would be swarming all over Palmer's house.

Obviously, the extraction of Tansy had been a success, but she wasn't happy about it. They'd stashed her in the SUV for safety, but they stood outside it now. Jack was restraining a frantic Tansy, holding her tightly by both arms. 'You can't go back in there until they're finished.'

'But it's my house! Mine! Daddy doesn't even live here!'

'It doesn't matter, Tansy. It's simply routine procedure. I'm sure there'll be nothing to find, and they'll let you back in shortly.'

'Let's go sit down,' I said, indicating a concrete picnic table the community had thoughtfully installed on the bank of the creek. As we made our way over to it, I took her arm gently and asked, 'Are you OK, Tansy?'

'No! I'm not OK,' she shouted, breaking her arm free from my grasp. 'Would you be? How would you feel if you got off a plane after an idyllic vacation only to find out that the police think your father is a serial killer?'

'Do you have someplace you can stay?' Izzy asked gently.

'This *is* my place! Dad doesn't live anywhere long enough to have a place. He rents one when he needs it.'

'How about your mother?' Izzy inquired.

'Dead.'

'I'm so sorry,' I said. 'I lost my mother when I was very young, too. I miss her every day.'

'I'll bet yours didn't die when you were two minutes old,' Tansy snapped. 'Basically, I killed her. She was simply too young to have babies.'

'How old was your mother?' I asked.

'Sixteen.'

It wasn't hard to do the math. If Travis Palmer was Tansy's father, then he must have slept with Tansy's mother when she was only fifteen. In no state, not even in the deep, deep South, was fifteen the age of consent. He could have been charged with statutory rape.

'I know what you're thinking,' Tansy said, 'but it wasn't like that at all. My parents had been sweethearts since junior high school. They were crazy about each other. When I was born, she was sixteen and he was eighteen.'

'Just kids having kids,' Jack muttered.

'Yeah, well that's the way it was, all hush hush. So, Mom was dead and I ended up being raised by my dad's mom. My mom's mom didn't want to have anything to do with me, for obvious reasons. I didn't even know I had a dad until he came home after graduating from the Naval Academy.'

'Fatherhood was a dismissal offense back then,' I said. 'And it's not particularly career-enhancing these days, either.'

'That's how Dad explained it,' she said.

'If you look anything like your mom, she must have been really beautiful,' I said.

Tansy blinked rapidly. 'They say that's why my grandmother hated me so. I look just like her daughter, red hair and all.'

Suddenly, the tears that had been glistening in her eyes spilled over and streamed, unchecked, down her cheeks. She sobbed until she was gasping for air, refusing the tissues I handed her and all attempts at comfort. 'And now I have nobody,' she hiccupped. 'Nobody!'

'You have your father,' I said. 'I think you were the only constant in his life, and he needs you now more than ever.'

She turned her tear-stained face to me. 'Do you think it's true? That he murdered all those girls?' She pressed both hands against her chest. 'It makes me want to throw up.'

There would be a time, not now, but in the near future, when I would introduce Constanza Palmer to her half-sister, Cheryl Lannigan. I prayed it would bring comfort to them both.

THIRTY-ONE

Pick Up the Pieces
(Average White Band)

I called Paul from Churchton to let him know I'd be late for dinner.

Jack and Izzy dropped me off at home around seven. I found Paul in the kitchen, presiding over a pot of stew.

'Oh, gawd, that smells good,' I said. 'I haven't had anything to eat since breakfast.'

Paul pulled out a kitchen chair, instructed me to sit down, and handed me a glass of Merlot he'd set out to breathe on the counter. 'Tell me about it,' he said.

So I did.

At four o'clock the following day, I was laying a linen cloth over the table in the dining room when Paul returned home from a meeting. 'And what to my wondering eyes should appear, but a dining room table?' he quipped. 'There was actually a table under there?'

'It's a miracle. I moved my laptop up to Emily's old room,' I told him. 'Temporarily, at least. All my paperwork is stashed in a tub in the basement. I'll get back to it some day.'

'It'll be nice to have people over again.' Paul checked his watch. 'What time did you say they'll be coming?'

'Around six. Mark said he's tied up until then, but you're to save him a beer. Izzy and Jack are coming together.'

'Together? As in together together?' He linked his index fingers.

'Officially, I know nothing,' I said. 'Last I heard, Jack's wife and kids were visiting her family in Albuquerque. But he hasn't spoken about them for weeks.'

'Could be a touchy situation,' Paul observed.

'Yes, it could, and that's why I trust the topic will never come up, at least not at dinner.'

'So, what *is* for dinner?' he asked, sniffing the air and making an elaborate show of it. 'I don't smell anything cooking.'

'That's because Nano Asian is cooking,' I said. 'They're delivering promptly at six. Now, if you'll kindly fetch the Chinese rice bowls off the high shelf in the pantry and bring me the plates that go with them, I'll let you be first in line for the dumplings.'

Paul returned with the dinnerware and helped me set five places. While he went off to fetch the soy sauce and rice wine vinegar we used as condiments, I aligned a pair of chopsticks on a napkin at the head of each place setting and provided everyone with a dipping bowl and porcelain spoon for the sauces.

By six o'clock, the Silent Sleuths had all arrived, as had the delivery guy from Nano Asian. Paul made sure everyone had an adult beverage of choice in hand and kept the conversation light while I unpacked the food bags and arranged the carryout containers in a semi-circle in the middle of the table.

'First things first,' I decreed once we were all seated around the table. 'Mark, will you offer the blessing?'

Mark bowed his head. 'Dear Lord, we thank you for this food. Bless it to our use and us to Thy service, and make us ever mindful of the needs of others. Amen.'

'That was beautiful.' Izzy sighed.

Not wanting to break the spell, I quietly picked up the sushi sampler and started it clockwise around the table.

After everyone was served, I said, 'Jack tells me that Travis Palmer is being arraigned in district court tomorrow. Two counts of first-degree murder. They are requesting no bail.'

'Two counts?' Paul asked, reaching for a dumpling with his chopsticks.

'Amy Madison and a young waitress from Buddy's Crabs and Ribs who was murdered in 1998,' Jack explained. 'That last one wasn't on our radar, but the DNA seems conclusive. And Travis Palmer was in Annapolis then, assigned to the Athletic Association, as you may recall.'

'Makes me sick,' Paul said. 'I hope the guy has a rotten lawyer.'

Jack reached for the shitake mushroom rolls and selected two pieces before passing the dish on. 'No such luck, I'm afraid. Big shot like that with big bucks? He can afford a good one. According to his daughter, Tansy, the lawyer works for a big criminal defense firm in DC. I'm blanking on the name, but it doesn't matter. The evidence is solid. Palmer's not going to walk.'

Paul took a bite of a California roll and chewed it thoughtfully. 'From what you've told me, after Anne Arundel County gets finished, there are several jurisdictions waiting in line to take a piece of him.'

'Yes, indeed,' I said. 'Including Montgomery County who will want to try him for Roberta Chapman's murder. And we're grateful to Mark for all the work he did dovetailing two very complicated timelines. Mark, you should write an article.'

'Not in a million years.' Mark picked up a spring roll and took a bite.

'Which jurisdictions?' Paul wanted to know.

I ticked them off on my fingers. 'After Anne Arundel and Montgomery counties in Maryland, there's Norfolk, San Diego, and Tampa to begin with. There's a similar case in Naples, too. Italy, not Florida. The *carabinieri* are taking the information Anne Arundel County sent them very seriously.'

'What makes a guy like Palmer tick?' Izzy wanted to know. 'Mark, you're the expert on that. Seems to me he had a victim type, in this case, redheads. If this were a bad novel, his mother would have been a redhead who neglected and abused him, so he's getting even by killing women who look like her.'

Mark rested a half-eaten spring roll on his plate. 'That's just a lot of psychobabble, Izzy. In my experience, the triggers for most serial killers are availability, accessibility and desirability, sometimes all three. Palmer must have found redheads desirable. They triggered his lust.'

While we thought over how that formula might pertain to Travis Palmer, Mark helped himself to a spoonful of rice and a serving of beef with scallions. He scooped up a bite, chewed thoughtfully, swallowed and said, 'I should confess that the reason I was a bit late today was because I was visiting Travis Palmer in jail.'

Our chopsticks had been clacking, but grew silent.

'What did he say?' I asked as I dug into the Singapore rice noodles with a serving spoon.

'Not much. He remembers meeting me up in Newport and seeing me hanging around the Officers' Club, but since he wasn't much of a chapelgoer, that was about the extent of our acquaintance.'

With the point of his chopstick, Jack skewered a dumpling and dropped it whole into his bowl. 'Did he confess?'

Mark shook his head. 'No. Clammed up, big time. And it concerns me that he seems to have no empathy for the victims or feel even the slightest bit of remorse. His lack of human connection is chilling.' After a moment, he added, 'If I were a betting man, odds are ten to one his lawyer will lay all the blame for Amy's murder on Nick. But when the other women were murdered, Nick was already dead, so that argument won't hold water going forward.'

Thinking about the evidence technicians who had been swarming all over Constanza Palmer's house the day before, I turned to Jack and asked, 'Did they find anything in the search that will help them with the case?'

'He didn't bring evidence of his crimes home with him, if that's what you're asking, but they did find three US passports under fictitious names, as well as a British passport in the name of Anthony J Parker. Also, a stash of bills, a mix of US and foreign currency, worth about three thousand dollars total.'

'Firearms?' Paul asked.

'No, not even a handgun.'

'How about in his car?'

'Not there either. A Swiss army knife, that's it.'

'Was he an undercover agent? A spy?' Izzy wondered as she picked at her serving of Singapore noodles. I swore she was eating it one noodle at a time.

'If he was, we will certainly never know,' Mark said, licking plum sauce off his fingers. 'It is so far above my pay grade that I'd need an extension ladder to get there.'

'Well, at least now the cops won't have any trouble getting samples of Palmer's DNA,' Izzy mused.

'And, another positive thing,' I pointed out. 'The third lecture in Travis Palmer's business school series has been cancelled.'

Paul faked a pout. 'Boo hoo. What are we missing?'

I had committed every word to memory. I closed my eyes and began to recite, as if the title had been written on the insides of my eyelids. '"Quandaries in the Economics of Dual Technologies and Spillovers from Military to Civilian Research and Development."'

Jack applauded. 'Very good, Hannah.'

'Good golly Miss Molly,' Mark chuckled. 'On that note, please pass the shrimp with cashews. All of a sudden, I'm starving.'

THIRTY-TWO
Ashes to Ashes (David Bowie)

A hot day in early August. The Silent Sleuths had agreed to meet at St Luke's Cemetery at two in the afternoon when the sun would be starting its inexorable journey west. I arrived around one forty-five to find Izzy already there, sitting ramrod straight on Mary Yardley's bench, her fingers laced together in her lap.

I paid brief tribute to the good general and his faithful steed, then joined her on the bench.

'We're back where it all started,' Izzy observed as I settled down on the cool marble next to her. 'Seems like one hundred years ago.'

I had to agree.

She leaned sideways and her shoulder bumped mine. 'I'm sure glad I ran into you, Hannah Ives.'

'Ditto, ditto, Isabel Randall,' I replied, bumping her shoulder in return.

Birdsong filled the growing silence between us, the *cheer-cheer-cheer* of a cardinal, if I wasn't mistaken, and the raucous *caw-caw* of a crow, probably expressing his annoyance at our presence. 'Are you writing Amy's story?' I asked my friend after a bit.

'Maybe,' she replied. 'But not right now. I need some distance.'

We turned our heads toward the sound of crunching gravel and the *squawk* of a parking brake being engaged. Jack Shelton hopped out of his SUV, adjusted his belt, and ambled between the cemetery gateposts. He paused for a moment at General Johnson's preposterous memorial – didn't everyone? – in order to read the inscription.

Moments later, a blue Neon with Mark Wallis behind the wheel pulled into the space next to Jack's SUV. Before coming our way, Mark walked around to the passenger side door of his car, twisted the handle and held the door open for someone.

Sensible low, black heels emerged first, followed by slim, stockinged legs, followed by the rest of an elderly lady dressed in a dark blue pants suit. She'd looped a scarf featuring a design inspired by Monet's garden around her shoulders and secured it there with a gold circle pin. Her hair was a finely spun bubble of cotton candy, and pearls the size of marbles decorated her ears.

Mark offered the woman his arm, she took it, and they made their way cautiously over the uneven turf towards our bench. As Jack hustled over to join us, Izzy and I stood to attention.

'Here's someone I'd like you to meet,' Mark said by way of explanation. 'This is Susan Oakes, Amy's mother. And, Mrs Oakes, this is Izzy and Hannah, with Jack appearing over the horizon. These are the people I told you about. This is our team.'

'Thank you, Mark, and it's Susan, please,' Susan said, patting his arm with her free hand. She released Mark's arm, then, starting with Izzy, she hugged each of us in turn. 'Thank you, thank you, thank you,' she repeated, as her rosy cheeks grew damp with tears. 'How can I ever . . .' She flapped her hand before her face, as if fanning the tears away.

I scrabbled in my handbag and came up with a packet of tissues.

'Izzy, Mark tells me you paid for Amy's testing,' Susan said as she used a tissue to pat her face and eyes dry. 'The least I can do is reimburse you for that.'

'We don't operate that way,' Izzy informed Amy's mother gently. 'Here, we pay it forward. Last year a three-year-old boy named Jaydn was found wandering alone in Quiet Waters Park. You could help us find and reunite him with family members.'

Susan nodded, reached into her handbag and pulled out a checkbook. 'How much?'

Izzy placed a restraining hand on hers. 'We'll talk about that later. Look, here's Mark.'

While we were talking, Mark had jogged back to his car. He returned carrying a horseshoe wreath, thick with white and yellow roses.

'Ready?' he asked Susan.

Susan nodded, stuffed the checkbook back into her bag and, once again, took his arm. With Mark and Susan in the lead, Izzy, Jack and I trailed down the narrow path that led to Amy's grave and formed a half circle around it.

Mark held the wreath out to Amy's mother who accepted it with both hands. We stood in respectful silence while she stepped forward and propped the wreath up on her daughter's tombstone. She stepped back, her head slightly cocked as if to admire the effect. 'Perfect,' she whispered. And with a smile aimed directly at me, she added, 'Amy was crazy about horses.'

I was already choked up, and then someone began to sing 'Amazing Grace' and I lost it completely.

I didn't know where the song was coming from at first. It took me a few seconds to realize that it was Mark, singing the old folk hymn in a clear, high tenor. His stunning voice swept over us, soared above the trees and into the summer sky. Even the birds stopped their idle chatter to listen.

When the song came to an end, Mark approached Amy's grave, rested his hand on her tombstone and prayed, 'Oh God, whose beloved Son took children into his arms and blessed them, give us grace to entrust Amy to your never-failing care and love, and bring us all to your heavenly kingdom.'

What more could I add but, Amen.